THE SECRET TO NOT DROWNING

THE SECRET TO NOT DROWNING

Colette Snowden

For Ingrid

First published in 2015 by
Bluemoose Books Ltd
25 Sackville Street
Hebden Bridge
West Yorkshire
HX7 7DJ

www.bluemoosebooks.com

British Library Cataloguing-in-Publication data
A catalogue record for this book is available from the British Library

Hardback ISBN 978-1-910422-11-3

Paperback ISBN 978-1-910422-10-6

Printed and bound in the UK by Short Run Press

1

There are four people in the room but only one of them is me.

I am the only one flat on my back, legs in the air, knickers somewhere on the floor. I am the only one focusing only on the paper towels stacked in piles from the floor almost to the ceiling. Little green bundles, ready and waiting for all those doctors and nurses to wash their hands and dry them again afterwards. That's a lot of hand washing. How many bundles of paper towels are there? How many towels per bundle? If, on average, each person uses two paper towels to dry their hands, how many hand washes are there stacked up in this room? How long will they last then? And why are they in here and not in a cupboard? Have they been put here especially for people like me to help them concentrate on something else? To help me and them drown out the sound of the doctor telling me something I already know.

He squeezes my hand. He wants me to look at Him but I don't want to. I don't want to look at Him. I don't want to hold his hand. I don't want to be here. I don't want to exist. I want to pull my hand away and pretend that there's no-one but me in the room. Just doing a paper towel stock-take. But I just lie there, letting Him hold my hand. He's holding it too tight for me to pull it free. And, anyway, what difference does it make?

"It's not good news I'm afraid." The doctor is talking to me but looking at Him.

"The baby hasn't developed since we examined you last week. There's no heartbeat. If the dates you gave us are correct, it may have all been over for several weeks."

He pauses for some kind of acknowledgement. I say nothing. He says nothing. The woman just nods and gives me one of those anti-smiles, the kind you'd give a small child whose hamster has died. I'm not sure why she's here. Is she supposed to be making me feel better? Is she making sure the doctor doesn't abuse his position? I don't like her. I wish she'd just get out of the room.

"Can I get dressed now?" I say.

"Of course. Of course," says the doctor, and the woman helps me get my legs down from the stirrups. She draws a curtain for me but there are still three other people in the room. It's quiet though, really quiet, and no-one says a word while I pull on my knickers, zip up my trousers and slip my shoes back on. I put on my cotton jacket, even though it's boiling in here and I'm too warm already. I just want to go.

When I was very small, my grandpa had a greenhouse where he grew flowers. It was so full that they spilled over through the windows. And when I went to visit, he always picked the biggest most perfect flower and presented it to me like I was a special lady.

I don't remember my grandpa or his flowers, but the story was told to me so many times that it became my earliest memory.

And I don't even care whether it's true or not. Who knows whether he picked a flower for me every time we visited or just the once, or even if he ever did it at all? Memories like those aren't about what really happened, they're about what you want to believe. I want to believe it and I want to always remember it. Even when it seems totally far-fetched. Even when it's impossible to think of sunny days and flowers and friendly grandpas. That's why I wrote it down on the thickest, most expensive paper I could find, and folded it carefully and put it away somewhere safe.

I unwrap it and read it sometimes and remind myself that somewhere, close to the beginning of time, even if it's not completely true, there were perfect moments like that and I was at the centre of them. And the paper is in the front pocket of my handbag now as He drives me home from the hospital. I take it out and read it again and He's so desperate not to be the first to speak that He doesn't even ask me what it is.

It's not that I don't remember what I was like before I met Him. I do. I was a cocky teenager. A little chip on my shoulder maybe, waiting for the world to pay up. Waiting for the world to sit up and take notice of me. And maybe it would have.

These days I look in the mirror and say to the woman I see: 'I am not you, I am not you, I am not you.' And she sneers back at me. She knows I'm lying.

Other memories of life before I met Him are much more concrete than the grandpa thing, verifiable even. I remember The Six Million Dollar Man and Charlie's Angels on the TV. I remember playing Charlie's Angels in the playground. I was always Jaclyn Smith. She was beautiful, but not the most beautiful because she was clever and tough as well. She wasn't the cleverest and the toughest: that was the short-haired one, Sabrina, the one that Julie the Weirdy Girl always wanted to be. But the thing about Jaclyn Smith was that she had everything – she could fight the bad guys in an evening dress while doing a crossword – and I planned to grow up to be her.

I planned to grow up to be her, but I never had much of a plan. I was going to get invited to all the best parties, have flings with pop-star heart-throbs, then stoically leave them in tatters because our lifestyles were simply incompatible. Then somehow I'd meet the man of my dreams and live happily ever after. Things were supposed to just fall into place.

Julie the Weirdy Girl had a plan. First of all her plan was to have a horse, and in the meantime she was quite content to gallop around the playground on her imaginary horse, neighing at people as she went past and leaping over their carefully drawn hopscotch. Some people assumed she thought she actually was a horse, but that would just be stupid. She was weird, no doubt about it, but she wasn't nuts. She planned to do well in her exams and go to university. She planned to be top of the class and be snapped up by the best law firm who would train her to be a hotshot so that she could make sure justice was always done, just like on TV. She was going to be champion of the downtrodden and friend of the needy. She didn't care what she looked like and she made no big plans for romance. She just wanted to be clever and make her cleverness count.

These days Julie the Weirdy Girl has a house and a car but no wedding ring. I see her sometimes in the supermarket, choosing wine from the top shelf where there's nothing under £10 a bottle.

When I see her I want to ask her, "Why didn't you warn me?" I want to say to her, "Why didn't you tell me to be Sabrina?" I want to ask her if it's too late to change my mind. But I don't speak to her.

She probably doesn't see me. She probably wouldn't recognise me anyway.

He's not looking at me, just at the road, as though He's not sure of the route back from the hospital and needs to concentrate. He doesn't know what to say, which is good, because I don't want Him to say anything. In fact, I don't care if He never says anything ever again. I know what He wants to say. He wants to say "I'm sorry" and fix it all. And then He wants me to say "It's OK." He wants me to say "It's not your fault." But it is his fault. How could it not be his fault?

We get home and He still doesn't know what to say and He hovers while I hang my coat up. Maybe He's waiting for me to cry. Maybe He's waiting for me to ask Him how He is.

"Are you OK?" I ask.

"I'll be OK," He says. "Will you?"

"I'm going for a bath," I say. How am I supposed to answer a stupid question like that?

"Good idea," He answers. Sure it is. Genius. He gets to escape from trying to find something to say and I get to go upstairs and spend some quiet time with the dead baby that's still inside me. Tomorrow they'll get rid of it.

I have never been a water-baby but in the bath I sink my head under the water and hear my heart beat thumping in my head out of my ears and into the water and I feel like I am the water and it is me. We are singing, me and the water, getting to know each other. "Keep me here with you, Water", I say inside my head.

Is this what it was like for my baby?

I'm thinking about what it would be like to be water all the time. To flow quickly in and out. To find holes to seep into. To part and reform when solid things got in my way. To trickle and drip in different directions at once. To know I could be ice, or steam or water. I'm thinking myself into water.

His hand grabs me by the neck and pulls up so that I can't breathe and I can't hear my heart in my head any more, I can only hear it banging in my ears.

"For fuck's sake Marion," He shouts and scoops all of me out of the bath like I'm seaweed.

2

On Mondays I swim. He knows I've been swimming because He can smell the chlorine on my skin. He knows how long it takes me to drive to the pool, pay myself in, get changed, swim forty lengths, wash my hair, get dressed and come home. He hears my key in the door and shouts hello from the living room.

"Good swim?" He says.

"Yes," I say. "The pool was busy tonight though," I say. Or something like that.

Then he watches me as I take my wet towel and swimming costume out of my swimming bag. He gets up from the sofa.

"I'll put that in the washing machine for you," He says and comes over and takes them out of my hand. He checks to see that they are wet. He kisses me on the cheek and checks for the smell of chlorine on my skin.

"See anyone you know?" He asks. He means, "Did you speak to anyone?", or "Did you meet up with someone?" or "Have you been fucking someone in the changing rooms?" I know what He means, He doesn't need to say it aloud. And I find myself feeling guilty and wondering if maybe I have looked at someone with a bit more interest than I should have done. Perhaps He's had someone go to the swimming pool to check up on me and make sure I'm not having some sort of aquatic affair that survives on a one-hour poolside liaison a week. But I know I've just been swimming and thinking and counting the lengths and watching the clock and taking note of my fellow swimmers – the regulars and the once-in-a blue-mooners. I know I've done nothing that even He could reproach me for. But still I panic that I won't be able to justify myself.

So I think of something to tell Him. I say "The old woman with the tattoo was there today. People should think about what their tattoos will look like when they're all old and wrinkly before they have them done." Or I say, "There was a pair of fat women there who swam about two lengths then just chatted at the side of the pool. What's the point of that? They could have just walked to the pub and got more exercise!"

And as I dry my hair I do think about the people I saw at the pool this evening. It's not a huge crowd – it's a Monday evening and a pool that's seen better days, so it's never going to be top of the 'exciting nights out' list – but it's a small private world that He knows nothing about, just the odd alibi I drop in here and there. Of course I don't know the people, not even the diehard every-weekers: they never say hello to me and I never so much as smile at them. But I know them well in a strange sort of way, their physical peculiarities, their swimming pool routines, what time they will leave. And I wonder about where they live, who is at home waiting for them and what they'll do when they get back there.

I wonder whether, for them too, the pool is as much a place for thinking as for swimming. Is that why they go? The bald guy with the dodgy leg that just drags behind him as he swims. The skinny girl with the goggles who just swims and swims and swims, expecting everyone else to get out of her way like she's some sort of Olympic champion. The old tattooed woman. The pervy old fella that showers for as long as he swims, gawping at the rest of us while he soaps himself over and over. The couple with ginger hair who stop for a chat between lengths. What do they think about while they swim up and down?

For me, each slow, deliberate stroke is like the ticking of a clock. A clock that replays the week in slow motion. I am not a swimmer. My technique hasn't progressed since, aged eight, I was awarded a certificate for the earth-shattering achievement of completing the 25 metres without drowning. But I can draw back the water with a strong, purposeful rhythm that's automatic enough that I needn't think about it. So while my body moves my mind rewinds and replays. It remembers what was said, it records a picture of where I was standing, what I was wearing, what His face looked like. It sets out a complete guide to what I felt like, how I responded to every detail and how I wanted to respond but didn't. And as I swim and count the lengths and check the clock to make sure I don't outstay my curfew, I let myself drift off into a parallel universe where things happen differently, I can make them happen differently, and alternative endings become part of the plot. I can invent scenarios that fit straight into my swimming pool diaries like the real thing. In this place, where sound is distorted and I am weightless in the water, who's to say what's real and what's not?

Then when I get to forty lengths, or sometimes forty-two in case I've lost count without realising it, I climb out of the pool, wash my hair, and climb back into my own skin in the changing room.

On Tuesdays He buys me flowers. Every Tuesday without fail. No matter what's happened in the day. No matter what's happened the day before. It would be nice to think that it's because he missed me on Monday evening. It's not. It's because we met on a Tuesday. He's kept up the Tuesday flower tradition ever since.

The flowers are often roses and are always pink. He says red flowers are vulgar. He says it's pink for nice girls. He says pink to make the boys wink. He pulls them from behind his back as though He were trying to surprise me, as though He didn't give me flowers every Tuesday. And He winks and says pink to make the boys wink. And He holds them out towards me and grins as though He were the first person ever to think of giving a girl flowers, as though these were the only flowers on earth.

And every Tuesday I smile back at Him and take the flowers. I hold them up to my nose and look at them and then at Him as I sniff them. I sniff them theatrically. And He grins in approval.

And I say, "They're beautiful. I don't know where you get them from. You always find the most beautiful flowers." Or something like that. I say "I must put them in water while they're still fresh." I go in the kitchen to put them in water. Sometimes He suggests a vase and follows me into the kitchen. And sometimes He doesn't.

Then I bring them in the living room and put them on the mantelpiece so that we can see them from anywhere in the room. And I stand back and say "lovely," or "gorgeous" or "perfect". And He repeats my word, whichever word I choose. Then He wanders up to them and re-arranges them in the vase, just one or two here and there. They look no different to me after He's finished. "That's better," He says.

One Tuesday, He buys me pink gerberas. And we sit on the sofa watching TV and He explains the subtext of the news to me, as usual. I ask the odd question so that He knows I'm listening but He mostly doesn't hear the questions, He just tells me what He thinks. But then I ask a question that He says is facetious. I tell Him it's not. I tell Him I lose track with African politics but it's too late. He doesn't believe me. And suddenly I find myself eating the flowers He's so carefully rearranged for me and drinking the water I'd put them in.

He pulls off the petals, one by one at first, then three or four at a time as He starts to run out of patience. He passes them to me so that I can eat them. He passes me the petals, then the heads of the flowers and then sends me into the kitchen for a knife and fork. Then He puts the stalks on the coffee table and cuts them into pieces with the knife and fork. He feeds me the pieces of stalk off the end of the fork. And I imagine that they're delicious. I imagine that they're a delicious, vitamin enriched, strength-giving vegetable and chew them slowly so that He has to wait to give me the next piece.

He gives up before the end of the second stalk and tips the table over, sprinkling the rest of the pieces of stalk across the floor. He leaves the house. I clear away the pieces of stalk and put the coffee table the right way up.

I don't feel sick; I don't even feel like crying. I just feel relieved that that's all there is, just a bit of indigestion maybe and some mess to clear up. Nothing broken, nothing that will leave a stain. Nothing that will leave a mark of any kind, permanent or otherwise.

And within an hour He's back. He has a fresh bunch of flowers, a perfect match for the ones I've eaten. He apologises. A bad day at work. "That fucking loser from accounts," He says. "Fucking jobsworth that just likes to make himself the big 'I am' by making everyone else feel small," He says. So I apologise for not asking Him about his day and sympathise about the loser from accounts.

And before I know it I have my nose against the mattress and He's telling me I'm a dirty bitch with a gorgeous arse.

On Wednesday nights He goes out. "To see a man about a dog," He says. He thinks a euphemism is better than a lie. Or maybe He wants me to guess. Or maybe He wants me to spend all night wondering and worrying what He's up to and if He's coming back. I've given up wondering. Instead I just use the time to do the stuff He doesn't approve of. I watch trashy TV, I eat toast with no plate, I bid for things I have no intention of buying on eBay.

3

There are other women. Don't ask me how I know, but I know. Where else would He be on Wednesday nights? What else would He be up to when He disappears off to 'visit friends' for the weekend and I'm not invited? They are the man He has to see about a dog.

Call it instinct if you like. Call it paranoia. Call it whatever you like, but I know there are other women.

There's a tall one. She's a blonde. A blonde in the old-fashioned 1950s sense of it. Blonde straight from the bottle and not at all bothered who knows it. She's high maintenance and He expects her to stay that way. Tells her off if her roots are showing. Loves to watch her put on her perfect make up and paint her filthy lips red like a whore. He has her stand naked in front of the full-length mirror while he watches her put her make-up on. And when she's finished creating a perfect red pout He has her kneel on the carpet, unzip his flies and smudge her perfect lipstick as He watches Himself come in her mouth. And He brings those red lipstick rings home with Him and makes sure I see them.

She's beautiful, there's no doubt about it. She turns heads wherever they go and He loves that. He keeps a close grip on her as other men leer at her and gives them a 'fuck you, she's mine' look as they pass.

She's beautiful, but she's not flawless. She brushes her peroxide hair forward to hide a mole on the side of her head. It's on a level with her eye, and He thinks of it as a third eye. It's like a kind of voodoo and He worries that she can see into his thoughts with it. She's careful to keep it hidden and most of the time it is. But sometimes, when He calls her name and she turns her head suddenly, or when they're busy fucking and she forgets to think about how she looks, her hair falls back and there it is.

He tries not to wince when he sees it. He tries to pretend that He likes it. And sometimes He even kisses it because He thinks it'll make her happy to know that He loves even her ugly mole. But when He kisses her on the mole on the side of her face she hates Him for making her admit that it's there.

Her name is Dorothy, after her grandmother. But she doesn't like the name or the grandmother and she insists that people call her Dee. So He calls her Dee nearly all the time. Nearly all the time, apart from when they're doing it. Then He calls her 'Dor-o-thee, Dor-o-thee, Dor-o-thee.'

Of course, she knows about me. She knows I exist, that is. She knows nothing about me though, only what He's told her, which isn't much and isn't even true. She thinks I'm a sap who doesn't understand Him. She thinks I'm some middle-aged frump that doesn't excite Him and forces Him to seek solace between her thighs. She's stupid, Dee for Dorothy. She doesn't even know Him. She doesn't even know that she's one of many. She has no idea that she's one in a long line. Not even the one of the moment. When He rings her to say He can't make it tonight she thinks it's me that's getting in the way, not some other deluded pretty young thing that's caught his eye.

She thinks He'll leave me one of these days. And maybe He will. But not for her. She thinks He'll leave me and they'll have a fairy tale wedding and babies and a perfect house with a kitchen-diner. She thinks He'll love her forever. But that's not what He does.

I wonder how I'd feel if He did want to leave me for her, or for any of them. I wonder what I would do. Maybe I'd be hysterical and rant at them and the neighbours would call the police. But I don't think so. I'd like to think that I'd just let them get on with it. I might even help Him pack. I might even make her a cup of tea and dig out a packet of biscuits so that we could have a civilised chat about how we were going to work it all out calmly. That would piss Him off. It would be worth making myself look like the pathetic sap she thinks I am just to piss Him off that much. It won't ever happen, though. I try to imagine it happening but even in my head it doesn't seem possible.

With Dee for Dorothy I imagine her deciding that enough is enough, it's time to force the issue. There'd be no clever games involved, just a this-is-what-I-want-and-this-is-how-I intend-to-get-it scene, something crass and obvious, like the red underwear she wears under her skin-tight jumpers.

It would be his birthday. He and I would be getting ready to go out. He would be helping me choose what to wear and telling me what jewellery to put on with it. And she would turn up at the door with a bottle of Champagne and an I've-come-to-take-your-husband-and-there's-not-a-thing-you-can-do-about-it grin.

I'd answer, and she'd say something like "I've come to see the birthday boy," and before I could reply He'd be there, pushing past me in the hallway in the hope of shooing her away before I worked out who she was.

But she's too quick for Him, old Dee for Dorothy. Way too quick. She'd be thrusting the bottle towards Him saying something like "happy birthday darling, I didn't think you'd mind!" But He wouldn't take it. He'd grab her arm and push her back towards the door and say something like "well I do mind you stupid bitch." So then she'd say something clichéd and impossible for me to misinterpret. She'd say "But I thought you wanted us to be together." And she'd sound pathetic and He'd hate her for it and be more angry than she'd ever seen Him. "Of course I mind, you stupid, selfish bitch," He'd yell at her and He'd hit her across the face so that she fell to the floor and dropped the bottle.

And He might even spit on her as He stepped over her and out of the house. And He wouldn't even look at me or say a word to me the whole time. Then He could come back later and we could both pretend that I hadn't seen any of it and it had never happened.

But while He was out having a drink and deleting Dee for Dorothy from his mind, the house would be quiet and I would need to clear up the mess. So I'd pick Dee for Dorothy up off the floor and take her into the living room to sit down. I'd open her bottle of Champagne and bring two glasses and we'd have a drink together and she'd pour out her heart to me as though we were good friends, even though she'd still hate me and I'd still hate her. And she'd cry and we'd drink until the bottle was empty and I would pat her on the shoulder and get to be the smug one who knows everything and has seen it all before, for once.

When she was ready to go, I'd like to think I'd pack a bag, ring a taxi for us both, ring the speaking clock in New York and disappear off into the sunset with her forever, leaving Him with the empty Champagne bottle and no note. That'd be great. That'd be perfect.

But I know that's not what I'd do in real life. I'd ring a taxi all right, but just for Dee for Dorothy. I'd put the bottle out with the recycling, wash the glasses and get on with some ironing, or something like that. And when He arrived back an hour later, I'd be ready to pretend that nothing had happened.

4

When we arrive at the hospital they're not expecting me. The woman on reception takes my name and I start to explain why I'm here but I can feel myself losing track of what I'm trying to say and she stops me.

"It's OK love," she says. "I'll go and find out what's happened to your file."

I hate it when people call me love, but I don't say anything.

And she seems nice, actually. She hands me a box of tissues and when I've taken one she pulls another couple out of the box and hands them to me. Then she gets up from behind the desk and comes round to lead me by the elbow.

He stands beside me, looking round as though He's weighing up whether the place could do with a coat of paint.

"Come and have a sit down in here while I track down your notes," she says. "Help yourself to water from the machine. The nurse will come through and see you as soon as she can."

So we sit down in this waiting-room-cum-living-room. It looks like a cross between the lounge in an old folks' home and a student common room. There are unwashed coffee cups on the table, the odd chocolate wrapper and magazines that are weeks old with 'shock break-up' and 'baby joy' headlines attached to pictures of harassed celebrities. I start tidying up. I can't help myself, but I can't find a bin to put the wrappers in and I don't know where to put the cups.

"Is there a bin?"

He doesn't answer me.

"D'ya want some water?" He says, standing by the water cooler with a little paper cone in his hand.

I don't answer Him either. He's not bothered. He's found a machine and he wants to use it. He fills up a little cone and knocks it back. Then fills it again and drinks it again. He takes another cone and offers it to me and I have to take it because he can't put it down, it's pointy on the bottom. It's a pointless, pointy thimbleful of water. But that's not going to curb his enthusiasm. Far from it, the novelty of drinking water from a big upside down barrel out of a tiny paper cone is too much for Him to resist. He just stands there like a little kid filling it over and over again and drinking and filling and drinking again. And I remember how endearing I always found that kiddiness. He could never resist kicking a ball or anything he could kick instead of a ball, like an empty toilet roll tube or a packet of crisps. And I know that when I'm not looking he still takes the top off a custard cream and licks out all the cream from the middle before he eats the biscuit.

While he's drinking an ocean one tiny cone at a time, I can't help joining the live TV audience in the corner of the room as they watch some know-it-all TV presenter put some hapless couple's life in order while they squabble in public. I find myself needing to know whether he really is the father of her son. I sip my water while I and the studio audience wait to hear the lie detector results that will prove whether she has, in fact, been having an affair with his cousin.

"I'm going to switch that drivel off," He says, finally abandoning the water cooler to hunt for the TV remote. "You weren't watching it were you?" He says as he switches it off.

Silence.

So we sit not watching the TV or reading magazines, or drinking water or talking or not talking and I try not to listen in to the woman talking on a pay phone just outside the room, but I can't help it.

She's talking way too loud, like a pensioner on a mobile phone, as though the sound of her voice needs to reach the other person by travelling down the wire on the end of the receiver. She's telling them in great detail about her fallopian tubes and what the doctor has said and what her options are and how she feels about it. Maybe she just doesn't realise that we can all hear her. Or maybe she just wants to share her misery with as many people as possible, like the mismatched couple on TV.

She's totally matter-of-fact. If she was having this conversation in another language and I couldn't understand the words, I might think she was talking about what she plans to cook for dinner. And the more she says the words 'fallopian tubes' the less real they are. They sound like some long-forgotten musical instrument from a Pacific Island and I can hear the advert for an album of fallopian tube classics on TV: "From the foothills of Fallopia, the haunting sound of the fallopian tubes brings alive all your favourite anthems from the world's greatest artists...."

"Is it Marion?"

The nurse walks into the room and knocks quietly on the open door as she comes in.

I start again trying to explain why I'm here but she stops me again. It seems that no-one actually wants to hear me talk about it. Maybe I need to go and use the payphone – but who would I ring? Perhaps there's not even anyone on the other end. It's just a prop so that fallopian tube woman can run through all the stuff that's happening to her without being politely interrupted by people who'd rather she didn't cry in public.

"I'm Maxine," the nurse says. "I'll be looking after you today. I'm sorry about the mix-up," she says, turning to Him as though putting us in a room with other people's dirty coffee cups is more of an inconvenience to Him than to me. "I've got your file now though, and we were expecting you, it's just been a bit crazy in here today. One of those days." And she grimaces in the hope that we can all roll our eyes together about how crazy it's been and how it's all OK now though, because they've found my file.

"We've got you your own room," she says, smiling and gesturing with her arm for me to walk with her out into the corridor. "It's a nice quiet one and it's just near the nurses' office so if you need anything just bob your head round and one of us will be along to help. As I say, I'm looking after you today but if I'm not around just ask any of the nurses." She smiles at me and I follow her past the reception desk and round the corner. He follows behind us, carrying my bag with my pyjamas in it.

"Here we are," she says cheerily, as she opens a door with a number 4 on it and a sliding sign on the front that currently says 'knock before entering'. I want to slide the sign back to see what the alternative message might be. I don't want people to knock before entering I just want them to go away, but it seems unlikely that the alternative message on the sign will say 'Fuck off and leave me alone'. Anyway, they're both waiting for me to walk into the room first so I don't mess with the sign on the door, I just go in and sit down on the bed as though I'm waiting for someone to finish using the bathroom so that I can go in and brush my teeth.

He plonks my bag down on the bed next to me and she carries on talking in her cheery tone. I wonder if they have lessons in getting the cheery tone right. Perhaps she practices in front of a mirror at home to make sure it's just the right side of keep-your-spirits-up and never tips over the edge into you'll-look-back-on-this-and-have-a-good-laugh-one-of-these-days. But she's nice though. Somewhere in the middle of telling me that I've got my own bathroom and I should run the hot water in the shower first because it can be a bit temperamental she stops talking.

"I know it's going to be tough," she says, "but you will get through it and we're here to help you. Honestly, if there's anything you need just press the button and we'll be here as quickly as we can."

And then she comes over to the bed and sits beside me and squeezes my hand. And I find myself wondering how she does this day in, day out.

She pats me on the knee and gets up to fetch a tissue from the window ledge, except it's not even a proper window, just a window onto the reception area. I am locked away here, I can't see out and no-one can see in.

"Tissues are just here," she says, offering me a handful.

"It's like a hotel," He chips in suddenly. "Where's the mini bar?"

Maxine forces a smile but I don't bother. Why should I?

"Hospitals make me nervous," He starts to explain.

"Everyone has their own way of dealing with things," Maxine says, kindly. And I hate her for giving Him excuses. Why should it be down to this complete stranger to squeeze my hand or offer me a tissue?

"I'll let you get settled in," Maxine says. "Would you both like a cup of tea?"

I smile at her.

"Coming right up," she says, and she opens the door just wide enough for her to fit through and closes it super quietly as though leaving an infant to sleep.

"Is the loo through here then?" He asks me, as though I know the place like the back of my hand.

"I think so."

And while he's in the toilet, I start unpacking my bag for something to do but there isn't anywhere to put anything. This isn't a room where they want you to spend very much time. It's a quick in and out job. Don't get settled, don't make a meal of it. Let's just sort it out and have done. I put my pyjamas under my pillow and line up my toothbrush, toothpaste, shampoo, soap, face cream and towel on the bed ready to take them into the bathroom when He emerges. Then there are two books. The one I couldn't get into when we were on holiday last summer and the one I bought when I went to get some new pyjamas for tonight. The blurb on the back says, 'don't buy this book unless you're happy for people to stare at you when you laugh out loud.' Hmmm. I can always leave it behind when I go. I won't be here long and by the time I go it'll all be over, the baby will be well and truly gone and I will be just the same. And so will He.

I put the books on the chair next to the bed.

He reappears from the bathroom.

"Okay?" He asks.

I nod. "Are you?"

"Actually I feel I bit dodgy," He says. And I think He might go on to tell me all about his symptoms and look for my sympathy, so I just pick up the things that I've laid out on the bed and take them into the bathroom.

When I open the door to the room He's sitting on the bed with my book in his hand but He's not looking at it. He's sobbing. His shoulders are shaking and, even though He has his back to me, I can tell there must be tears. I don't know what I'm supposed to do. I slip back into the bathroom, flush the toilet and turn on the tap which shoots out water like a waterfall and splashes me all down my front.

When I get back into the room again, the tea that Maxine promised us has arrived and He's lying on the bed as though He's just been snoozing the whole time.

"Just checking it's comfy enough for you," He jokes. But He doesn't get up and I just perch on the end of the bed with my cup of tea while he idly reaches for the books I left on the chair and reads the back of each of them, raising his eyebrows but saying nothing.

"I might head off," He says after a while.

I look at Him and don't know what to say.

"You don't need me here, do you?" He adds. "The doctor'll be in to see you soon and I'll just be in the way."

I can't find the words to say 'don't leave me here alone' so I just keep on saying nothing.

"Unless you want me to get anything for you?" He asks hopefully. The perfect get-out: He can be caring and helpful but still be allowed to leave.

I can't sit here and watch Him pretend not to be upset and I can't deal with Him being upset either.

"No," I say. "You get off. I'll be fine. I'll give you a ring later."

And He kisses me on the forehead and goes.

5

Sometimes I have dreams that start off as dreams and end up as nightmares. But it never ever happens the other way round.

I'm walking this dog in the park. We haven't even got a dog, but in the dream it's my dog and walking it is a normal thing to do. I don't know the park in real life, which is odd because we live round the corner from a park and if we did have a dog I'd walk it there, obviously. It does have bits of places I know but it's not an actual park that I could name and it has this weird mini fun fair in it and there are people queuing all over the place to get on the rides. But in the dream I don't care about the fun fair, I'm just walking the dog and enjoying the sunshine and kicking acorns off the path as I walk. The dog is small and cute and people keep smiling at me and the cute little dog running like fury to keep up with my walking pace. It's not even on a lead, it's just scurrying along beside me like we're some kind of Crufts champions putting on an obedience display for the judges.

And then as we're walking along, without warning the dog jumps up at me. It starts to bite me and it's suddenly much bigger than it was before. It looks like a wolf now and it's biting me and snarling and pushing me to the ground. And a crowd gathers. All the people who were out walking their dogs and all the people who were queuing for the fun fair gather round to watch me being savaged by this big, wild dog. But not one of them comes to help me, they just watch. They don't look at all horrified or concerned. They just watch.

I wake up to find I'm bleeding all over the bed. The clock on the wall says it's twenty past eleven. That means I've been here for six hours.

I call for the nurse.

"I'll help you get yourself sorted out," she says. And she takes charge and I feel like a kid that's been sick in the playground being looked after by the teacher.

"D'you need the loo?" she says and hands me something that looks like a bowler hat made of recycled cardboard. "Just wee into that for me love," she says, "then we can make sure we know when you've passed everything."

She gives me one of those smiles and I just hold onto the cardboard bowler hat and watch her while she strips the bed.

"It's OK, love. I'll sort this out. You just get yourself to the bathroom."

So now I'm like some weird phobic in the bathroom. I steel myself to sit on the toilet with the bowler hat underneath me and when I've finished I reach forward and take a handful of paper towels to drape over the bowl. I don't want to see what's in there. I know what's in there, if not now, then next time I go, or the time after that.

I carry the bowler hat back into the bedroom and the nurse has made the bed for me and brought me a fresh jug of water

"I'll take that," she says, holding her hand out for the bowler hat, "you get yourself back into bed. You look pale. Are you OK? D'you you need any pain relief?"

"Got any Rohypnol?" She forces a smile and so do I.

"I can offer you an injection that will help relax your muscles and reduce the pain," she says. "It might help you sleep."

But I don't want to sleep. I can't just sleep while my baby leaves me, what kind of mother would that make me?

"I'll leave you then," she says once I'm back in bed. "But don't forget, if you need anything, just buzz."

She gives me another one of those smiles and reaches over to turn the lamp off but I ask her not to.

"OK then love," she says, "but you try to get some sleep." And she opens the door silently and slips out.

In the quiet I can hear the sound of my own breathing. How many breaths will it take until morning? If I hold my breath can I stop time passing? Can I stop this baby, dead as it is, from leaving me? I look at the clock. It's hardly moved since the last time I looked at it.

This room is stuck in time. It looks like it's been 1983 in here ever since about 1987 when it was decorated to look like the living room of a suburban semi. If I turn on the TV there'll probably be an episode of *Dynasty* or *Knight Rider*. It's all calm and matching with pastel scrolls that repeat around the room. If I squint my eyes they turn into dragons chasing each other around the walls and I swear I can see them moving, nose to tail, in an endless circuit. It takes me back to the curtains in the bedroom I had as a kid. Dark green and brown and navy with a big, repeating floral pattern. In the daytime they just had big flowers on, but at night they were covered in witches and ugly bogeymen and all kinds of monsters.

There's nothing scary like that in this room, unless you count the reminders of the decade that taste forgot. But I'm scared. I'm scared of being alone here and I'm scared of leaving here and having to just go back to normal.

I close my eyes. Those dragons are driving me nuts. I need the loo but I don't want to go. How long can I lie here, needing the loo but not going? If I were on a bus I could hang on. Pretend you're on a bus. Pretend you've only just got on and it's half an hour until the bus gets where it's going. Now stop thinking about it. Stop thinking about it. Think about something else.

I pick up one of the books that I brought with me but I can't concentrate. Maybe it's a slow burner. I skip to chapter two but I still have no idea what the story is. Chapter three. Last page. I need the loo. I'm going to have to go to the loo.

So I pick up another bowler hat and go into my little en-suite where the fluorescent light fitting flickers and hums. I quickly switch it off again. I can see as much as I need to from the light in the main room. In fact that's better. I can only just see well enough so the chances of seeing something I don't want to are slim to nil. I feel odd. Woozy. I love that word. I wonder if it's a real word. Who invents the words that aren't real words?

Woooooozy. That's more like it. My belly is aching and my legs are all heavy and prickly so I end up sitting there on the loo for a good few minutes just in case I stumble when I get up and make a mess. I sit there with a huge handful of paper towels in my hand ready to cover the bowl as soon as I stand up. Then I finally place the bowl carefully on the floor while I wash my hands and congratulate myself for being so brave. I am doing this on my own. He can't touch it.

I press the button by the bed and Denise the nurse, a different one, comes to take the bowler hat from me. She asks me if I need anything and smiles before slipping off to perform the thankless task of looking at what's in the bowl. I'm glad I'm not her. Fancy having to look through other people's business like that. Fancy having to come to work and find the right thing to say to a bunch of women who are totally miserable and don't want to talk to anybody. I'm rubbish at things like that. I can never say the right thing. I'm lucky if I manage to get through a day without saying completely the wrong thing.

I lie back in the bed again but I can't get comfortable sitting up, the pillows are too thin and the bedstead is metal and digs in to my shoulders. So I lie down and decide to give myself a break from the book for a while. I can just have a think while I lie here. It's good to have time for a bit of a think. But I find I haven't a thought in my head apart from the baby.

It's the ceiling tiles that come to my rescue. They surely can't be polystyrene but they look like it. Big white squares all across the ceiling, each with lots of little holes in. I start trying to count how many tiny holes there are in each tile but the dots play tricks on my eyes and I keep losing count. I try again. Maybe if I just count the number of dots going across the tile and multiply that by the number of dots going downwards, then I'll be able to work out the number of dots per tile and then I'll be able to count the number of tiles and work out the number of dots in the whole room.

Maths never was my strong point and I never do get to the answer because suddenly I can hear the sound of a phone ringing and apparently it's morning.

A nurse pops her head round the door.

"Hiya", she smiles, "I'm Jess, "I'll be looking after you today. Though we should be able to let you go home pretty soon," she adds. I'm not sure whether to feel relieved or bereft.

She comes and perches on the side of my bed and tells me that I've passed everything they need to see during the night and it reminds me of passing my driving test. "I'm pleased to tell you that you've passed..." For a minute I think she's going to be like the driving examiner and pull out a clip chart and run me through everything bullet point by bullet point but she just starts asking me about arrangements for being picked up and whether I'd like to use the phone in reception.

And suddenly I find myself crying. How stupid is that? I've managed to get through the whole night on my own without crying and then I blub in front of a complete stranger. She looks round for tissues but the box is empty so she raids my en-suite for toilet paper.

The toilet paper sort of disintegrates and I sniff and force a smile which she takes as her cue to let go of my hand again and get on with the business of getting me out of here.

"I've got a few leaflets to give you," she says. "Is there someone at home to take care of you?"

"My husband will be working but I think He'll be home in the evenings," I say. "And I think He was going to ask my mum if she would come and stay for a couple of days."

"Perfect," says Jess, smiling again. "And if you need to talk to someone outside the family there's a helpline number on here. They're very good."

She takes a pen out of her pocket and puts a big asterisk next to the helpline number on a leaflet before she hands it to me. "You know, lots of women find they fall pregnant straight away after miscarrying. It's like nature putting things back the way they were supposed to be."

I muster a smile.

"Now there's no rush," she says. "When you're ready you can come and use the phone on reception to ring your husband about picking you up and then we'll take it from there. OK?"

"Thanks," I mumble.

6

When He gets to the hospital I'm in the shower and He's cross because I'm not ready to go. I couldn't help it. Once I was under the water I just didn't want to get out. The water is warm – on the hot side of warm – and I stand with my back to the flow of it with my head dipped forward, letting it splash off the back of my neck and trickle down my back. It's a tiny little cubicle and the shower head isn't very big but the water pressure makes it belt out like a torrential downpour; the noise of my shower rain against the hard floor and Perspex door is like the sound rain makes in my mum's conservatory. I turn round and open my mouth and let the water gush in and trickle out again.

I wasn't going to wash my hair but there was a bottle of shampoo already in there. Someone else must have left it behind – perhaps they were being chivvied along by an impatient husband and just left it by accident. It's posh stuff and it smells so lovely that I decide to use it. It's nice to smell the unfamiliar and step out of the shower smelling like somebody else so I do take my time, just like Jess said, and I think 'sod Him.'

"I thought you said you'd be ready to go when I got here," He snaps at me as soon as I walk back into the bedroom.

I think about saying, "I didn't expect you to get here so quickly," but instead I just say "Sorry, I won't be long."

"Well, just get a move on," He sighs. "We've got about another fifteen minutes free parking, then we have to pay for two hours."

I wonder if expensive shampoo woman had to pack up her things and throw her clothes on in record time to avoid shelling out £2 on the car park. Probably not, I'm guessing. If she can spend a tenner on a bottle of shampoo, two quid on a car park is neither here nor there for her. It's no big deal to Him either, it's just an excuse to hurry me out of here because He hates being in the hospital. He'd rather whinge about the cost of parking than trot out the old cliché about how the smell of hospitals turns his stomach. Not that this place smells like a hospital at all. All I can smell now is the perfume from the shampoo, but even before that it smelt mostly like school dinners.

I wonder if shampoo woman's husband asked her how it went. Perhaps he even stayed the night with her on the put-you-up bed in the corner. They offered the bed to Him but He said it was best if He went home. My mother's coming today so He thought He'd better make sure the place was presentable for her. There's no way He's so much as plumped a cushion, I know that. And He knows that I know it was just an excuse. But He won't say anything and neither will I. And anyway, I only wanted Him to offer to stay. I didn't want Him to actually be here. What would have been the point of that?

I get dressed quickly and start shoving things into my bag. He starts putting things in too, trying to be helpful, but it's just annoying. He puts my wet towel on top of my pyjamas so the whole lot will be damp by the time we get home. But I don't say anything. I decide to give Him the benefit of the doubt: He's just trying to be kind.

"Thanks," I say.

"It's all over now," He says. And that's it.

"Let's go then," He says. But I need to check that I have everything, so I ask Him to wait while I check in the bathroom and He offers to have a quick scout around in the bedroom for me. Anyone would think I'd been here for a fortnight the way we're hunting for things we might accidentally leave behind, but I can't quite think what I brought with me so it's not easy to do that quick mental checklist of everything I should have packed. And I feel like I'm leaving something behind. I've got that I've-forgotten-something feeling. I want to be home but I don't really want to leave.

In the bathroom I collect my toothpaste and toothbrush and the make-up bag I haven't even opened. I quickly run the hairbrush through my hair then tuck it under my arm while I have a last look round. In the shower cubicle the borrowed shampoo is still sitting there. I should leave it for the next person to find, a bonus little treat on a bad day. But I want to take it home. I really want to take it home. The smell of it will remind me of here. I want to be able to open that bottle and remember the baby I had that will never be born. I want to smell something that takes me back here and reminds me that I have spent this night all by myself and I'm OK. I wrap it in a paper towel, take it back into the bedroom and tuck it in the top of my bag. Ready.

On the way out I pop my head round the door of the nurses' office to say goodbye to Jess and let them know we're leaving but she's not there. Just in with one of the patients, apparently. I can wait if I want. Clearly, I can't wait: the car park beckons.

"I'll just get off," I say, "but if you could let Jess know that I've gone and tell her thanks for everything."

"OK, love," says the nurse, "I'll tell her."

He carries my bag back to the car and we get back there just in time to avoid paying for the car park. He puts the key in the ignition and then stops to squeeze my hand. I give his a faint squeeze back and He gives me a nurse's smile. "OK?" he whispers.

I nod. What else can I say?

There are flowers in a vase in the hall when we get home, and it's not even Tuesday.

"Lovely flowers," I say and He's pleased that I've noticed. He dumps my bag in the hall and tells me He's just got time for a cup of tea before He goes back to work. I thought He might have taken the day off. I'm sure they would have offered to let Him take the day off. But He needs to get back, He says. He's waiting for someone to return his call this afternoon and He's already missed them once, He mustn't miss them again.

Fair enough.

So He sits down and checks his watch again while I put the kettle on and take my bag upstairs. The pyjamas are wet from the towel, so I take everything out and unpack it there and then and take the damp towel and pyjamas downstairs to put them straight in the washing machine. He's made us both a cup of tea by the time I get down there. In fact He's already drunk most of his.

"I just don't know how I should feel," He says. And I think He's talking to me but He's not, He's talking to someone on his phone with that silly earpiece thing that makes Him look like He belongs on the flight deck of the Starship Enterprise.

He jumps when He sees me as though I've caught Him genuinely talking to Himself, not just looking like He's talking to Himself.

"Who was that?"

"It was Jimmy. He just rang to see how we're doing. How you're doing, you know."

Jimmy is our friend. His friend, to be honest. He's around all the time and I know exactly how he likes his tea and which are his favourite biscuits – dark chocolate digestives – but I never really have a conversation with him.

"Nice of him to ring."

"Will you be all right while I'm out?" He says. And I wonder what He would do if I said 'no'. Should I try it? Should I say 'no' and see if He stays home with me and just lets someone else take his stupid fucking precious phone call? But even if I say no He might just go back to work anyway and then where would I be? Still on my own with a very pissed-off husband, that's where. I know it's a rhetorical question so I just give Him his rhetorical answer and He glugs the last of his tea.

"I'll be off then," He says. And He gives me a kiss on the cheek and squeezes my hand again. "You will be OK, you know,"

He says. He sounds like a hypnotist giving me an instruction while I'm in my trance. When He clicks his fingers, then I will be OK. Perhaps I'll do a chicken walk every time I hear Kylie Minogue on the radio or curtsy every time I see a picture of the queen, but when the music stops I will not pass go, I will not be forced to go on the run for a crime I didn't commit and I will not in any way fall to pieces. I will be fine. I'm waiting for Him to click his fingers but He just picks up his keys, grabs his coat off the banister and goes.

And for a minute I do feel as though I'm in a trance. I can't think what I came into the kitchen for and I'm just standing there with a pair of damp pyjamas and a towel in my hand trying to think what to do next. But in the quiet I can hear the steady beep beep beep of the answering machine and that brings me right back into the room.

It's my mum, calling to tell me what time she expects to arrive. She hates talking to the machine. She rambles on in the stroppy answering machine voice she uses to indicate how pissed off she is that you've dared to be out when she's called. But actually she hardly ever rings and generally times her calls for when I'm likely to be out and then I have to remember to ring her back, because the only voice more stroppy than her answering machine voice is the voice she uses when I've taken more than 24 hours to call her back. She's coming by train, she says, and will get to the station at about six o'clock this evening and will someone ring her to tell her that they'll be here to pick her up.

I need to ring her. And I need to ring Him to let Him know what time we're expecting her. And I need to put these sodding pyjamas in the washing machine. And I don't know what to do first. Decide what to do and just do it, that's what I need to do. So I put the pyjamas and the towel in the washing machine, make another cup of tea, drink it and then ring her.

7

There are other women. Don't ask me how I know, but I know. Why else would He keep his phone switched off when He's out? Why else would He change his underpants when He gets home? Maybe I'm just paranoid, but I'm pretty sure I know.

There's an older one. She's quite a lot older than Him, ten years older at least. But she doesn't look it. She has wrinkles on her face. More wrinkles than me, but they're the right kind of wrinkles. They're the sort of wrinkles that come with great nights out and laughing with friends. They are the marks of experience. Her wrinkles tell you something about how she's lived and what she knows. She knows plenty.

She's strong but she's not invincible. She thinks she's so capable and that's what makes her vulnerable. Little Miss Independent who can turn her hand to anything, she thinks. Nothing bad ever happens to her, does it? She's good at life and woe betide the person who tries to prove otherwise. But then one day someone does. She's mugged. Someone snatches her bag when she's out shopping. And for once in her life she's one-nil down to the low-life scum she crosses the street to avoid. She's a loser. Her handbag is gone and her dignity with it. From here on in she can be as clever and middle class as she likes but she'll always know that some thug spotted her and saw her as an old lady. The knowledge shakes her up much more than being jostled and robbed by some chancer on the street. Even before she takes stock of what she's lost in that bag, it dawns on her that she'll never be able to even the score. A line has been crossed and she can't step back over it.

And while everyone else just walks past and leaves her to it, He stops to offer help and see if she's OK. It's not like Him. He's not one of your natural have-a-go-heroes. Don't get involved, He always says to me. But that day He's a real knight in shining armour. Her very own Sir Galahad. And – let's give Him the benefit of the doubt – I think He genuinely offers her help out of some sense of civic responsibility. From across the street He sees what the mugger saw, a vulnerable old lady, a victim. But close up He sees that she's not that old after all. He sees that she's beautiful. He reads her wrinkles and sees that she likes to have fun. Within seconds He's already planning the fun they could have together.

And she would never normally let herself be picked up by some bloke she's just met in the street like that. But she's vulnerable now. The mugger has made her feel old and weak. She needs someone to make her feel confident again. She needs an ego boost and the flattery of this younger man who has raced to her rescue is just what the doctor ordered.

And He does flatter her. He flatters her right there in the street and insists that she lets Him take her home. He rings the office with some lame excuse about how the central heating system is leaking at home and He's got to try and sort an emergency plumber. He winks at her while He's lying to his colleague on the phone. He makes her part of the charade. He makes it clear to her that He's bunking off for her benefit. She knows what He's up to and He gives her a chance to speak up and let Him know that she's not interested. But she is interested. She wants to be a naughty teenager right along with Him. She says nothing when He tells her He'll ring the office to arrange the afternoon off. She doesn't stop Him when He hesitates on the phone and she laughs with Him when He hangs up.

He walks her to her car and insists on driving her home. "I'll pick my car up later," He says. He tells her she has a nice home and suggests she has a drink for the shock. So she tells Him where the whisky is and He pours two large glasses. And when she's drunk hers He comes over to her and says something like "Let's have a look at you. Someone should check you over to make sure you've not been hurt..." and that's where it all begins. He pretends He's looking at her and touching her just to make sure she's OK. And she lets Him.

And long after the crime number and credit card cancellations, she lets Him keep the role of rescuer, counsellor, flatterer. She lives alone in a nicely turned out semi in a good area. Divorced, but amicably so, with a few bob tucked away and an ex-husband who makes sure she doesn't go without. So when He starts to pop round for coffee she's happy to invite Him in for a chat. And before too long He's sending her considerate text messages to check she's OK and starting to drop in with a nice bottle of wine on his way home from work. And, sometimes, when she asks Him if He'd like a bite to eat, He stays for dinner. They are friends, she tells herself. But she doesn't believe it any more than He does. He is just biding his time and she knows it. And she's grateful for the attention and the compliments.

Before long she's fishing for the compliments. So when He turns up unannounced and she says "Look at the state of me, I look so flat and haggard this evening," He tells her He can't see any wrinkles on her face. And when modesty makes her insist that they're there and point them out to Him, He tells her that her wrinkles are beautiful. And that's when He finally kisses her. He kisses her wrinkles. He kisses her crow's feet gently, smooths the back of his hand across her laughter lines and makes them disappear.

And she takes Him upstairs where He can see all the pots of creams and potions that she uses to try to keep the wrinkles at bay. None of them have really worked. Only her confidence and easy acceptance of the way she looks has helped to make them fade but, as soon as He sees the pathetic attempts she's made to keep the years at bay with her fancy jars of oily gloop, they all seem to jump back into place. Suddenly He looks at her and sees a woman that's far too old for Him. He's appalled by the sinews in her neck and the little lines pointing the way all around her mouth to her thin, dry lips. He knows straight away that He can't kiss those lips. He won't be able to do it whatever she does. No amount of lipstick or dim lighting can bring her back to being the woman He followed up those stairs just a few moments ago.

But she's waiting for Him now. She's waiting to reward his patience and his flattery with whatever He wants. He's trapped. If He just leaves now, what will she think? She'll think He's not up to the job. He can't have that. But she's starting to unbutton her long-sleeved blouse. Undoing each button slowly while looking Him straight in the eye like the seductress He thought she was only five minutes ago. He knows He has to do something. He's scared to catch sight of her body under those clothes. Scared it will be saggy and wrinkled. So He grabs tight hold of her wrists to stop her from undressing any further and leans her over the dressing table with her nose face down against all her face creams. He pulls her skirt up and over her back like a cape, pulls her knickers down and holds on to her tiny waist. Then there's just his own face in the mirror and the tiny, girlish waist in his hands.

And afterwards He's sorry but He has to go. He'll ring her. He'll see her soon. He kisses her on the cheek and He's gone and she doesn't know why. She doesn't know what to think.

She texts Him that evening but He doesn't reply, He just deletes it. He doesn't call her, He doesn't pop round for coffee. He doesn't drop in on his way back from work. And after a while she doesn't even bother texting Him any more.

8

I want to lie down and sleep for a hundred years.

Instead I am standing in the living room ironing pillow cases. In the other room, the washing machine is spinning the duvet covers and the floor is juddering as it whirrs round.

When I was small I used to watch my mum doing the ironing and I was fascinated. There was something much more exciting about ironing than any other jobs around the house because it involved dangerous equipment that I'd been warned never to touch. The iron was exotic. It let out huge clouds of steam and created a smell of clean that was home on a rainy Sunday with Little House on the Prairie on the TV and a big mug of hot chocolate. Even now the smell of warm fabric conditioner makes me think of those little girls in their petticoats running down a hill.

My mum ironed everything. Not just my clothes, but towels, bedding, my dad's handkerchiefs, even his underwear. The handkerchiefs were the most intriguing. In other people's houses they had tissues, kept in boxes on the sideboard and thrown away after their snotty child had had their nose forcibly wiped. Not in our house. In our house, if my dad wasn't around you were sent upstairs for a piece of toilet paper to wipe your nose with – guaranteed to fall to pieces on first contact with snot. If my dad was in, he would first tell me off for sniffing and then reach into his pocket for his handkerchief. The hankie he pulled from his pocket looked nothing like the neatly ironed and folded thing I watched mum place carefully in the ironing basket. When it came out of his pocket it would be more grey than white, and totally crumpled. He would look at it carefully, isolate a corner and then hand it to me with his assurances. "This bit is clean," he would say, followed by stern instructions to 'blow' and another rummage to find a second 'clean' bit before he proffered it again and demanded that I 'blow' a second time.

I asked my mum once why she spent her time ironing my dad's handkerchiefs when he was just going to screw them up in his pocket and make a mess of them. She gave me an impatient look, she sighed crossly and she said: "That's my job." She folded the ironed hankie in half and pressed the iron down firmly on it again. "He might not notice that I do it for him, but he'd notice soon enough if I stopped."

And that's why I'm standing here ironing these bloody pillow cases. Because even if my mum doesn't notice that I've ironed the sheets she'll be sleeping in tonight, He'll notice if I don't.

It's OK anyway, it gives me something to do. Mum won't be at the station until 6 o'clock, so I have plenty of time to make sure that the house is spotless before she gets here. I've already cleaned out the fridge and wiped down the inside of the kitchen cupboards. All the bins are empty, I've wiped the skirting boards upstairs and down with a damp cloth and hoovered behind the sofa. And now I'm getting the bedrooms ready. Clean sheets. Not just for her in the spare bedroom but for me and Him too, so that she can't give me that face when she wanders into our room on some flimsy pretext.

And I know my ironing won't be good enough for her, despite the hours I spent absorbing her little tricks and habits from the sofa. I haven't time today to be a perfectionist and, anyway, there are some skills that you could study all your life and still never master. Ironing is like that for me. But at least I'm making the effort, there's got to be some Brownie points in that. So I'll iron the bedding and iron the clothes I'll wear for when she arrives and put some make-up on and brush my hair. She'll see that I'm bearing up.

And at some point before then I need to find time to make a cake and get something sorted for dinner. I love to bake. The smell of it in the oven makes me think 'this is how life should be.' The magic of putting a tin full of sloppy mess into the oven and bringing out a cake all soft and risen is still a little miracle to me. And I'm good at it. I'm Little Miss Domestic Goddess and no-one can tell me any different. Not my mother. Not even Him. Of course, whatever I bake, she won't eat it. I'll bake it because she'll want to see that I've made the effort. If someone's coming to stay, even if it's your mum, there's got to be a homemade dessert. But she won't eat it because she never does. She'll be watching the calories – at least in front of me – then she'll maybe agree to accept a small slice of cake from Him after I've gone to bed. And they'll enjoy it in secret while they talk about me. And she'll love every mouthful and wish she could have more but she won't mention it to me.

I'll need to cook something that can be left in the oven while we go and pick her up from the station, so that it will be ready pretty much straight away when we get back. Otherwise she'll just start dropping hints as soon as we get through the door and He'll start getting under my feet making her a piece of toast because she 'must be starving.' So I chop and assemble and wrap things in foil so that I can produce it all Blue Peter-style later – 'Here's one I prepared earlier' – and even if they say nothing at all I'll know when I carry their cleaned plates into the kitchen that they've enjoyed every last mouthful.

***

I want to lie down and sleep for a thousand years.

Instead I'm getting changed into a skirt and top and putting on make-up ready to go to the station. I'm wiping mascara off my cheek ready to start again when I hear his key in the door. He's come home early to make sure the house is just so for my mother's arrival. I should have got changed earlier. I should have known he'd get home early to make sure everything's shipshape.

He calls to me up the stairs. "Thought I'd get back a bit early in case you needed a hand with anything."

I flush the toilet to give me an extra minute or two's excuse for not coming down the stairs straight away and run the tap while I finish with my makeup.

I apologise for taking so long to come downstairs. He's already in the kitchen with the kettle in his hand and He offers me a cup of tea. I know He'll switch the kettle on and leave me to make the tea, but still, it's nice to be asked. And He smiles at me and asks if I'm OK and I let myself think that perhaps I might be…or I might be soon.

"You look nice," He says, as I stir the milk into the tea. "Is that new?"

I tell Him how I picked it up in the sale and it wasn't expensive but He's not listening, He's looking in the fridge for a quick snack before dinner.

"What's for dinner?" He asks.

"Stuffed chicken breasts," I answer. "They're in the fridge." And He rummages around in the fridge to see them.

"And what's for afters?"

"Chocolate cake." I open the tin to let Him have a look at the cake I made earlier. "I just need to put the fudge topping on it."

"Are you OK?" He asks me again and I want to say "No I'm not OK, of course I'm not OK, what do you think?"

"We'll have to go in about half an hour," I say instead, and He checks his watch as though my ability to tell the time cannot be trusted.

"So we will," He says, "I'll just grab a quick shower." And He downs the remains of his tea in one gulp and takes the stairs two at a time.

I'm not sure what to do now. I could finish the cake but it might take longer than I've got and then I'll be in trouble for not being ready to go when He's ready to leave. So instead I wander aimlessly round the house looking for things I can tidy away, or dust I can clean, or pictures I can straighten. I should sit down and relax. Plenty of rest, that's what they said at the hospital. But I can't just sit down. I have to keep busy.

I'm emptying a few tissues out of the waste paper basket when He calls me upstairs and I know there must be something that I've missed.

"I thought we'd just have a quick scoot around just to make sure everything's ready for your mum," He says. And his tone is still friendly and there's still a good chance that it might all be OK.

"You know what she's like," He says. And He's still on my side, still coming to my rescue so that I can put things right before I have to suffer the embarrassment of my mum noticing something I missed.

So we walk slowly round each room together, inspecting the place like old-school hospital matrons looking for dusty corners and hastily turned down beds. We both know there'll be something she spots that I haven't noticed. There always is. And however hard I look I won't see it before she does. I won't see it and neither will He. But we look all the same. We look so that I won't have to suffer the embarrassment of my mum looking at me with that disdainful expression. We look so that He won't have to suffer the embarrassment of my awkwardness when my housekeeping skills just don't measure up.

He's happy with the bathroom and with our room, but when we get to the bedroom where mum will sleep He's not impressed. He looks at the duvet and lifts it to see the sheets and the pillow cases. He stands on a chair and runs his finger along the picture rail then looks at it in disgust. He tells me I'm a disgrace. He tells me I should be ashamed to offer my mother a crumpled bed in a filthy room.

And I stand in the bedroom where my mum will sleep, wishing she was here already. I'm wishing for my mum and watching the carpet while he tells me what a disgrace I am.

I want to shout back to Him. "I was in hospital last night." I want to scream "Who fucking cares about crumpled fucking sheets!" but, of course, I don't say any of that. "They are clean," I say, "I washed all the bedding this morning and I did try to iron them."

But it just sounds pathetic and I wish I hadn't said anything at all. He looks at me and spits a sarcastic, "Well as long as you've tried, I'm sure your mother won't mind." And then He smiles. Does He think it's funny? Does He think He's funny? Does He think I am?

I'd like to wrap that sheet around his neck and pull it hard at both ends until He's the one that's crumpled and gasping for breath on the floor.

He puts his hand on my shoulder. What if He knows what I'm thinking? He puts his finger under my chin and lifts my face up to look at his.

"We'd better get going," He says, "we're going to be late. You look lovely."

So He can't see inside my head but He's right about the time. We are going to be late if we don't get a move on because He spent so much time in the shower and He insisted on dragging me round the house to double check everything comes up to scratch. I was ready. I was ready early. But somehow, thanks to my shoddy ironing skills, we're late now.

So we drive in silence again. He takes a strange, long-way-round route to the station. I want to tell Him which way to go to get there quicker but He hates that. He'll just get angry with me, so I sit there quietly allowing Him to make us even more late by going all around the houses. I look in my bag for some change for the car park.

"What are you doing?" He barks at me. "Don't distract me while I'm driving." And when I tell Him that I'm just looking for change for the parking He says, "Don't be stupid. The one advantage of being late to pick her up is that we won't have any waiting around. It's free for the first fifteen minutes and it'll only take her five to give us a dressing down for not being there when the train arrived."

But actually, there's no dressing down at all. We park up and go into the station at a trot to look for her, expecting to find her huffing and puffing and all agitated on the concourse. But instead she's busy chatting, totally relaxed. She even looks a bit annoyed that we're here to get her already.

9

I've always loved railway stations. They are magical places. Places with endless possibilities. What if you just turned up there with a bag full of your stuff and a few quid in your pocket? What if you just turned up at the station and you'd told no-one where you were going? Maybe you don't even know where you're going yourself, but you've just jumped on any old train and off you go? Where would it take you? You could just get off anywhere you liked the look of. Just jump off at any station and be whoever you liked when you got there. If I win the lottery that's what I'm going to do. I'm going to put the money in a bank account that no-one knows about and go to the station and just head off somewhere. I won't even look to see where the train stops; I'll just get on and get off whenever I feel like it.

Mum usually hates railways stations. She says that they're filthy places where every corner has puddles of vagrants' wee. She says it's all overpriced coffees and cardboard sandwiches and you have to pay to use loos that aren't even clean. But as we walk towards her she spots us and looks properly disappointed that we're on our way to get her. She waves, only half to say hello. The other half is to wave us away for a bit longer so that she can carry on chatting.

As we get closer I can see who she's chatting to. It's Julie the Weirdy Girl. Julie from school. I see her out and about sometimes, in the supermarket mostly, but I never quite manage to say hello to her. They're chatting like old friends. Catching up. And I remember how my mum and her mum were friends when we were at school. How they used to chat outside the school gates for ages and expect us to play together. How Julie and I used to weigh each other up and play our separate games in the same space outside the school. I did want to play with her but I couldn't find a way of talking to her so we used to just rub along, looking like friends but never really being friends.

As we get closer, He asks me who it is that my mum is talking to.

"It's a girl I knew at school," I say, "I think she's called Julie."

I don't want Him to think that it's a friend of mine. I don't want Him to start quizzing her about what I was like, or things I did or who I hung out with. I'd rather Him think that she's just some vaguely-remembered girl who was in the same class. I don't mention that I see her from time to time myself and never speak to her. I don't say "Isn't odd that when I bump into her we never speak but when she bumps into my mum they chatter away like best buddies." I just brace myself for the awkwardness when we get to them and Julie and I will be forced by politeness to speak to each other. I just hope that she doesn't say "I've seen you lots of times but you always blank me," or anything like that.

She doesn't.

When we reach them it's difficult for anyone to get a word in edgeways because Mum is so enthusiastic about this chance meeting. She can't wait to tell me everything that Julie has just told her. She can't wait to introduce Julie to Him. She's delighted, on my behalf, that I'm married and Julie is not. She is point-scoring by proxy, visualising the look on Julie's mum's face when she finds out that middle-of-the-road Marion has bagged a husband whilst Brain of Britain Julie is still on the shelf.

So Julie and I smile at each other in silence and it's actually much less awkward than I would have thought. Probably less awkward than we used to be together when we were kids waiting for our mums outside school, or circling each other at other kids' birthday parties. And while we stand sharing a doesn't-she-witter-on moment and my mum fills us in on the marriages and babies of everyone I went to school with, He looks Julie up and down as though He were a Special Branch officer looking for evidence of wrongdoing.

I wonder what he thinks her face will reveal. If He's looking to see what kind of bad influence she was or what secrets she could tell Him about me, He's looking in the wrong place. Hers is a face that should tell Him that she can't be bothered what people think. She has lipstick on but that's all, and it's probably just because she's dressed for work and lipstick is part of the uniform. Her hair is less wild than it was when we were at school but it's still curly, still tucked behind her ear on one side and still a wishy-washy colour that you'd be hard pressed to put a name to. It still looks like it hasn't seen a hairbrush in days. Those makeover shows would have a field day with her. She probably doesn't watch them. She probably doesn't even know they exist.

"I thought you still lived around here," she says to me when my mum pauses for breath. "I've seen you I think, once or twice, but I was never sure it was you so..."

Her sentence trails off, partly because I'm nodding in acknowledgement that I've seen her too, partly because He's audibly sighing with irritation at this unscheduled delay.

"So you two go way back?" He says.

"Kind of," she says, smiling at me. "We went to primary school together; we used to play together sometimes."

"And our mums were friends," I add. "Weren't you, Mum?"

"We were, we were," she joins in, "but I lost touch with so many people when I moved away. It'd be great to get her number from you, Julie," she adds.

He actually tuts then, realising that we'll get a ticket unless He moves the car from the waiting zone into the proper car park.

"I'd better move the car," He says and waits for one of us to respond with a 'no it's OK, we're coming now'.

But then my mum says "Perhaps Julie would like a lift?" and He wasn't expecting that. Not at all. These are the curve balls that my mum is allowed to throw. I could try that kind of trick but I know how long I'd spend trying to make amends for it later. I know it's not worth it. I've given up recklessness like that. For my mum there are no consequences, apart from the apologies I'll have to make on her behalf and she won't even know about those. As far as she's concerned, it's no bother.

To my amazement, Julie jumps at the chance.

"That'd be great if it's not too much trouble," she says.

"Oh, it's no trouble," my mum chips in before He gets a chance to say anything, so He has no choice.

"No, it's no trouble," He says sarcastically, but she chooses to ignore his sarcasm and just smiles. She smiles at Him but I know the smile is for me really. She has scored a point for me and, somehow, she knows it.

So He marches on ahead of us and my mum practically has to break into a trot to keep up with Him.

"Sorry," I say to my mum and Julie. "We put the car in the waiting zone. You only get fifteen minutes. He's worried about getting a ticket."

My mum gives me that 'I wouldn't put up with it' look she does so well.

Julie just says 'It's fine.' Maybe she doesn't know how it works. It'll be fine while she's in the car but at some point this evening it won't be fine. Or maybe she's right. Maybe it will be fine. It wasn't me who offered her the lift or me who accepted it, so maybe it will be fine.

Julie and I are sitting in the back of the car like two school kids with my mum in the front with Him. Mum says she gets car sick in the back. She says it disorientates her. Normally that makes me cross and I end up seething in the back, dethroned from my own front passenger seat. But today I'm happy to sit quietly in the back while my mum cranes her head round the head rest to speak to Julie sitting next to me.

And while she tells Julie all about the many health concerns that plague her, I glance down at Julie's hands holding her handbag on her knee. The bag is leather. It's a bit old and worn but good quality. 'Well loved' you might say. But I'm not looking to see the bag, I'm looking to see whether she's wearing a wedding ring. I want to see whether I am more or less normal than the Weirdy Girl. Why should I think that being married should make her more normal or being unmarried keeps her weird? I don't know, but that's what I'm looking for. I'm looking for clues to see whether she is better at life than me or not.

There is still no ring there. Not even an engagement ring. There's no jewellery on her fingers at all. No nail varnish either. But her hands are nice. A bit bony, but soft. You can tell that they're soft even without touching them and the nails are not long but not bitten, just right. They're probably her best feature, these soft, long-fingered hands, but they give nothing away.

There's no jewellery on her hands but there's a charm bracelet on her wrist and I'm counting the charms on it. One for every birthday, maybe? There are fourteen, so maybe that's one for every birthday since she was 21? Or could it be one for every birthday and every Christmas for the last seven years? Maybe they're love tokens? Maybe the love of her life buys her a different charm every time they go on holiday together, to remind her of her special memories every day. Maybe she has a charm bracelet instead of a wedding ring and instead of one little gold ring to last a lifetime she gets a new little piece of silver every few months.

I can't help wondering about it and before I know it I am reaching out to touch one of the little charms and my mum and Julie both look at me at the same time. I feel like I've committed the world's most atrocious faux pas.

"It's lovely," I say and I blush. But she smiles at me. It's fine, she doesn't think I'm odd, she's just pleased by the compliment. Anyway, I tell myself, why shouldn't she think I'm odd? I think she's odd.

"A boyfriend bought it for me years ago," she tells me. "I think the idea was that he would buy me a new charm every birthday.

Unfortunately, we never got past the first couple of charms but I love the bracelet and if I spot one I like, I just buy it."

"Doesn't it make you a bit sad to be buying the charms yourself when you thought he'd be doing that for you?" I ask.

And I blush again, especially when Mum chips in with an admonishing 'Marion!' to make it clear that I should have thought before speaking.

But Julie doesn't mind. "Maybe it should make me sad," she says, "but it doesn't. It sort of reminds me of him, but in a nice way. If we'd still been together now he'd probably just be buying me the charms because he felt he couldn't stop, but this way I know that the ones he bought for me he bought because he really wanted to."

"Which ones are they?" I ask. And she shows me two: a little silver horse and a tiny enamelled lily.

And I think I'm going to ask her whether she has a boyfriend, or if she misses Charm Bracelet Man, but suddenly He is back in the car with us.

"Does someone want to let me know where I'm going?" He pipes up. "I'm just heading home at the moment but if Julie wants dropping back at hers I'll need to know where it is."

So we just stop talking and Julie directs Him from the back seat until we get there. It's not that far from our house. In fact it's a street that I sometimes cut through on the way home from the shops if it's sunny. It's not a short cut. If anything it's a long way round, but it has beautiful trees on either side, really old horse chestnuts. Her house is not one of the biggest but it's one of the nicest. It has blinds that have been custom made to fit the windows and a front door that's been stripped down to the bare wood with a stained glass panel at the top.

"What a lovely door," I say when we stop, and He gives a snigger under his breath because I've said something so banal again. But Julie grins.

“That’s my favourite bit of the house,” she says, “in fact that’s what made me buy the place. I knew it was the right one as soon as I got to the front doorstep.”

“Women!” He says disparagingly and she just laughs.

“Let me give you my phone number,” she says, and she takes a business card from the front of her well-loved handbag then scribbles a number on the back.

“That’s my work number, my mobile and my home number there now,” she says, and as she hands it to me she gives my hand a little squeeze with her soft, bony fingers. “You’ll give me a ring so we can catch up properly, won’t you?”

And I don’t even need to answer her, because Mum says “Of course she will” so it’s done for me. And Julie can just get out of the car and dash to her front door as though it’s raining. She dashes towards that beautiful front door grasping that scruffy bag by one handle and turns and smiles and waves before she disappears inside. Even from inside the car I can hear the door slam shut behind her and I turn the card over to where she’s scrawled her home number and wonder if I will ever ring her. And if I do, what will I say?

“Right, home,” He says. “At last.”

“She’d look so much better if she just sorted her hair out,” Mum says as we drive away and then she finally stops peering from the head rest and rummages in her bag for a boiled sweet to keep her going until dinner.

10

"How are you bearing up?"

He's taken her bags upstairs and finally I'm allowed to be a little girl with a grazed knee running in for my mum to kiss it better. But she can't kiss it better. She doesn't even know where it hurts. And I can't tell her.

"I'm OK," I say. "I'll be OK."

And then she hugs me and I cry big body-shaking sobs and she tells me it will all be OK.

"There'll be other chances, you know," she says and now I know she isn't going to make it better. Her grazed knee treatment was always TCP, waterproof plaster and out you go again to play. 'You don't grow up tough without getting a few bruises along the way' she used to say when I just wanted a hug and someone to feel sorry for me. But the cure-all for everything in our house was a quick kiss-it-better and stop-feeling-sorry-for-yourself. "There's plenty have it much tougher than you, miss!"

I want to say 'there's only one chance at life for that little person and it's already gone.' But I can't tell her to piss off home so I just say, "I'll be OK mum. I think we all need to eat though, don't we?"

"I do," He chips in as he comes down the stairs. "What's for dinner?"

So He pours three glasses of wine and takes two of them into the living room for Himself and my mum and leaves me on my own with mine in the kitchen. He loves a captive audience and Mum does captivated very well. She'll listen to his stories of office politics and the dickhead from accounts (renamed 'bird brain' for her more sensitive ears). She'll let Him explain to her how the management team have got the business strategy all wrong and wouldn't know a commercial opportunity if it jumped up and bit them. She'll marvel, sympathise and agree. She will never interrupt and she will fill every pause with a relevant question that gives Him the chance to explain how He would run things better. They will not talk about me. In fact they might even forget that I'm in here. Until they remember how starving they are, anyway.

I'm peeling potatoes and thinking about Julie the Weirdy Girl. I shouldn't call her that, it's unfair. Who am I to call her weird? I should never have called her that. I'm sure she knew, too. People always know their nicknames even if no-one ever calls it them to their face. Mum always told me not to call her that. "How would you like it?" she would say. I wouldn't have liked it, but that's not the point. No-one would have called me that. "No-one would call me that because I'm not weird," I would tell her. But perhaps by not weird I just meant ordinary. Maybe I was just bland. I never had a nickname and it didn't bother me then, but thinking about that now gives me a niggling paranoia that I was just too boring to deserve one. The thing about Julie though, is that Mum could tell me off for being cruel by calling her Weirdy Girl, but she couldn't contradict me. Julie was weird, even if it was weird in a nice way. "Just don't let her hear you saying it," Mum used to say. "It could be hurtful."

Just thinking it was hurtful enough, I'm sure. Just behaving it was hurtful. And I liked her even though she was weird. I was her friend as much as anyone. But she just brushed it off. She expected people to think she was weird and in a way I even think she liked it. I think she cultivated it. Better weird than boring.

I don't think I hurt her with the nickname but I did hurt her. Not on purpose though. Definitely not on purpose. How was I supposed to know, when my mum told me I'd be weird if I'd been through what she'd been through, that I wasn't supposed to share the information? I thought I was defending her in the playground. Pleading her side, producing mitigating circumstances as she galloped round the edges of the playground instead of standing in a line doing clapping rhymes like the rest of us.

"When Suzy was a teenager a teenager Suzy was, and she went 'ooh ah, I lost my bra, I left my knickers in my boyfriend's car.'" Clap-clap, clap-clap-clap, clap-clap, clap-clap, clap-clap-clap...

While she trotted round us in her own horsey world: "Clip clop, clip clop, OK Snowdrop, ready for a canter."

I can't help laughing to myself, remembering the stupid shades of normal behaviour in the playground, but He pops his head round the door to see how dinner is coming along just as I'm grinning at the thought of all that senseless clapping.

"Having fun in here?" He says.

So I stop smiling and put the kettle on for some water to boil the potatoes.

"It should be ready in about ten or fifteen," I tell Him and He picks up the bottle of wine without saying anything else and closes the door behind Him.

And with the potatoes on I take the meat out of the oven and peel the carrots with the uneasiness of guilt weighing heavily on me. The guilt is at least twenty-five years old but it still makes me feel queasy in my stomach. I never meant to make Julie the centre of everyone's gossip but I did, and the sinking feeling I had aged eleven when I was told I was a bully comes straight back to me when I think of me in that playground. Even when I try to think of something else, I can't shake it off.

So I don't want to think about Julie and all of that, and I don't want to think about the hospital and the baby and all of that, so I'm trying to find something to distract me. What's on the TV? I won't be able to watch it: Mum's here so we'll keep it switched off unless there's something she wants to see. I won't be able to watch it but I can run through what's on tonight. What day is it? What day is it? I can't even think what day it is.

And before I know it I have cut my finger peeling the carrots and it won't stop bleeding. It's bleeding all over the carrots and I can't stop it. I wrap a piece of kitchen roll round it and try to carry on peeling but the paper just keeps falling off and my finger just keeps bleeding and I can't peel the bloody carrots. I'm crying and I don't want to cry, I just want to peel the fucking carrots, get the dinner on the table and have them both tell me what a good job I've done. But now the potatoes will be too soft by the time the carrots are cooked and how am I going to be able to serve everything up without getting blood on it?

I abandon the kitchen roll and just run my finger under the tap. The cold water stings and runs pink into the sink. The finger is numb and the water runs clear but as soon as I turn the tap off it starts bleeding again. I just stand there watching it, reaching for the tap and hesitating with my uncut hand halfway between the tap and my bleeding finger.

Maybe He hears me crying. Maybe He just uses that radar He has to sense when I'm weak enough to snap in two. But anyway He comes back in the kitchen, glass of wine in hand.

"What on earth's the matter?"

And when I tell Him that I've cut my finger and show Him the little nick, which miraculously stops bleeding the minute He looks at it, I feel stupid.

"You stupid woman," He says. "You shouldn't be trusted with sharp objects." He smiles when He says it but I'm not convinced He's joking. He sends me up to the bathroom to look for a plaster.

"Sort yourself out," He says. "D'you think your mother wants to see you like this? Just take your wine with you, calm yourself down and I'll take over in here."

So now He's the hero of the hour. He's the cavalry. I take my place at the table with my mum and He serves the dinner that I've cooked as though He's Fanny bloody Craddock.

"I've buttered the potatoes and the carrots, Jean," He says as He puts them on the table. He hasn't put them on the plates,

He's brought them to the table in the white serving dishes that we got as wedding presents and never use. "I know you don't get to keep that trim waistline without keeping an eye on the calories, but it's only a bit and they taste so much nicer with a little bit of butter."

My husband is flirting with my mother and she is sitting there lapping it up while I sit here letting Him pass off the meal I've cooked as his own. My blood is boiling. I want to pick up those fancy serving dishes and hurl one at each of them. But I don't. Of course I don't, they were a wedding present after all, and it'd be a shame to smash them after I've kept them nice all this time. He can see I'm cross, though. Even He can see that.

"Are you OK Marion?"

"I'm fine," I say, "My finger's just stinging where I cut it."

"She always was clumsy," Mum smiles, helpfully.

Too boring for a nickname, too clumsy to be trusted with sharp knives. Great.

"Lucky I was here to save the day," He smiles back at her. And He serves my mum and then Himself and then hands the dishes over to me with a "help yourself."

The food is lovely but I don't feel hungry. I don't want to be here. I would like to be swimming in the cold, silent water at the swimming baths. I would like to be in that big echoing space with a bunch of familiar strangers where the only sounds are the gentle splish splash of my muscles pushing me through the water and the counting and thinking inside my own head, driving me on. I wonder whether Julie would sit at the table forcing herself to eat food she didn't really want just so that she didn't make a fuss. Just so that she didn't get accused of making a fuss. I wonder what Julie would do if she were me?

"I'm quite surprised at how friendly Julie was, aren't you?" Mum says, pointing towards me with a piece of potato on the end of her fork before she puts it in her mouth.

"It was good to see her," I say. "She hasn't changed a bit."

I'm hoping that Mum will just agree with me and move on and leave me to force down my dinner in peace. But even if she wanted to let me off the hook, He's never going to let her leave it there. The can of worms has been opened... too late to do anything to close it again now.

He lets me carry on eating for a few seconds without asking anything. He watches me chewing on my food, waiting for me to volunteer some information. But I don't know where to start. I know the best thing to do would be to get in there early. Find a way of cutting the conversation about Julie short and move on. That would be the best thing to do but I don't know where to start. And while I'm panicking and thinking 'How can I do this? How can I steer Him away from this?' I can see Him enjoying me squirm. And He knows exactly how long He can leave it before my mother moves us off on another tangent. He leaves it just a few long seconds and then He asks:

"So why shouldn't Julie be friendly towards Marion?"

He asks my mum, not me. He knows she loves to dig up a good anecdote. He knows she'll always give Him the long answer. And she does.

"Marion used to call Julie 'The Weirdy Girl'," my mum tells Him. "She wasn't the only one, they all did. You know what kids are like..."

He nods. He knows. Of course He does. He used to be one.

"Well, they were friends really, and so were me and Joyce, Julie's mum." She pauses for a piece of broccoli. "So I wanted her to stop using that stupid nickname. I mean, those things can be hurtful, can't they?"

He nods. "They can. Of course they can."

"So I kept telling her to stop it but it was like a bad habit with her," my mum goes on. "She was terrible for bad habits, weren't you Marion? You should have seen the lengths I had to go to, to stop her from biting her nails. She would have bitten them right down to the quick and had them bleeding if I hadn't worked so hard at helping her stop."

And I spot my chance. This is the tangent I've been looking for. Here's where I can draw my mum away from Julie and get her talking about something else instead.

"Yeah, but look at them now," I say, holding my hands up for them both to admire my nails. Not long but not bitten, just a sensible length. "No-one would ever guess, would they–"

"Go on Jean," He interrupts.

"You used to go mad at me about chewing my hair as well Mum, do you remember?" I say. "You used to tell me that I'd get a hair ball in my stomach and die if I didn't stop chewing it. Do you remember?"

"I do," she says, "and you never listened about that either."

She pauses for a sip of wine and He jumps straight back in again.

"So what happened with Julie?" He asks.

And then she tells Him. She tells Him how she had told me that I would be weird too if I'd been through what Julie had been through. She pauses to tell Him how she always used to try to drum it into me that there were plenty of people worse off than me and I should spare a thought.

"She wouldn't just take that at face value where Julie was concerned though," my mum says, pushing a token, calorie-laden potato to the edge of her plate before putting her knife and fork down carefully across the middle of it. "So in the end I had to tell her about Julie's real mum being an alcoholic and her being put into care and her mum ending up in prison and Julie ending up being adopted.

"Joyce wasn't her real mum, you see, she adopted her. And heaven knows she had her work cut out for her and she used to confide in me about what a tough time Julie had had and the nightmares she used to have sometimes and how hard it was listening to her cry for her real mum when all her real mum had ever done was neglect her."

My mum takes a breath, picks up her fork again and uses it sideways to cut in half the potato she had left. While she pauses to eat this half a potato, I try once more to change the subject.

"It doesn't seem to have done her any harm in the long run though, does it?" and I'm about to start talking about how nice her house looked and how I sometimes walk down that street because the trees are so lovely but He knows there's more to be said.

"So go on Jean," He says, topping up her glass. "What happened after you told Marion all about it?"

I can feel my stomach churning and there is nothing I can do. I can't ask her not to finish the story. I want to say 'just shut up will you.' I want to say 'you never told me it was a secret, Mum. You should have told me not to say anything.' I think about spilling my wine 'by accident' – after all, I am notoriously clumsy – but we're too far down the track for that. At best I could delay the end of the story, but now that He's seen me squirm He'd come back to it anyway. So I don't try to put off the inevitable; instead I just sit at my place pushing carrots around my plate.

And she tells Him. She tells Him that I blabbed the whole story to the whole school. She tells Him that I spread gossip that had Julie crying in lessons and refusing to go to school in the morning. She tells Him how the school called her and asked her to come in and discuss how I had been bullying one of the other children by spreading gossip about her. She tells Him how Joyce turned up at our house in a rage, screaming at my mum for telling me and screaming at me for telling my friends. She tells Him how difficult it had been for her to have her daughter branded a bully. She tells Him how disappointed she had been in me.

I can't speak. I have that burning in my throat, the same as I had in the headmaster's office when it all happened. If I open my mouth I will cry and I'm not going to cry. That's pathetic. It was a long time ago. Ages. I was just a little girl then and I didn't know that I was hurting anyone. I didn't mean to do it, I want to stand up and yell 'I didn't mean to do it, you know! I just wanted to make the other kids understand she was weird for a reason' but I can't do that. It's a lame excuse anyway.

I just sit in my seat squeezing the place on my hand where I cut it when I was peeling the carrots. I make it bleed again. I make it hurt like hell. That's where it hurts, just in my hand. Just in my hand and nowhere else. And tears come to my eyes despite my best efforts to stop them.

"Are you OK?" He says, looking towards Mum to enlist her interest.

"It's just my hand," I tell Him. "It's hurting where I cut it before."

"Sounds like an excuse to get out of the washing up to me," He jokes to my mum, handing me his plate. So I take the plates into the kitchen, take off the plaster and wash the blood off my finger for a second time, letting the cold, cold water get colder and colder and pour over my finger until all the red in it has gone and it's just clear and cold. Then I make some coffee and take in the cake.

It takes a few trips to bring in the cake and the coffee and the cups and the plates and all of that and they're just chatting about something completely different by the time I sit down. She's waxing lyrical about how lovely her spring bulbs have been this year and He takes the opportunity, while they're on the subject of flowers, to get in a mention of the ones He bought me to welcome me home from the hospital.

"You've got a good one here," she says as I pour the coffee. "There aren't many women whose husbands still buy them flowers after so many years."

"Not just for special occasions either," He chips in, blowing his own trumpet. "Every Tuesday too, without fail."

"She's a lucky girl," my mum says to Him, smiling at me.

I don't say anything.

"Well it's nice to know there's still plenty to discover about each other after so many years," He says. "I didn't know I was married to a bully and a gossip."

He's not going to let it drop. She has handed Him a stick to poke at me again and again and He's having fun. He can prod me and poke me as much as He likes and I can do nothing to stop Him. The only thing I can do is pretend I'm not bothered. But I'm not very good at that. He can tell when I'm bothered and He knows I am now.

I pick up the knife to cut the cake. "Just a small piece for me," says my mum, bang on cue, and He and I almost share a smile.

"And watch yourself with the knife, Marion," He smiles at her, changing his allegiance once again. "It's sharp you know."

It's OK, though. I can rise above it. I don't even have to visualise stabbing Him, Psycho style, at the dinner table because soon he'll be tucking into my cake and He won't be able to help but enjoy it.

But when I cut into the cake it's still soft in the middle. Not exactly raw, but undercooked and a bit gooey. It might still be OK. It could still be OK. It's a chocolate fudge cake, who's to say that it's not supposed to be like that? So I cut it anyway, a small piece for her, a big piece for Him and a normal piece for me. I hand them out and hope for the best.

My mother can see that it's gooey where it's not supposed to be and she does her best to save me the embarrassment. She eats from the outside edge then uses the old waistline excuse to leave the rest untouched on her plate.

"It's so rich," she says, "I can feel the inches appearing with every mouthful."

He's not going to let me off so easily. He prods it and pokes at it.

"Is this cake supposed to be so mushy?"

I tell Him it's not. I tell Him I was in a bit of a rush getting everything ready today.

"Why," He says, "what else did you have to do? You've been off work all day."

"I know. I'm sorry. I think it's probably because I've been upset and your mood kind of shows in the cake when you're baking."

"Bullshit," He coughs under his breath so that I can hear it and my mum thinks he's just choking on the inedible cake.

So I stop making excuses and just try to make out like it's not that bad. I eat all mine and make a show of enjoying it.

"I quite like it like this, actually," I say.

"Well I think it's revolting," He says and pushes it away. "I'm sorry Jean," He says, "I'll see if we've got any biscuits."

And when He leaves the room to look for biscuits my mum makes excuses for Him.

"He's probably just a bit upset. You know, about the baby. And worried about you too."

"Probably," I say.

I clear the last plates and cups, load the dishwasher and switch it on. I make his sandwiches ready for the morning. I ask them do they want a cup of tea and I tell them I'm going to take mine upstairs with me to bed.

"Your mum's come all this way to see you, Marion," He says.

But she lets me off the hook. She says I'm bound to be tired after everything I've been through. She gets up out of her chair and gives me a big hug and tells me to sleep well. He lets me bend down to give Him a peck on the cheek.

"I'll try not to wake you when I come up," He says.

11

Sometimes I have dreams that start off as dreams and end up as nightmares.

I am meeting Julie the Weirdy Girl for lunch and I can't wait. I have this strange kind of 1950s throwback dress on, with orange flowers on it. It's not like anything I actually own. It's nothing like anything I would wear in real life. But in the dream I think I look fab. In the dream I feel sure that Julie will like the dress. I'm meeting her for lunch but I'm taking my own cake. I made the cake and it's in my kitchen but it's not like homemade cake, it's more like something that you would buy at some fancy deli and it's already sliced up and in one of those little white cardboard boxes with the flip top lid like they have at the baker's.

I leave the house and I've remembered the cake and the sun is shining but as soon as I get in the car I realise that I have no idea where I'm going. I thought I knew before I left the house but now I have no idea and I switch on the engine and start driving but I'm just driving round hoping that I might spot the place. In the end I have to stop because I'm crying and I'm getting nowhere and I know I'm never going to find the place. So I stop and I decide to eat the cake since I'm not going to make it for lunch. So I open the box and eat the cake and the address is written on the bottom of the box. It was underneath the cake all along. So I drive to the place and dash inside but she's not there. She's not there and people are staring at me because I have cake all down me and I'm dropping crumbs all over the floor.

"Up you get," He says.

It feels like it can't possibly be morning yet. I'm so tired and it's so dark.

"How can it be morning already?" I ask, hauling myself out of the bed.

"It's not," He says. "It's just time for you and me to have a chat."

My mum has gone to bed. He's waited for her to turn in, finished the second bottle of wine and then come in to wake me up.

We go downstairs and He asks me if I want a cup of tea. He puts the kettle on and we stand and listen to it boil. He says nothing and I don't want to interrupt Him. It boils and clicks off and He does nothing, so I make the tea and He says thank you. And then He starts.

"What can you see that's wrong in here?" He says.

I look round the kitchen to see if I can spot what He's talking about. I look round where I've cleared away the plates, wiped down the surfaces, swept the floor.

"I don't know," I say.

"Look again," He says. "See if you can spot the bleeding obvious."

So I look again. The light is still lit on the dishwasher. I put it on before I went to bed and it hadn't finished by the time I went upstairs. I try that. But that's not it. Yes, it's bloody stupid. Sure, it's a fucking fire hazard and we could have all been frying in our beds thanks to me, but that's not it.

I see the piece of kitchen roll I used to wrap round my finger when it was bleeding. It's still in the sink, all wet with my blood still on it. I walk over and pick it up.

"That's disgusting," He says.

And I just say 'sorry' because I don't know what else to say. I put it in the bin and hope that's an end to it. But that's not really it either.

"What about this?" He says. And He hands me the tin with the rest of the cake in it. I just take it. I am standing in the kitchen in my pyjamas holding a tin full of cake and I just don't know what I'm doing here. It must be about one in the morning and I've got about two seconds to figure out why He's handed me the cake.

"So?" He says.

"I'm sorry."

"What are you keeping it for?" He asks me. "Why on earth haven't you put it in the bin? Are you saving it to poison us with all over again tomorrow?"

"It wasn't that bad," I say. It might not get me a fast track to the fast lane of the WI but it could still give Mr Kipling a run for his money. I don't say that last bit out loud but even the bit I did say was nil points, wrong answer. I should have just kept to 'sorry'.

"You thought it wasn't that bad, did you?" He says. "You liked it did you? Eh?"

I want to say 'it's only a cake, get a grip', I want to say 'fuck off and make your own cake next time', but what would be the point?

He takes the lid off the cake tin and picks up a knife. He cuts the cake up into pieces. Not pieces so much as bite-sized chunks. Then he hands it to me.

"Eat it," He says.

"I can just throw it away," I say, "It's no big deal."

But it's a big deal to Him, apparently. It is a big deal when your wife feeds you raw cake in front of a guest in the house, He says. It is a big deal when your wife is purposely giving you shit to eat that she knows will make you ill. "If it's no big deal, then why don't you just eat it?" He says. And He's almost whispering so as not to wake my mum. He holds it out to me and punctuates his words with the tin full of cake thrust towards me. "Just. Fucking. Eat. It."

So I eat the cake. It's one in the morning and I'm in my pyjamas in the kitchen eating cake. It's a big cake with only three slices missing. Only two and a half slices gone really, since my mum had such a small slice. It's mushy and slightly bitter from being undercooked and it's sticking to the roof of my mouth but He's not going to let me off with just some of it. He stands in front of me while I eat every last little bit.

So I take myself back to my childhood self. I am nine and my mum is frugal – some might even say mean – with treats because my dad has left and money doesn't grow on trees. And neither does cake. So one angel cake opened on a Sunday after tea has to last all week. But when I've cleared everything and she's not looking I might just be able to sneak into the kitchen for an extra, extra-slim piece of cake and she'll be none the wiser. My nine-year-old self would love the chance to eat all the leftover cake. My nine-year-old self can't believe my luck. And I find that I can chew and quite enjoy it while I look contrite. I am tired and I just want to sleep but cake won't kill me. Who ever got tortured to death by cake?

When I've finished He takes the tin and tells me to hold out my hands. So I hold out my hands and he pours the crumbs from the bottom of the tin into my hands and tells me to eat them too. When I've finished he says:

"Look at the state of you, you've got cake all over your face. Go up and get yourself cleaned up. I'll be up in a minute."

So I'm wiping my face with a flannel and looking at the stupid cow in the mirror and thinking out loud to her: You stupid cow. Why don't you just tell Him where to stick the stupid fucking cake?

And I can't look at her then. The crying makes her face so ugly. All red and blotchy. Mouth all contorted. What am I doing? How did I get here? No wonder that baby didn't want to stay with me. No bloody wonder. I feel like I could cry my body inside out if only I had the energy. But I haven't. I feel worn out. I feel woozy and just too tired to cry any more. So I brush my teeth for the second time tonight and as I put my toothbrush back in the little pot on the sink I challenge myself to some kind of rebellion. I tell myself not to leave it at that. Don't let Him win outright. Do something to fight back. But all I can think of is that I won't ever bake a cake again. How pathetic is that? The only rebellion I can muster is to deprive Him of homemade cakes. As if He'd care. As if He'd even notice.

I want to lie down and sleep for a million years.

Instead, I lie awake in the bed listening for the sound of Him coming upstairs and trying to be still enough that He'll think I'm already asleep. I can't sleep, how can I sleep? But I can make sure I'm not crying when he gets here. If I slow my breathing right down and keep totally still He might just think I'm asleep.

He knows all the tricks though. He knows I'm not asleep. Or anyway, even if He thinks I am He doesn't care. I hear Him closing the living room door. I hear his feet on the stairs. I hear Him peeing loudly into the toilet and then leaving the bathroom without washing his hands. He gets into the bed letting the cold air in and comes all the way across onto my side.

"Are you awake?"

I don't answer. Maybe if I just say nothing He'll give up. He doesn't.

"Are you awake?" He says louder. And I can't even pretend to be asleep any more because even if I had been asleep He would have woken me up.

"How's your finger?" He says, as though a cut on my finger is the worst thing that's happened to me in the last twenty-four hours.

"My finger is fine," I say.

"Hey," He says, "I'm only asking. I know you're hormonal," He says, "I know you've been through a lot in the last week or so.

"I'm just trying to look after you. You needn't have cooked tonight if you didn't feel up to it. We could have got take-out. You could have asked me to cook. That's why I came home early, to help you get ready for your mum. I have been trying to help but you make it a bit difficult for people to help you sometimes. I did step in to finish the dinner when you hurt yourself, though didn't I? I do love you."

I say nothing and He can't stand the silence.

"You push yourself too far," He says. "You push yourself too far and then end up getting everything out of proportion. You didn't need to make a cake. You could have just bought one. But, oh no, you had to go and make one and it had to be perfect and we all had to sit around pretending it was perfect even when it wasn't.

"You could have poisoned all three of us with that bloody cake," He says. "Why can't you sometimes just admit to yourself that you're not Wonder Woman and buy a fucking cake from the supermarket like everyone else?"

He pauses again for a response. I try not to say the word, and it makes my throat burn, but sometimes it's easier just to stick to the script.

"I'm sorry," I say. "I'm really sorry."

And He thinks I'm sobbing because I can't believe how silly I've been. But I'm just crying because I'm so angry with myself for saying sorry. For walking straight into the sorry trap and being completely unable to stop myself. In a parallel universe somewhere maybe there is a Marion who doesn't apologise. Maybe she tells Him to make his own fucking dinners from now on and means it and never steps foot in the kitchen ever again. Good luck to her.

In the meantime I am here in this bed with his arms around me, crying more and more because I can't stop crying. I am telling myself to stop. Telling myself that once I stop crying this time I will never let Him see me cry again. Never ever. Not in a million years. I tell myself that this is the last time He will see me cry but I don't believe it. Even I don't believe it.

And then He tells me that I look lovely when I've been crying. It's his usual preamble. He'll rub my face with the back of his hand. He'll run his fingers down my neck, over my shoulder and down my arm to my hand then He'll guide my hand towards Him so that I can feel just how lovely he thinks I look. I let Him.

I play along with his whole seduction routine until he gets to the bit when He says:

"Are you OK?"

And instead of just saying 'yes', I say, "Not really." I say, "It's taken it out of me, all that stuff at the hospital, and I didn't sleep much last night and I'm bleeding and everything."

He might have persevered had it not been for the bleeding. He smiles at me sympathetically but his whole body recoils from me.

"I'd better get a tissue," I say, moving to get out of the bed, "I've got snot everywhere."

And that does it. Blood and snot together is much too much for Him to deal with and He turns over to go to sleep with a whispered, "Sleep well," and not so much as a peck on the cheek.

So I wander off to the bathroom and blow my nose on a piece of toilet paper and drink a glass of water from the not very clean toothbrush holder. I dare myself to look in the mirror. She has red eyes and her skin is a bit puffy but it's still me. I am in there somewhere and just to remind myself I press down hard on the finger that I cut when I was peeling the carrots.

It hurts. It bleeds again and I can still feel it.

12

I'm sitting on the sofa with my legs curled up under me keeping everything crossed for a happy ending.

But I know there won't be one.

This is one of those Hollywood tearjerkers from years ago. One that pretty much everyone has forgotten. Not a classic. Not a notorious turkey. Just one of those films that have faded into the past along with all those black-and-white starlets who look a bit familiar but you couldn't actually name them with any real confidence. I don't even know what the film's called. I didn't see the beginning. I don't even care what it's called.

It's watchable, it's good in fact. But this sort of thing is out of fashion. There's just me and a thousand grannies retreating to the sofa for a Friday afternoon alone with a packet of biscuits and some smouldering looks from Stuart Grainger – or maybe it's Alan Ladd. Whoever he is, he's torn between leaving the love of his life with her nasty husband or rescuing her from his clutches and standing by her as she faces the shame of running off with another man. Maybe he should just sort her out with a bank account and a plane ticket then it would be win/win. For her at least. But there's no point talking to the TV, or even willing him to work out a happy ending. He's been on to a loser from the start. And sure enough, the minute he finally gets his act together and helps her escape the marital home the husband finds out, picks a fight with him and poor old Stuart, or Alan or whoever he is, ends up in the dock for murder.

But she's standing by him. She's there in the courtroom keeping everything crossed too. I'm not the only one still keeping hope alive that there might be a happy ending. And she's looking pretty good for a woman whose boyfriend has just killed her husband. No mascara panda eyes for her. She's all suited and booted and she's had her hair done and everything. Not like me. I'm curled up on the sofa in a pair of jeans that are ripped at the knee, my grandad's old Aran cardigan and my much-loved kingfisher-green legwarmers.

My legwarmers have never seen a ballet class: the nearest they've ever got to any strenuous activity is when I used to dance round the room in them when the kids from Fame were on the TV. But they were there in the 80s and everyone wore legwarmers pushed down round their ankles over their jeans whether their legs needed warming or not. Not everyone had a pair in such a great colour but everyone had a pair. Now they don't. I bet I'm the only person I know who has a genuine pair of teenage legwarmers. But I love them. They take me back to a place when looking great was as simple as pulling a woollen tube up over your jeans, scrunching it down and tucking it into your ankle boots.

He hates them. He says they should never have been allowed in the first place and it's ridiculous for me to wear them now. He says it's self-indulgent nostalgia for me to keep them and I should just throw them away. He's thrown them away before now and I had to retrieve them from the outside bin, all damp and stinking of potato peelings. He doesn't know I got them back. They are contraband legwarmers. I can only wear them when He is out. I can only wear them when it's just me and a packet of biscuits and Stuart Grainger and this stoical woman who is clutching the railing dramatically in the courtroom but doesn't cry in case it gives her away.

And there it is. Happy ending officially off the cards completely. He's been sentenced to death and she's in a cab leaving the courtroom clutching the letter he told her to read if he was convicted of murder. And they do that thing where you hear her voice as she starts to read it in the back of the cab but then it changes to his voice, declaring his love, telling her she's not to blame and asking her to leave and start a new life far away. He's enclosed a cheque with the letter and the address of a friend who can help her. He's thought of everything and she gives up being stoical now and just cries into her dainty little hanky and asks the cab driver to take her to the station. The End in big fancy letters, followed by a full cast list. It was Stuart Grainger – at least I won't have to wonder about that for the rest of the day. And strangely, I'm not crying. I'm unmoved by her drama and his imminent death. I was bothered while I was watching it but now that the credits are rolling I find that I couldn't care less. I can feel nothing for anybody, not on the TV, not even if they were in my own living room. All I can think about is my little baby and how my mum has gone home and I am going back to work on Monday so it's all officially over. The End, run the credits, nip to the loo in the ad break, put the kettle on. Move on.

My mum left a day early, making excuses about a toothache that she'd have to nip in the bud. She rang the dentist from here and had to be home to see him today otherwise it would be two weeks. Fair enough. Thank the Lord. It was a relief actually. I did a dutiful show of looking a little upset about it, not enough to make her feel guilty, just enough to make her feel like I was bothered. In truth, I couldn't stand any more shopping for nothing in particular. Any more cups of tea – "No, you sit down, I'll make it." Any more standing in the kitchen while I was cooking, chatting to me so that I couldn't concentrate and stirring, turning, fidgeting things on the stove. She decided on a strategy before she got here, I think. She took the relentlessly cheery approach with lashings of take-her-mind-off-it on the side. So I have new shoes and mascara, birthday presents for birthdays that aren't coming up for three or four months, a freezer full of food and a new hair cut. I have the world's cleanest bathroom which has been completely cleared of all disused medicines and long-forgotten bubble bath and body lotion gift sets. I have empty linen baskets, ironed knickers and carpets that are freshly vacuumed. Even under the sofa.

Now that she's gone I feel like moving the sofa and crumbling a biscuit over the carpet then pushing it back into place. But I have eaten the full packet of biscuits. I am having a private little rebellion that no-one will ever know about but me. I have not had a shower, I am wearing legwarmers and an ancient cardigan, I've wasted two hours of my life watching an instantly forgettable film and I've eaten a packet of biscuits for lunch. Perhaps I'll go and turn down the pages on some books. I might even have a drink of milk swigged straight from the bottle (which I'll then put back in the fridge). And later, when I brush my teeth before bed, I plan to squeeze the toothpaste from the middle of the tube.

I'm tying knots in the empty biscuit packet to see how many I can do and I hear his key turning in the door. I am sitting in the living room in my legwarmers and cardigan with a knotted biscuit packet in my hand and he appears at the living room door.

"So this is what you get up to when I'm not around."

Anyone would think He'd caught me devil-worshipping or piercing my own belly button. I feel like I've been kept back in detention and the headmaster has caught me enjoying myself when I'm supposed to be considering the error of my ways. He's waiting for me to say something but I don't know what to say.

I don't know what to say.

He waits.

The next film is starting in the Friday afternoon black and white double bill. The music is very loud. It makes me jump when it comes on.

"Can we turn that thing off?" He says and He just strides across the room and switches it off. And then He walks across to me and takes the knotted biscuit packet out of my hand.

"What's this?" He asks.

Bloody stupid question. It might be tied in knots but you can tell it's an empty biscuit packet. Anyone could tell it's an empty biscuit packet.

I don't say anything. He doesn't expect me to. He doesn't want me to.

"And what are those?" He asks and He points to my legwarmers with the knotted biscuit packet. It's exhibit A raised to accuse me with exhibit B. If I didn't know better I'd think He was having a laugh. He looks like He is. If my mum walked back in the house right now, having forgotten her handbag or something, she would think He was just having a laugh and He would play along. But He's not.

Again I don't answer and again He doesn't expect me to. I could leap to the defence of my legwarmers, but there's no point. It wouldn't change anything.

"I thought I threw those out," He says, sneering at them. "Didn't I throw them out?"

And that's my cue to speak. But maybe I don't want to speak to Him. It's not like He's offering me a conversation. So I just nod.

"Pardon?"

He's not going to let me off that easily.

"Yes." I think it's best to keep it short and to the point but maybe that's not the best plan today because He pauses to wait for me to say some more.

I brace myself for what He's going to say next and it feels like we're both holding our breath. But it's his phone that breaks the silence with its Mission Impossible theme tune ring-tone. If only these legwarmers would self-destruct in 30 seconds we'd be fine. If only He would.

It's Jimmy.

"Probably best not tonight," He says, "Marion's still, you know, a bit fragile and that. Yeah, she'll be alright. She's a tough old bird. Tough as old boots," He looks at me while He's talking to Jimmy. He's talking to Jimmy but talking to me too.

"Tough as old boots but higher bloody maintenance. All right, no worries. I'm sure I'll get a pass to come out at some point over the weekend."

He puts his phone back into his pocket and looks me up and down, letting his eyes rest on the legwarmers.

"Fine," He says eventually. "If they mean that much to you, keep the disgusting, flea-bitten things. If that's what you need to do to get through it all, hang on to your youth with a revolting pair of sad, fat-girl legwarmers, you do that. Just don't let me see them on you again though, eh? Same goes for that moth-eaten cardigan."

Not the most generously expressed change of heart I've ever heard, but it's better than wrestling with potato peelings in the outside bin again, so I'll take it.

"D'you fancy take-out for dinner?" He asks and I just say yes. Why not? And He even asks me if I've got any requests. And He even kisses me on the cheek before He picks up his keys and pulls the front door closed behind Him.

And while He's gone, I take off the legwarmers and take them upstairs and squirrel them away at the back of my knicker drawer. And there in the corner of my knicker drawer, just where I left it, is the little card that Julie gave me with the printed name and telephone numbers and email address on the front and the hand-written home number scrawled on the back. I look at the name, Julie S. Woodburn. I don't know what the 'S' stands for. I wonder what it stands for. I wonder which number it's best for me to ring.

I try the home number. She's bound to have an answering machine. Bound to. And I don't want to end up trying to explain who I am to some secretary if I ring her on her work number. And I don't want to disturb her while she's chatting to someone or in a meeting or something by calling her on her mobile number.

I count the rings while I wait for her to answer. They are so slow compared to the ridiculous pace my heart is beating. Stupid. What's it doing that for? Four... Five...

"Hello?"

"Julie?"

"Yes. Hello?"

"It's Marion," I say, "you know, from school. I saw you the other day at the train station. You did say to ring you."

"I did," she says, "and you chose just the right time. I'm not usually home this early but I had a meeting this afternoon and decided to come straight home. You must've known."

I don't know what to say next but it's OK. It's like she really was waiting for me to call. Like she's thought what she'll say when I do.

"I don't have any plans for tomorrow," she says. "Fancy coming round for lunch?"

"OK," I say without even thinking about it. Without even thinking what He'll say. Normally Saturday is supermarket day but my mum's been visiting so the cupboards are already full to bursting.

"Brilliant," she says, and she sounds like she's genuinely pleased. "About half twelve then. Do you remember which house it is?"

I hear the front door close. He's back. He shouts hello up the stairs.

"Yes," I say "that's fine. He's just got back, I'd better go."

"OK," She says, speaking more quietly as though there's a danger He might hear her. "See you tomorrow."

And the phone clicks as she hangs up and I turn around to see Him standing in the doorway.

"Who was on the phone?" He asks.

"My mum," I answer. I don't know why I don't just tell Him. Maybe I know He'd be cross. Maybe I just want a secret to replace the legwarmers.

"So what's fine?" He says.

Think quickly Marion: what's fine? "She left her bra here because I put it in the wash for her the other day," I tell Him. "I've said I'll post it back to her." End of conversation: he doesn't want to think about my mum's bra. Stroke of genius.

"The food's in the kitchen," He says. "Let's get it while it's hot."

13

There are other women. Don't ask me how I know, but I know. Why else would He always suspect me of eyeing up anyone and everyone? Why else would he always think that everyone we know is having an affair?

Maybe I am looking for someone else and I just don't know that I'm doing it. Maybe everyone we know is having an affair. But I don't think so.

There's a crazy one (obviously!), she's an adrenalin junkie. She did all the textbook crazy-girl stuff back in the day. She bungee-jumped in Australia, she went white water rafting. She backpacked, she hitchhiked, she walked home alone through the dodgy park near her flat where all the druggies and the weirdos hung out. Well into her twenties she was like a five year old kid who thinks she'll live for ever. Who thinks bad things only happen to other people. Bad things only happen to people on the telly, not to anyone you know in real life. She was like that as a teenager, like that as a student, like that in her post-student haze when she could still drink until two in the morning then wake up God knows where next to a complete stranger and still make it into work for nine with her hair tied back and her shoes on the right feet.

But now she's at least thirty-two, maybe even thirty-five. Maybe pushing forty even. It's hard to know. She still dresses like she did when she was twenty. Not like any other twenty-year-old you'd see now. She's not pretending to be a twenty-year-old, she's just stuck in a time warp. She just can't leave her twenty-year-old self behind. And in an ideal world she'd still be taking home the skinny, self-obsessed twenty-somethings she used to sleep with back then and she'd still be playing the stupid drinking games and daring and double-daring them to do something daft. She'd still be taking pictures of them asleep in her bed to put in her scrap book. But they're not interested in her any more. She can fool herself that she's still a slip of a girl. She can skip meals. She can give herself bubble gum days when she's allowed to chew gum but swallow nothing except water to keep her skinny little backside in her skinny, skinny jeans. She can abseil, pot hole and run a thousand miles for charity but she can't compete with the genuine article. She can dress like she did years ago, act like she did, feel like she did but no-one's interested any more. No-one except Him anyway.

He's happy to travel with her on her nostalgia trip. He encourages her. He makes her feel like she's the most exciting person on earth. He's good at that, up to a point. He goes to hers for nights in drinking vodka or tequila or her secret recipe cocktails that she mixes up in a blender in the kitchen and carries through to the living room, spilling them on the carpet because she's too drunk to hold them steady and too drunk to care about the spills. It's a rented flat anyway and a carpet that's seen better days. She doesn't care about it. She doesn't care about anything much. She doesn't even care about Him. But she cares about how he feels about her.

She thinks He loves her. And she has good reason to. He professes his love to her long and loud every time He sees her. But He's never sober when He says it. And He never sees her unless He's bored and He's got nothing to do. She's his last resort girl. She's his confidence boost. He rings her to tell her He's coming round and she always says yes. Or He just turns up and she's there and she's glad to see Him and she never turns Him down.

But then one evening He turns up at her flat and she's not there. She's nowhere in particular. She's gone late night shopping or something. She's gone out for a drink after work and just stayed out because she felt like it. And why shouldn't she? She didn't know He was coming round. It'd be different if she knew when to expect Him, but He's being unreasonable. She's not a mind reader. She has a life of her own. And why shouldn't she be out with other people once in a while? She thinks it's fine. She thinks it's fine to say all that to Him. But He soon lets her know that it's not.

He tells her that she's a sad case. That she's mutton dressed as lamb. He tells her that He's only interested in her because she's an easy lay and a good excuse for a night on the piss. He tells her that they stay in because He doesn't want to be seen with her in public. He tells her that she's boring, inane, dull as digestive biscuits.

She listens and says nothing. She just sits there while He tries to make her angry and lets the words float over her like they're nothing. She lets Him rattle on like He's nothing. Like she can't even hear Him. So soon enough He runs out of steam. It doesn't matter what nastiness He comes up with, if she's not bothered, what's the point?

So in the end He just gets up out of the chair and pours Himself another drink. "One for the road," He says. And she holds out her glass for another one too but now it's his turn to ignore her and He pointedly screws the lid back onto the bottle and puts it back on the table. He doesn't say a word. He just behaves like a little kid who doesn't want to share his toys with his ex-best friend.

But she doesn't care. She's got something up her sleeve. She's a resourceful woman and she's kicked tougher men than Him out of her flat before now.

She walks calmly to the bottle and pours herself a drink. And while He's trying hard to ignore her to get back at her for ignoring Him, she reaches into the pocket of the coat that He left hanging on the chair by the table.

And she walks back to her own chair, large glass of vodka in one hand, car keys in the other. She sits down, glugs the drink and says in a strong clear voice, "Let's go for a drive."

It takes Him a minute to realise what she's saying and to cotton on to the fact that it's his car keys in her hand. And in that minute she's at the front door and heading out to the street to where he parked the car earlier.

She's already in the driving seat by the time he gets to the car and she's starting the engine. He has to decide whether to get into the car with her or just let her drive off. For a moment He considers standing in front of the car and blocking her way but even through half a bottle of vodka He can see that she's going to drive whether He's standing there or not. So He gets in the passenger side and fumbles around trying to fasten the seatbelt as she speeds off.

And He's contrite now. He tells her He's sorry. He tells her that it was just the drink talking and He didn't mean any of it. He's actually scared. He has no idea where she's driving to or what she plans to do when she gets there.

The truth is, neither does she. She doesn't have a plan but she's enjoying putting the fear of God into Him. And she's still saying nothing. He's apologising like He's never apologised before in his life. He's making promises about a weekend away in Paris, telling her He loves her, telling her He'll leave me and she can hear every word but she's not prepared to listen to any of his bullshit.

She's hooning around corners like a joyrider. She's having fun. She's loving every minute of her improvised rally circuit and loving it even more that He's squirming in his seat thinking that's she's lost it.

She hasn't. She's drunk and she's angry and she's upset but she's not a psychopath. But she hasn't got a plan. She doesn't really know how she's going to end this whole fiasco without doing a full-on Thelma and Louise. And she knows He's not worth that. He's definitely not worth that.

So she just drives them into a supermarket car park. She revs up to crash through the barrier but then just crashes the car into a post instead. She's not hurt anyone. She's not done anything she's going to be arrested for. She's just given Him a big bill for the crumpled bumper and smashed headlight at the front of his car.

She switches off the engine and hands Him the keys. "Nice knowing you," she says. "Explain that to your wife, why don't you?"

And as far as she's concerned, they're even.

14

I'm playing the 'what if?' game.

What if I'd gone to University and moved away from here? What if I'd met someone different? What if I hadn't phoned Him up and persuaded Him to give it another go the first time we split up? What if we'd gone backpacking around the Far East instead of getting married?

It's a great game. I can come up with different answers every time I play. I can play out the sort of life I might have had if I changed just one thing. But it's not real. In real life I was never going to do things differently. People like me never do.

I'm thinking about the game, imagining myself in some floaty summer frock wandering around a marketplace in India, and I don't notice the traffic lights changing before I step out into the road. The road was empty a moment ago but now there is a truck coming straight at me and I know I should get out of the way but there are cars coming in the other direction too and the pavement seems a long way off. The truck driver sounds his horn loudly. It sounds like a ship's foghorn. And he must have put his foot down on the brake at the same time because it screeches to a halt just in front of me. It's like some silent movie clip where the heroine is tied to the railway track and the train stops just in time. Except my hero is no handsome movie star, he's a big, fat truck driver. And he's not going to whisk me into his arms and kiss me. He's going to yell at me for being so bloody stupid.

He gets down from the cab and there are cars beeping behind him and pointedly swerving past his truck to get to where they're going, staring at me as they drive past.

I think he's going to yell. I'm bracing myself for a good ticking off but instead he just puts his arm round my shoulder and leads me onto the pavement.

"Are you all right love?"

I just nod at him. I can't believe he's being so nice.

"Stay there," he says, "I'll just get the truck out of the way and put my hazards on. Just stay there."

So I do as I'm told and a minute later he's back with a flask of tea in his hand.

"They say you need sweet tea after a shock," he says, opening the flask and pouring a cup. "I always drink mine sweet. You should have some."

And he hands me the tea and I want to ask him why he's being so nice but people are still staring at me and I think I should just politely sip the tea and get going.

But the tea is hot so I can't drink it too quickly and he seems not to care that his wagon is causing traffic chaos around us. He must be able to see what I'm thinking on my face because he puts his hand on my shoulder and says, "Don't worry love, it's Saturday, they can't have anywhere all that urgent to get to."

I smile at him and he smiles back and I just can't believe he's being so nice. Why is he being so nice? It's funny that a complete stranger can be so kind and yet I know if my own husband were with me He'd be yelling at me for being so stupid and be more concerned about the five minutes added on to everyone's journey than the fact that I nearly just got squashed like a beetle underfoot. Maybe I'm doing Him a disservice. Maybe He'd be finding me somewhere to sit down and telling me to sod the lot of them. But I don't think so.

My truck driver is still hovering next to me and I can tell he wants to head off.

"I'm fine now, honest," I say, giving him back my cup of hot, sweet tea, which is still half full.

"Nonsense," he says, "I'll give you a lift home."

"I was just on my way out, actually," I tell him, but he's not taking no for an answer.

"You were nearly on your way out permanently just then, love," he answers. "I think you need to go home, don't you?"

Is that a rhetorical question? He might think I need to go home but I don't want to go home. I really don't want to go home. I want to go to Julie's for lunch like I've planned. She'll be waiting for me and I'll be late now and He thinks I've gone shopping for shoes and He'll have a fit if I turn up at the front door in the cab of a great big truck. I'm not even sure it would fit down our street. I'm not even sure I can trust this guy. Just because he's been nice to me, it doesn't mean he's actually nice does it?

"Come on love," he says again. "Will there be anyone in when you get home?"

It's clear that he's not going to give up so I just lie.

"My sister will be there," I tell him.

"Great, you hop in and we'll get going."

"Thank you so much," I say and I direct him to Julie's house and thank him again before I climb down the steps of his truck, scraping the back of my leg on the metal edge of the step as I go.

"No more playing in the traffic," he grins at me as he leans over to close the door of the cab.

"No," I say. "Thanks again." And he just drives off and waves and that's it.

I'm still a bit dazed. I have a funny kind of invincible feeling: the truck didn't get me, so nothing can. It's a good feeling to have. I was nervous as hell this morning. Lying to Him about where I was going. Wondering what to wear so that I look nice but not like I've dressed up to look nice. I thought maybe she was setting me up to get me back for all that stuff all those years ago. But now I'm not bothered. If the truck didn't get me, Julie can't get me. Nothing can get me. I am Wonder Woman. I am superhuman. I am ready for anything.

But when I knock on the door of Julie's house there is no answer and I wasn't really ready for that. I knock again and I'm embarrassed now. I can't see them but I can feel the curtains twitching in the houses all around. I arrive in a big noisy lorry on Julie's quiet, tree-lined street and then I walk up to the front door and just keep knocking even though she's evidently not even in. 'Who is this freak?' they must be thinking. Valid question. I'd be thinking that myself if someone turned up at my neighbour's house in a whacking great big truck and carried on knocking even though there was no answer. I almost expect one of them to come out and invite me in for a cup of tea or a nip of something stronger. I'm wondering whether it's my day for good Samaritans.

But after three progressively louder knocks on the door with no response and only silent curiosity from the neighbours, all my paranoia about why Julie really invited me comes flooding back and I just need to get out of there. So I dash back up the path as though I've just forgotten something important and that's when I trip. I'm not even sure what I trip on, my own feet probably. And that's when Julie finally appears at the front door.

"God," she says, "are you all right?" and she strides across to me and makes me take her arm so that she can lead me into the house like I'm some old pensioner who insists on trying to manage without a walking stick.

I'm sitting on Julie's settee with a glass of wine in my hand – definitely much more effective for shock or whatever than the truck driver's sweet plastic-flask-flavoured tea. She's telling me about the disaster she's had with the risotto. She left it for a minute while she went to the loo but then she got distracted and emptied the bin in the bathroom before she went downstairs and by the time she made it back into the kitchen the whole thing had caught and burnt itself to the bottom of the pan. So when I knocked on the door she was out the back scraping the charred remains of our lunch into the bin and that's why she didn't hear me knocking.

"And there's me thinking that you're good at everything," I say. It must be drinking wine in the afternoon. I never normally say things like that to people. And straight away I can feel myself blushing and I wish I hadn't said it.

But she just laughs. Not in a horrible way. Not in the way that people laugh if you walk into a lamp post or come back from the loo with your skirt all caught up in your knickers. Her laugh is a thank you.

"Thank you," she says. "Thank you. People who only know me at work think I'm good at everything. But most people who've ever seen me do anything in a kitchen assume that I'm completely crap at pretty much everything. And they might have a point."

I make all those noises that people make when they want to politely contradict someone who's telling them how rubbish they are. 'I'm sure that's not true, I can't believe that for a minute, I bet you're good at lots of things.'

But she seems determined to make sure I know just how rubbish she can be. She tells me about the time that she invited people she works with round for dinner and everything went pear-shaped. One of them was vegetarian and she didn't know and had nothing to offer her apart from a plate of vegetables and a lump of cheese. For the rest she had cooked roast duck and proudly brought it to the table ready to carve and it had looked great and smelled fantastic until one of her guests noticed that the giblets were still there, stuffed inside the duck in a plastic bag that had now melted all over the inside of the carcass.

"If I'd just known my limits and carved the stupid thing in the kitchen," she says, "no-one would ever have known and I'd just have had the vegetables and cheese embarrassment to deal with."

She carries on, telling me all about her cooking disasters and the times she's arranged to meet up with people then completely forgotten, or invited people round and got the days mixed up. We laugh and drink more wine and I can't believe I'm laughing so much. I can't believe that Julie the Weirdy Girl has ever laughed this much in her life before. This isn't her. This isn't the solemn girl I knew at school, galloping around, semi-joining in, mostly knowing everything about everything and going on about it and getting on people's nerves. How did she grow up into someone who can laugh like that? How did she grow up into someone who can celebrate how totally crap she is and laugh out loud about it?

We're laughing and she has tears pouring down her face and I'm listening to her endless stream of anecdotes trying to think of one of my own. And I remember the cake.

"I had a disaster with a cake when my mum came over to stay last week," I say. "It looked cooked on the outside but it was still all soggy in the middle."

"I bet it was still nice," she says. I wonder why she's being so kind. "So did you eat it?"

"Yes," I tell her. "My mum and my husband had a little bit after dinner and I ate the rest."

And now I've totally broken the spell. My story isn't funny. And even though I haven't given the punchline, she still seems to know that it's an anti-joke. She's stopped laughing. She's stopped laugh-crying and we're sitting there in awkward silence.

"I'm dying for a wee," she says. "Then I can offer you my speciality beans on toast." And she disappears off up the stairs leaving me alone to snoop around her living room.

It's what you might call tidy-cluttered. There are piles of stuff but it's all in neat, meant-to-be-there piles. The magazines are with the magazines, the newspapers are with the newspapers and there's a box with bits of torn-out stuff that she must want to keep for something. The piece on the top is an interview with a playwright all about the new play she's written and the production that's in rehearsal in London. I read the first couple of paragraphs, the intro. It just rattles on about the girl, how young she is, what she's wearing, how she's clutching a latte and chain smoking and twiddling her hair round her finger.

Fancy being twenty-two and writing a play that's good enough for people to put on in a London theatre and then having them just rattle on about your hair-twiddling habits when they come to interview you. If I were her I'd be cross about that. I'd love to be her.

There's a table by the window that's like an old fashioned desk. One of those huge solid things that weighs a ton, with drawers down each side. It's covered in papers and Post-it notes. There are even Post-it notes stuck to the drawers. Julie must have a lot to remember. I try not to read them but you can't help trying to read little notes like that, just lying around, can you? It doesn't matter anyway because I can't read them even when I give in to temptation and have a proper look. Her writing looks lovely, all curly with little squiggles. But you can't read it. I bet even she can't read it. The top of the desk, under all the papers and everything, is a big sheet of glass and under that are postcards. Tons of them, all spread out so that you can see the pictures but not lined up straight. They look as though someone has piled them up neatly then spread out the pile with their arms and plonked the glass on top. I wonder if that's what she did? I wonder if these are postcards that people have sent her or ones that she's collected from places she's been. I'm dying to read what's on the back of them.

She comes back in the room.

"The beans are on," she says. "Now, would you like the speciality of the house: grated cheese on top, or are you a beans on toast purist?"

I wasn't listening. I was looking at a picture of Venice and wondering if she's actually been there.

"What?"

"Beans on toast," she says. "I was just wondering whether you'd like them with or without cheese? You know," she says, "Instead of the risotto disaster?"

"Yes," I say, "cheese would be nice, if there's enough."

"There's always enough cheese," she says, "I practically live on cheese on toast."

But she's not going back to the kitchen, she's coming across the room to see what I was looking at. And now I'm embarrassed for snooping.

"I'm so sorry," I gush. "I'm sorry. I don't know why I'm so nosey. I just thought the pictures looked interesting. I really wish I'd travelled more."

"You make it sound like all travel is banned as of this afternoon."

I don't answer. He hates airports. Says He'd rather be in the car getting somewhere than sit in an airport for hours then take your life in your hands when you finally step onto the plane. He says there's plenty to see in this country and we might think about going abroad when we've got bored with it here. He says I'm crabby in hot weather anyway. One day maybe I'll go to the airport with £500 in my pocket and get on the next flight to wherever. I'd like to think I would. It'd be great to do that and not even care that you hadn't packed all your little essentials. But I can't really see me doing it.

I don't answer. So she jumps in again.

"God," she says, "don't worry. I always thought postcards were fair game anyway: they don't even arrive in an envelope, so normal rules don't apply."

I still feel embarrassed and it must be obvious because she tries to make me feel better yet again.

"I have a terrible bathroom cabinet habit," she says. "It's so hard not to, don't you think? Especially if you can half see things through the door or there's stuff standing on top. You start looking and then you start wondering what else they have in there and before you know it you know their full medical history, including the piles and the athlete's foot, and you wish you hadn't been so nosey."

"I'll make sure I check yours out while I'm here," I say. And I can't believe I've said it. But it's fine. She laughs.

"Oh shit," she says, "the beans!" and she darts off into the kitchen to rescue the pan full of beans that she put on the stove before she came in to make my excuses for me.

We eat slightly charcoaly beans on not very warm toast with cheese grated on top at the table in the kitchen. There's a tablecloth on it and I wonder if she has a cloth on the table all the time or just because I was coming over for lunch. My mum always says that you should keep the standards day in, day out, that you would expect to have if the Queen came to tea. I always used to wonder why she said it, because the Queen was never going to come to our house for tea and I couldn't imagine anyone less exciting as a tea-time guest anyway. But maybe Julie's mum had the same housewives' motto as my mum did. Maybe my mum even learnt it from her. It's funny to be in a house where I don't know the rules and no-one is bothered whether I stick to them or not.

"Eat up," Julie says, putting brown sauce on top of hers and offering me the bottle. "I've got cheesecake for afters. Shop bought, don't worry. And then we can have a look at the postcards in the living room, if you like."

15

I have always envied people who like coffee. Proper coffee. I've always wanted to like it, but the taste of it never lives up to the smell. And because I'm not from a family of coffee drinkers or a coffee-drinking marriage, I don't understand the mysteries of coffee making. I'm not in the club. I can swoon at the lovely smell of every Starbucks I ever pass from outside on the street but they would probably refuse me at the door if I ever tried to go in. I have some kind of invisible sign on my forehead that says 'She Only Drinks Instant' and the coffee fraternity would snub me if I came anywhere near.

Julie is not like that. She sweeps her plate into the washing up bowl and is tinkering with the coffee machine even before I've finished my beans on toast. She is measuring out coffee from a packet and measuring water into a jug then pouring it into the top of the machine. There are handles and nozzles and little knobs everywhere. It's like a circus act. Any minute now it will play a tune, doves will fly out of the top, there'll be a blinding flash and the machine will transport us back in time to some 19th century freak show where I'll try not to stare at the bearded lady while Julie takes a bow for demonstrating her fabulous machine.

I don't like real coffee (not for the want of trying), but I don't tell her that. I like that she assumes I like it. I'll just have to drink it. Or accept it and then pretend I forgot to drink it. That's what I'll do. I'm just thinking that that's what I'll do when she asks me do I take milk.

"Yes," I say, "I like it with lots of milk." Genius. With any luck I won't even be able to taste the coffee very much. With any luck this could be the start of me actually beginning to like real coffee.

What Julie said about being rubbish in the kitchen clearly wasn't true. I'm watching her with the coffee machine and she's like a concert pianist. She plays it by heart, she's barely looking what's she's doing but the whole room smells of coffee now so she must be pressing all the right buttons in the right order.

She hands me a cup of milky coffee. Hers is black.

"You don't take sugar do you?" she grimaces. "I don't think I've got any."

I tell her I don't and she sweeps her brow in an over-the-top display of theatrical relief. She's funny and I like her more than I can ever remember liking her as a kid.

"Come on then," she says. "Come and have a proper look at the postcards on my desk. I can take the glass off if you like."

So we're sitting on the floor, me kneeling up and her cross-legged like they used to make us sit in school assembly. She has dumped all the paper work that was on the desk in three neat piles on the floor and I've helped her lift the big sheet of glass off the desk so that we can get at all the postcards underneath. There are even more than I'd thought. They are heaped on top of one another so some of them were almost completely hidden by others before we took the glass off. I am looking the way my mum always taught me – with my eyes not my fingers – but she wants me to dive in. She picks up a couple and hands them to me to show me. I still feel like I can't touch them. Even with her implied permission I feel like I mustn't move anything in case she can never get them back the way they were before.

And then it's as though she can read my mind.

"Don't worry," she says, "They're not in any particular order. I get them out and look at them and then put them back any old way whenever I feel like it," she says. "I like it that the order they're in changes sometimes. I work at this desk, I see it every day but I look much more when the pictures have been moved around. Even if I move just one or two just a little bit, it's amazing what I might see that I'd forgotten all about."

So, with her permission, I finally start ransacking the display of postcards on her desk. I take one, look at the picture and then look back down across the whole lot and choose a few more. I feel like that woman off Countdown, picking up cards to allow the contestants to play the game. I feel as if we are playing some kind of game and she'll be quizzing me later on which cards I picked up and why. Maybe she will.

She lets me look through the cards I've picked without saying anything. She lets me turn them over and glance at the back without saying anything. And when I look up to see whether she minds if I read them she just nods towards them. She wants me to read them. She's asking me to read them.

All the cards I look at are addressed to someone called Linda. They're just postcards from people's holidays. Just stuff about the weather and the food and this place they visited that was nice and what fun the kids had on the beach. There are no great secrets in them. Nothing special.

And then she starts to tell me. She tells me how the postcards belonged to her mother. Not her mother that I know, the one who knows my mum. The postcards belonged to her birth mother. The one who had Julie taken away from her. The one whose life was a mess. The one that Julie could barely remember but missed like hell all the same.

"I didn't know the whole story," Julie says, looking through the postcards but not really looking at them. "I didn't remember what she was like at all. I just wanted to know her and wanted to be able to ask about all that stuff. So eventually, when I was about twenty, I decided to go and look for her."

She tells me that it took her nearly two years to find her mum. Two years of knocking on doors and talking to neighbours and ringing up strangers and nearly giving up. And at the end of it she'd expected to find a mum that was an alcoholic and a jailbird.

"To tell you the truth," Julie says, "I half expected her to be dead." She pauses over a postcard of Loch Lomond as though she's found some detail on the picture that's not quite right. "Actually," she says, "I half hoped she'd be dead," and she looks right at me like she's trying to read my face, like she's trying to see whether I think she's awful. But I don't. I think I'd probably feel the same in her shoes. But I don't say that. I don't say anything. I don't think she wants me to say anything. She just wants me to be on her side. So I just smile at her to let her know I want her to carry on telling me the story.

So she carries on. She found her mum alive and well and living in a leafy suburb with two cars on the drive, a cat in the window and matching hanging baskets either side of the front door. She found her mum and drove to the house and parked outside four times before she got out, crossed the street and pressed the doorbell. She stood at the door counting to ten, getting ready to turn around, get back in the car and never go back but her mother opened the door and she couldn't have lied even if she'd wanted to.

"My mum recognised me straight away," Julie says. "I look just like her. I look freakishly like her."

And then she tells me how her mum had invited her inside but stepped out to look left and right to check that no-one had seen, like some cartoon spy. She tells me how her mother chatted to her about her life and how she had turned it round with the help of a lovely man. How she'd got a job as a waitress when she left prison and the restaurant owner took a shine to her and they ended up married and running the restaurant together and living happily ever after.

"And then when she'd told me all her good news, she just cried and cried and cried," Julie says. "She said she was sorry for being such an awful mother and letting me down. And that she wished she'd tried harder to make a good job of being a mum. And that she wished she'd been able to hold on to me.

She said she'd thought of me every day and prayed for me to have a happy life."

And now it's Julie that's crying but it's just kind of in the background. I don't think she even knows she's doing it, but I can see the tears while she's talking and I'm wondering how much more there can be. But there is more.

It seems that Linda had never told her husband about Julie. She'd never told him about the stint in prison or the drink problem or anything about her old life that he might not like.

"So... what?" I ask, "She just wanted you to go and leave her to it?"

"No," Julie says, "she just didn't want to introduce me to her husband. So we meet, just the two of us, every two or three months or so. For lunch or just for a coffee or a walk sometimes.

"The postcards are hers. Were hers. From the customers at the restaurant. She wanted to give me something personal of hers, but it had to be something that her husband wouldn't notice so she gave me the cards that she'd collected over all those years. They're just random bits of kind thoughts from all her friends. Not even friends some of them, just customers. They used to display the postcards in the restaurant. People used to go in and look for their own postcard on the wall."

She stops talking and I think she might start properly crying now.

"They're nice," I say, "I like them."

"I like them too," she says.

And she looks at me and has nothing else to say about it.

I feel like I owe her something.

"I was going to have a baby but it's died and I just can't believe that it's gone for good," I say.

16

When I walk into the office everyone looks up and no-one says anything. I feel like I have stuck in time. I feel like I am the freeze-frame on the titles of one of those cheesy American cop shows. I'm just standing there, feeling those twenty-odd eyeballs all on me, feeling like I should just put one foot in front of the other and get to my desk and sit down. But I can't work out whether I can actually do that or whether I should just turn round and go home. Luckily, someone puts a hand on my shoulder. It's my line manager, Heidi. She's a huge woman and the weight and size of her hand on my shoulder make me think, as I always do, how little her name suits her: nothing dainty and little blonde pig-tailed here. Heidi doesn't say a word. She doesn't move me towards the desk but her hand on my shoulder has pressed the 'go' button. Suddenly my legs start moving again and they choose to move me towards my desk.

There are flowers on my desk and for a minute I think they might be from Him. It's only Monday but they still could be from Him. But they're not. The card reads "Thinking of you at this difficult time, from all your friends in customer support." I look round the room to nod my thanks to everyone as though I'm some aging film star modestly accepting an award for life-time achievement, but there's no-one to nod to now. They've all stopped looking at me sympathetically and they're just getting on with their work. Heads down, engrossed, committed. They think I won't want them to make a fuss. They're right. I don't want them to make a fuss but I still want someone to say something.

Heidi tells me to get myself settled in and then she'll run through where everything's up to with me. Mandy has been handling my work while I've been off, so the three of us will get our heads together in about half an hour or so, OK? OK. I've only been away from this desk for two weeks but it feels like a lifetime ago. It feels like centuries. I want to go home, but what would I do there? Watch crappy TV and eat biscuits and feel sorry for myself. "You'll be better off here," I tell myself and, as though she heard me, Mandy chips in: "It'll be good to occupy your mind with something. You'll soon get back into the swing of things." I want to say, "This is my job, you know. I do know what I'm doing. It's hardly rocket science." But I remind myself that Mandy's nice and she's just trying to say the right thing, like the nurses. "Give yourself five minutes to have a cup of tea and look through your in-tray and you'll feel like you've never been away," Mandy says and it sounds like a good thing.

She's right too. Once my big entrance is over and everyone's overcome the urge to give me a standing ovation just for making it to my desk, it does feel like I've never been away. I'm in the kitchen making three cups of tea (one for me, one for Heidi and one for Mandy – don't forget the soya milk, she's trying to go dairy free to please her vegan boyfriend), and the kettle still carries on boiling and shudders so that you have to switch it off at the wall and there are still no clean teaspoons and someone has finished the last of the tea-bags again without putting out a new box. I've never been away and nothing has changed, and yet everything has changed. How is that?

The three of us sit down together and just as Heidi starts to tell me about the delayed deliveries because of a backlog in the Wolverhampton depot her phone rings with an urgent call and I'm left with Mandy again. "You OK?" she whispers and I just nod. What else am I going to do? So she tells me what a nightmare weekend she's had trying to sort out a dinner party for her boyfriend's vegan mates and the disaster with the nut roast that just crumbled when she took it out of the tin and the woman who had a nut allergy that couldn't eat it anyway. "And she turned out to be Guy's ex-girlfriend, which he managed to keep quiet," she said, perhaps a bit louder than she meant to: she looked a bit shocked when everyone on the work station behind us turned round to listen in. "Fancy inviting her," she whispered, making it clear to them that this was a private conversation with me, who is never in on the office gossip.

"I hate cooking anyway," she says, "what about you?"

"I love it," I say. It's like we're just meeting for the first time today and I've worked with Mandy for nearly two years. She waits for me to keep talking.

"I love baking most of all," I add. "I love putting a big dollop of stuff in the oven and bringing out a cake. It's like magic, don't you think?"

"It would be bloody magic if mine came out looking like an actual cake," she says and she laughs so loud that all the people behind us turn round again and give us one of those 'shhh!' looks that teachers use. So then she pulls a face like 'aren't we naughty?' and we giggle quietly like kids.

"You'll have to bring some cakes in for us all to pig out on one lunchtime," Mandy whispers. "Or maybe just for our pod...."

I can see Heidi coming back over to the table and I nudge Mandy to let her know. She hands me a piece of paper and points at it as if she's explaining something, but what she says is: "Make sure it's got proper butter and lots of cream and stuff in it won't you, this soya crap is bloody killing me!"

So we run through all the ups and downs of the last two weeks and Heidi runs through the schedule for this week and I go back to my desk and just get on with it. And every now and then Mandy hands me a boiled sweet or puts her head over the little wall thing that separates my desk from hers to pull funny faces while she's on the phone or make her hands chatter chatter if she can't get the customer to finish the conversation. Mandy's always been like this, but not usually with me. Maybe someone's told her it's up to her to cheer me up. She's not doing a bad job, actually.

At lunch time I wander up to the shops like I usually do to pick something up for lunch and get some fresh air. My phone rings and I end up having to empty out half my handbag on someone's garden wall to find it, by which time it's stopped ringing and I've got a text message. 'Hpe ur OK & wrk not 2 awful. Jx'. I don't know whether to ring her back so I just put the phone in my pocket and carry on walking to the shop while I decide what to do. And once I've bought my sandwich I think I'll just text her, then she'll know I've got her message but I won't interrupt her by ringing because she might be busy. I get the phone out and think about what I can say in the text but before I even start pressing the buttons it rings again.

"Hi", she says, "It's Julie."

"That's funny," I say, "I was just about to text you."

"Did you get my text from before?"

"The one from a couple of minutes ago? Yes. That's why I was going to text you. I'm just out getting a sandwich," I add, not knowing what else to say. "I've treated myself to a vanilla slice."

"You certainly know how to live it up," Julie laughs, "I'll give you that. Are you OK?"

"I'm OK," I say but even as I'm saying it I know I sound unconvincing. "It's not been that bad. It's nice to get my head back into work in a way and everyone's been lovely and everything but..."

"But you still needed the vanilla slice?" she asks and I know that she knows exactly why I need it. I haven't finished being self-indulgent yet. I'm still in need of big hugs and a good old sob, but the closest I can get to all of that is my vanilla slice.

"Actually I could do with a large gin and tonic but I don't think lunch time drinking's such a great idea on my first day back."

"How about tonight then? After work?"

"I can't," I say, and it's such an automatic response that I don't even stop to ask myself whether there's a way I could do it. "I'd love to," I say – I want her to know that I'm pleased that she asked – "but I can't."

And if she were me she would leave it at that but Julie is not like me.

"Why not?" she says. How long has she got? I'm about to say something, I don't know what I'm about to say, but before I get any words out she says: "Is it because of him?"

"He doesn't like me going out," I tell her, "and anyway, I go swimming on Mondays."

And I think she's going to leave it there.

"I'm sorry," she says, "I've got to go in to a meeting now, they're waiting for me. Hope the rest of the day goes OK for you – we'll speak soon."

"Thanks."

"Enjoy the vanilla slice."

"Thanks," I say again but she's already hung up so I just lock the key pad on my phone and fling it back into the bottom of my handbag.

I walk back to the office with that horrible unease you get when you feel like you've said the wrong thing but you can't put your finger on exactly what went wrong. Julie said she had a meeting and she probably did have a meeting but perhaps she just thinks I'm too much like hard work and she can't really be bothered. Why should she? It's not like we were best friends at school, even before I set everyone's tongues wagging about her. It's not like she owes me anything. It's not like I've asked her to look after me either. She's got her own stuff to worry about, I'm sure she has, and her own friends and everything.

Mandy greets me from her desk with a big smile and a 'T' sign made with her two index fingers.

"I'd love one," I say and I sit down at my desk to eat my lunch.

By the time she gets back from the kitchen carrying a mug of tea each for me and her and one for Amy who sits behind us, I've almost finished my sandwich and I'm thinking about my vanilla slice and whether I'll need to go and find a plate and a knife to eat it. It seemed like a good idea in the shop but now it just seems like a good way of getting bits of flaky pastry in the gaps between the keys on my keyboard.

"Ow, oww, owww, owwww!" Mandy says as she plonks the two mugs of tea she was carrying in her right hand down on the desk. "I knew I should have made two trips. Sorry it took so long. I was just telling Liz about the whole vegan nightmare thing. She reckons I should just meet him half way and go veggie. But I don't think he'd go for that. What do you think?"

"I think you should just eat this vanilla slice and not worry about what he thinks," I say. "What he can't see he can't complain about." And I hand it over to her and she swaps me for a cup of tea which is now less than piping hot but I don't care. She's grinning from ear to ear and she doesn't think it's weird that I've given her my cake, she just thinks it's great.

"Oh my God that's fantastic," she says. "Did you get this for me?"

I nod. It's much nicer for her to think that I got it for her than that I just went off the idea and palmed it off on her. And she's so pleased. Anyone would think I'd just handed her a winning lottery ticket.

"You are a complete hero," she says. "Everyone's entitled to a little lapse every now and then, aren't they?" And she doesn't go and get a plate or a knife or anything, she just pulls open the wrapper and lifts it to her mouth. She hesitates. "Sure you don't want to go halves?" she says.

I know it's a rhetorical question really, and I'm enjoying her excitement much more than I would have enjoyed the cake, so I shake my head and she takes the most enormous bite she can. Crumbs of pastry shoot out across her desk and a big blob of vanilla cream splodges onto her t-shirt but she just laughs. I think for a moment how He would react if he saw me behaving like Mandy. He'd go ballistic. He certainly wouldn't think much of her. But who cares? I like her and she likes me, even if it is only for today and for the sake of a vanilla slice.

"Mmmm!" she says with her mouth full and nodding violently towards my handbag.

"What?"

"I think that's your phone," she says, displaying a mouthful of half-chewed cake.

So I pick my bag up from the floor and empty it out again onto the desk to find my phone. There's a text from Julie.

"How about a quick G&T after swimming?" it says.

17

There are other women. Don't ask me how I know, but I know. I know from the names He mumbles in his sleep. I know from the door He closes quietly before He picks up the phone to dial out. I trust my hunches and my can't-put-my-finger-on-it funny feelings. I used to be a Charlie's Angel didn't I? Trust me, I know.

There's a slobbish one. She's not fat, though, she's thin. Too thin. And she doesn't look like a slob, not from the outside. To anyone who doesn't know her she looks like a high maintenance, well-groomed, seriously vain type. And she is. She takes care over her appearance, spends ages trying on outfits just for going out to work or meeting up for coffee. These shoes, or maybe these shoes, or maybe those shoes with that bag but not with that jacket. Blah, blah, blah. But then when she's finished strutting up and down in front of the mirror admiring herself, she just dumps the lot on the bedroom floor and gets up in the morning and rummages through the pile for the bits of it she wants to put on. She likes it when people notice her but she couldn't give a shit what they actually think.

Her flat is nice: it's an apartment, one of those city centre conversions with bare brick walls and beams and a balcony overlooking the canal. It's posh but it's a mess. There are piles of paper all over the table where she ought to be eating her dinners, or laying out nice romantic meals for Him, even. But she never uses the table for meals and she never tidies it up, she just carries on adding to the pile with receipts and letters and bits that she's cut out of newspapers. There are newspapers stacked up in the little fireplace where there's never been a fire and books lined up all around the walls and a bin that's full of crisp packets all folded up into neat little triangles. But there are no pictures on the walls, no ornaments and no vases. He could never buy her flowers, she has nowhere to put them.

She eats breakfast cereal in bed. Not just every now and then when she's feeling poorly or having a bit of an off day. She eats breakfast cereal in bed pretty much every day. And not just for breakfast. She eats it for dinner too. Or ready-made sandwiches or packets of crisps or those little boxes of raisins that kids have in their packed lunches. She watches the news on her flat-screen TV while she munches her way through crunchy nut cornflakes every morning; she has fruit for lunch on the hoof while she's working and she has a bowl or two of cereal or maybe an egg mayonnaise sandwich for dinner. And if she has nothing much planned in the evening she'll just put on her pyjamas, grab the remote and flick through the channels until she finds something she wants to watch while she chomps on a bowl of Rice Krispies and talks at the TV, gesticulating with her spoon.

He met her at the all-night garage at two in the morning. He was just on his way back from somewhere, putting fuel in the car for the morning. She had just nipped in for some milk. "A funny time for breakfast," He'd quipped while they waited for the guy behind the counter to change the till roll. "Any time's a good time for breakfast", she said and He took that as an invitation and before she knew it she was inviting Him over for breakfast the following evening and He was certain that He'd turn up to a full on feast of bacon and eggs with whatever he fancied from the bedroom menu for dessert. But she doesn't cook. She might oblige with whatever else He wants, but she never, ever cooks.

When He got to her swanky apartment He couldn't quite believe it. He couldn't stop Himself from tidying the odd pile of papers here and a few stray books there. She was irritated by Him but she let it go. She offered Him a glass of wine and He followed her into the kitchen where she had to wash a wine glass from the collection of dirty glasses sitting by the sink waiting to be cleaned. And while she ran it under the hot water tap He opened the fridge to get the wine and let out an audible gasp. All that was in there was the wine, a bottle of milk and a week's worth of pre-packaged sandwiches.

"Have you just got back from a trip?" He asked.

"No", she said. She just handed Him the glass, which was cleaner now, but if He was in a restaurant He'd still ask for another one. But He took it and let her fill it up and didn't ask any more questions.

If she could be bothered to explain she would tell Him that she used to cook, once upon a time. In fact she was a great cook. She loved it. She'd cook pancakes for breakfast and bake pies and make her own pasta, kneading it and wringing it through the pasta machine until her arms ached and the workbench was covered with strand after strand of perfect linguine. She made cakes too, lots of cakes, and flans and pastries and trifles and home-made ice cream. She set the table for every meal with a cloth (freshly ironed) and place mats and coasters, and she tidied the kitchen as she went along and cleared up after every meal. She kept the house spotless, got the vacuum cleaner out every day and moved the sofa so that she could clean under it and behind it. And once a week she got down on her hands and knees and wiped every skirting board with a damp cloth.

That was her alter ego when she was married, years before. And she didn't do it because her husband expected her to, she did it because she expected him to want her to. But all that baking made her fat and all that cleaning gave her dishpan hands and a lingering smell of bleach. He didn't like it and he didn't like her. And he told her so, just before he ran off to start a new life in the South of France with her best friend, the skinny one who couldn't so much as boil an egg but loved to shag alfresco on sunny afternoons.

Understandably, she was upset when he left and spent a couple of weeks in bed consoling herself with family-sized packs of Maltesers and cheese-and-onion crisps (her husband had never liked the smell of those either). But after her hibernation she discovered that she missed the friend more than the husband. She wasn't that bothered about the husband at all. All that domestic goddess stuff was just a distraction from the fact that she couldn't really give a shit about him, so she made a decision: she just wasn't going to do that stuff any more. So she gave up cooking and she gave up cleaning and she gave up worrying what anyone thought of her. So when He grimaced at the sight of stray Sugar Puffs in the bed, she just grimaced back at Him.

He fucked her anyway. But He never went back.

18

There are hardly any pictures of me as a child and in all the photos I've ever seen I have a dirty face. Back in the days when you had to pay for the film and for the processing whether your pictures were any good or not, people used to wait for the 'Kodak moment' before they bothered getting the camera out. Apparently most of my Kodak moments involved eating chocolate or ice cream or licking the bowl after we'd been baking. In those pictures I'm proud of my dirty face and you can almost hear me yelling 'CHEEEEESE' from the grainy old print. I would like to be that girl again. That girl who is caught in the act of being totally oblivious to social conventions like clean faces and table manners. That girl who doesn't care what anyone else thinks.

But that's not allowed when you're a grown-up. Certainly not in my house. So when I get home I say nothing about laughing with Mandy, or the vanilla slice, or the phone call from Julie. I just ask Him does He want a cup of tea and He says, "Ooh, please, I'm gasping." And I stand by the kettle waiting for it to boil, putting teabags into cups and getting the milk out ready, thinking about how I'm going to squeeze in a quick drink with Julie and get back here at the usual time without Him knowing.

I hand Him his cup of tea and He asks me what's for dinner.

"Chilli con carne."

It was going to be lasagne but there's only one piece of lasagne in the packet so I had to do a quick re-think. Thank goodness for the versatility of minced beef; He hates it when I have to nip to the shop for an ingredient we've run out of before

I can cook. Thank goodness I checked the cupboard before I brought the teas through.

I wait for Him to ask me how it went at work but he's just flicking through what's on TV tonight with the remote, waiting for me to ask Him the same thing.

"How was work?" I say.

And as though He hasn't heard me He carries on searching through the schedule for something He might want to watch later and I find myself sucked into the screen too, trying to read fast enough before He presses the button again and I'm cut off mid sentence.

Eventually He presses the button one more time and the screen goes black and He looks up at me.

"Work was fine," He says. "OK. Well, as OK as it ever is. You know."

And then He launches into a story about that fucker from accounts and how he's got everyone's back up and how they're thinking of going to the boss now to complain about him because it's bordering on harassment and something needs to be done.

I nod and gasp in all the right places and He cheers up just for getting it off his chest.

"Anyway," He says. "How was work for you? First day back and all that. Was it OK?"

I tell Him about the awkwardness when I first arrived and about the flowers and how nice everyone was.

"Great," He says. "So back to normal then."

"Back to normal," I repeat.

"So are you going swimming tonight then?" He says.

"Yes," I say, feeling like He knows I'm planning to meet up with Julie even though He can't know.

"Great," He says, "Cos I think I'll go out. There's nothing on the telly and Mike's trying to get a team together for a pub quiz."

"Oh. OK. Do you want me to come down and join you after swimming?" I don't know why I ask the question, I know He'll say no and I don't even want Him to say yes.

"No," He says, "You'll be knackered after swimming and quizzes are not really your thing are they?"

Then, just so that I can't reply to his rhetorical question, He gets up from the chair, announces He needs the loo and dashes off upstairs yelling "How long 'til dinner? I'm starving!"

"About half an hour," I yell back and get out my phone to text Julie the good news.

***

I feel stupidly nervous when I get to the swimming baths. It's not that long since I was last there but I feel like everyone will be looking at me and wondering why I've been away. Maybe they've even been talking about it over the past couple of weeks, maybe I should have a story ready in case anyone asks. They won't ask. We never do more than nod at each other. Why should they ask?

The guy at the reception kiosk is new, new to me anyway. He's good-looking in a sporty kind of way and he's much less miserable than the woman who's usually on the front desk. He even says please when he asks me for the money and smiles as he gives me the change. You stay away for a couple of weeks and suddenly the place goes all friendly and polite.

But poolside everything is reassuringly the same. Same old faces in the pool. Same po-faced lifeguard counting down the minutes until he finishes his shift and texting his mates while he's supposed to be poised ready to save a drowning pensioner at any minute. Same old dodgy smell coming from the gents' toilet, same creaky doors on the changing rooms with the same illegible graffiti. It's one of those old-fashioned municipal pools with the changing rooms down the side and the pool in the middle. No lockers, no wheelchair access, no fancy Jacuzzi, just a big, echoey room with massive, round lights, like flying saucers, hanging from the ceiling.

I take out my swimming costume. It has been folded in the bottom of this bag since I washed it after my last swim nearly four weeks ago. I think about my baby and how the swimming costume would have stretched to cover my bump. But I'm not going to cry, I'm just going to swim. So I put it on and I sling my towel over the door so that I can see which changing room is mine, then step out of my cubicle and take a look at who's in the pool. The bald guy with the dodgy leg is there, and skinny goggles girl and the old tattooed woman, and there's one or two semi-regulars who I've seen here before but not every week.

The bald, dodgy-leg guy nods at me as I walk down the stone steps into the pool, then he launches himself off again as I shiver. There's a funny kind of noisy quiet, with just the exaggerated sound of splashing echoing through the room, and the odd cough and the sound of my brain banging around inside my head. But as I finally throw myself forwards into the water and start swimming, the quiet suddenly explodes into the sound of loud voices and laughing as a group of teenage boys burst into the room and the door handle slams against the wall and everyone in the pool stares to see where the racket is coming from.

We don't usually get teenagers in: there's no water slide, not even a diving board, and the average age must be at least fifty, so it's not exactly in the teenage hotspot top ten. But I'm glad that I'm not exiled with the pensioners and the oddballs for a change and, anyway, they stop being quite so loud when everyone stares at them.

It doesn't last though. When the first one comes out of his changing room, he just jumps in and starts swimming. The second one finishes getting changed and jumps in, swims up behind him and grabs him by the ankle and drags him under. So he comes up yelling and pushes his friend under, just as the third one arrives to join in the mutual ducking. By the time all five of them are in the pool it's all noise and splashing. Then they start jumping in, then they start pushing each other in and everyone who was already in the pool when they arrived is squeezed into about a third of the space down at one end and skinny goggles girl gets out and gets changed without even having a shower.

And all the time, the attendant just watches them as though by the power of staring alone he can stop them from behaving like thugs and restore peace to the pool. I keep thinking, 'in a minute he will go and tell them.' 'In a minute he'll do something.' But he just lets them carry on pushing each other in and jumping on each other's heads and making ridiculous amounts of noise.

A guy in a suit comes in, a manager I think. He's obviously heard the noise and wonders what's going on. So he and the pool attendant have a tête-à-tête and then they both stand and stare at the kids in the pool, while the adults in the pool stare at them and wait for them to do something and the hooligans completely ignore everyone. And when the power of staring doesn't work, they clearly don't have a plan B because they do nothing. And since I can't swim because half the pool's a war zone, I just get out, collect my shampoo from my cubicle and head for the shower.

So I'm standing in the shower, washing my hair and watching what's going on. And the old bald fella with the leg comes and stands in the showers next to me. I've never seen him get out of the pool before. He's always in the water when I arrive and still in the water when I leave, but today he's got out and for the first time ever in his life this guy that I see every week, pretty much, actually opens his mouth to speak to me.

"They shouldn't be allowed to get away with that," he says. "It's dangerous, don't you think? It's dangerous."

I mumble my agreement through a haze of shampoo suds but, even though I do genuinely agree with him and think it's ridiculous that they can carry on like that with no-one stopping them, the first thought that jumps into my head when the old fella stands next to me in the shower is: 'I wonder if I can see what's wrong with his leg?' So I reach down for my conditioner so that I can look at his leg without making it obvious that

I'm looking at his leg. But it seems normal. No shark bite. No hideous wasting disease.

"Don't you think, love?"

He's still talking to me and I have no idea what he said because I was too busy thinking about his gammy leg.

"Yes," I say. "Someone should say something."

"But they're not going to, are they?" Gammy-leg Man says, nodding towards the pool attendant and the man in the suit, who are still watching the boys pushing each other into the water.

"No," I answer, "and telepathy's not going to do it, is it?" and he gives me one of those hospital smiles.

He's hoping I'm going to do something. He's waiting for me to do something and it occurs to me that I actually could.

I flip my shampoo bottle closed purposefully. "Somebody should say something," I say again to Gammy-leg Man and with my shampoo bottle in one hand and my conditioner in the other I march towards the pool attendant and his useless sidekick.

"Yes love," says the one in the suit. He's too warm in his suit and his collar is too tight and his belt has been pulled in too far so that his fat belly flobbles over the top of it. He's sweating. He's wondering what I'm going to say. I'm wondering what I'm going to say.

"Don't you think you should be stopping them from doing that?" I say.

"Our health and safety guidelines advise us not to put members of staff at risk," he says and he can't even look at me while he's saying it because he knows it's the lamest excuse anyone has ever uttered.

"Oh," I say. I can feel the eyes of every swimming pool regular in the place looking at me and waiting for me to sock it to him. "And what do your health and safety guidelines have to say about the health and safety of your customers?" I pause to give him chance to answer but he's not got anything to say. "Do they say anything about protecting them from yobs while they're on the premises? Do they tell you that you'd be liable for any injuries incurred on your premises if you haven't done everything you can to prevent them?"

The sinewy pool attendant in the stupid baggy shorts thinks he might interrupt me but I'm on a roll.

"Perhaps you don't think they pose any danger to anyone? Perhaps you think they're just a bit of a nuisance and it's not your job to sort it out? It is your job though, isn't it? Or, let's put it this way, it certainly isn't our job. Surely you have rules about behaviour in the pool and surely they've overstepped the mark, so it's your job to chuck them out, or at least have a word and ask them to behave? Isn't it?"

I give him a proper chance to answer this time and realise that the pool has gone spookily quiet. Even the thugs have stopped pushing each other in long enough to eavesdrop and suddenly I feel like I should have left it to someone else to speak up, or at least got dressed before I started going all superhero citizen.

"They seem to have stopped now, anyway," the sweaty suit man says, lamely.

I turn round to look at the yobs and they give me a round of applause.

"Are you OK love?" says the old tattooed woman behind me.

"Thanks," I say, "I'm fine."

"Thank *you*," she says. "It's not her job to sort out their behaviour," she says to the pool attendant and the sweaty suit man, "is it?"

And then she speaks to the gang of lads across the pool. "No-one wants to stop you having fun, lads, just spare a thought for those of us who want to chug along quietly and do a few lengths, will you?"

One of them gives her a double thumbs up while another says, "Sorry ladies," and that's that.

"It wasn't that difficult was it?" she says to Tweedle-Dum and Tweedle-Dee.

They don't reply.

"Sorry for losing my rag," I say to them.

"Don't you apologise, love," says Tattooed Woman. "Just you get yourself changed."

So I do as I'm told and the quiet yobs are still watching me and Gammy-leg Man nods and smiles at me from the shower.

As I get changed I keep replaying what I said and what I could have said and I find myself grinning and I can't stop. I didn't really stop the boys from behaving like hooligans and I didn't deliver the killer blow to the pool attendant and his sweaty sidekick, but the hooligan taming and the Tattooed Lady's outburst wouldn't have happened if it hadn't been for me.

Look at me, I'm an actual grown-up. Frame me and put me on the wall.

19

I arrive at the bar all out of breath from rushing because I was convinced I was going to be late, but I'm forgetting that I got out of the pool early and when I scan the room looking for Julie I can't see her. I'm not sure what to do. My mum would tell me to wait outside. But it's cold outside and that's not what Julie would do. That's not what Jaclyn Smith would do, either. She would order something on the rocks and sit down and flick her hair at the barman. My hair's too wet to flick and I'd feel stupid asking for anything on the rocks but I'm not going to wait outside. I sit at the bar and when the barmaid comes over and says "What can I get you, love?" I ask for two gin and tonics and explain that I'm a bit early and I'm waiting for my friend. The barmaid doesn't care but she stands there while I finish speaking and listens politely before tottering off on her ridiculous heels to press the two glasses up against the optic, one, then the other.

I would like to wear heels like that. Tart's shoes. Fuck me shoes. Shoes that would make me as tall as anyone. Shoes that could have somebody's eye out if you ever needed to defend yourself in a dark alley – you'd need to square up and fight: there's no way you could run away fast enough in those things.

I'm thinking about the shoes and looking at the scruffy trainers I have on when I get one of those sudden uneasy feelings that you get sometimes when a thought flits in and out of your brain too quickly for you to remember it but not quickly enough for you to dismiss it and move on. I'm worried that maybe Julie won't turn up and I'll be left here drinking two gin and tonics on my own and looking stupid. But that's not it. That's not it. What is it?

It's the pub quiz. That's it. He didn't tell me where the pub quiz is. The feeling I have is the fleeting question: what if it's in here? I look around. I can't see Him but I can't get the thought out of my head. I call the barmaid over and ask her for two packets of ready salted crisps and when she puts them on the bar I ask her, "Do you ever do pub quizzes in here?" she says, "Yes, love, Thursdays. That's £1.20 please." I give her the money and she teeters off again. Phew.

I look at my phone. No missed calls. No Messages. 21.02. I told her that I get out of the pool at nine and I'd get to the pub as quickly as I could after that. She'll probably get here about ten past. It might be quarter past. They might have a newspaper or something.

I look round. The place is full of after workers. People in suits, people not in suits but not in weekend going-to-the-pub clothes either. People just stopping off for a drink before they go home, without thinking there's anything odd about it. I still have that queasy feeling and I'm trying to put it down to nervousness that Julie might not turn up. But that's not it. I'm sure she will. She will. So what's the feeling?

And then I see someone who looks a bit like Him. Just a bit. It's in the way he waves his arms about when he's talking. The guy doesn't look like Him, he's taller and he has less hair but there's something similar about him that ties a knot in my stomach. What if there is no pub quiz? What if 'pub quiz' was just a euphemism for going out for a drink with some woman or other? What if He is here with all the other men flirting with colleagues while their wives put their dinner in the oven on a low light and look forward to presenting them with it all dried out and mushy. What if He's here?

I try to look like I'm not checking every face that comes through the door and peering at the people sitting at every table but I'd make a terrible undercover cop. Charlie would be disappointed in me for sure. For every table where I can't see Him I start to feel a bit more paranoid and I'm telling myself ‘relax, relax, relax’ but it’s not working. And then I see a familiar face.

“Julie!” Embarrassingly, I’m so delighted to see her that I pretty much somersault off the bar stool, sending my bag flying and the contents scattering across the floor.

It turns out that she’d been there the whole time, since before I came in, having a drink with some people from work. They’d been busy talking about work stuff and she hadn’t seen me come in. Well, she’s seen me now. Pretty much everyone in here has seen me now and I’m amazed not to have had a ripple of applause. Instead I get a half-interested-in-the-answer ‘You all right love?’ from the girl behind the bar and a leery smile from the guy on the bar stool nearly next to me. Clearly he thinks I’ve had a few too many. So, dignity thoroughly irretrievable, I smile back at him and say:

“Tricky sport, bar stool gymnastics. Need to keep working on that dismount.”

And he laughs and so does Julie behind me, gathering up my keys and half a dozen long-forgotten lipsticks. And it’s not that bad.

“Do you want to meet my work friends?” Julie asks. What do I say? If I say yes I might end up having to chat with them for the next hour and if I say no, she might think I’m rude.

“Don’t feel you have to,” she says, “they’re nice but we won’t sit with them. We always end up talking about work stuff and you’d be bored stiff. I’ll just go over and get my things and then you can teach me some of your bar stool moves.”

So I wander back to her table with her and they all smile at me while she introduces me and she goes round the table telling me their names and they wave at me when their name is called, like kids at school with her taking the register.

“Right,” she says. “Go home. Especially you,” she says, pointing to a thirty-something with an almost empty and a completely full pint in front of him. “See you tomorrow.”

And she links arms with me and drags me back across to the bar whispering in my ear.

"He thinks his wife might be about to tell him she's pregnant," she whispers, "and he doesn't want to hear the news!"

The two gin and tonics are still on the bar and leery smile guy is still looking at us and still smiling.

"I think he thinks we were whispering about him," I say.

"Let him," says Julie. "We are now!" and she laughs and glances across at him and laughs again.

I start to wonder how many she's had before I got here, but when I give her the gin and tonic she lets out a massive sigh.

"Oh God I'm dying for this," she says. "I'll only ever have one when I'm driving so I've been on orange juice until you got here so that we could have our G&T together. I like orange juice but it's not a drink you look forward to at the end of the day, is it?"

"Not like hot chocolate with whipped cream and marshmallows...."

"Now you're talking. With a glug of Bailey's in!"

And as if we've rehearsed it we throw our heads back with a big, guttural 'mmmmm' and leery guy grins at us and we burst out laughing and I've completely forgotten any possibility that He might be in here.

"What's up?" she says. So I tell her that I'd had a bit of a panic that He might be in here and I might get in trouble for coming out for a drink instead of going straight home after swimming.

"Give over," she says. "What are the chances? Anyway, you're just having one G&T with me and I'm hardly little miss wild child. Far from it, I'm usually in bed with a book by ten o'clock. It's not like you're lap dancing on the bar and shagging a stranger in the ladies loos."

I can't quite believe she's said that and neither can leery man, apparently. He's now stirring his drink with a straw and trying not to look at us. Maybe he thinks he'll hear something more interesting that way.

I change the subject and tell Julie all about what happened in the pool. I start with the bit when the boys started pushing each other into the pool and Julie says that they could have hurt one of us, not just each other.

"Exactly!" I say. And I tell her all about how the pool attendant and the manager did nothing and about Skinny Goggles Girl getting out and Gammy-leg Man in the shower and me going over to talk to the pool people.

And I think she's going to say something but she just leans back on her stool and puts her hand on her hips and opens her mouth wide in theatrical shock. I wait for her to say something.

"Go on," she says. So I tell her how everyone was looking at me and about Tattoo Woman coming to back me up. And when I've finished I just say, "And that's it, then I came here."

"That's fantastic," she says.

"Not really."

"Yes really," she says.

"I think I maybe had an out-of-body experience or something."

And she laughs. But she's not really laughing.

"What?" I say.

"Nothing," she says.

"What?" I ask again.

"Do you remember when we used to play Charlie's Angels and you were always Jaclyn Smith and I was always Sabrina?"

"Yes." I'm smiling but she's still not. "You always wanted to be the clever one and you always thought of a way of bringing horses into the story so that you could gallop off and rescue someone."

"I didn't always want to be the clever one," she says and I think she might be about to have a go at me for bullying her into being boring old Sabrina with the rubbish haircut but she says: "I sometimes wanted to be Sabrina but I sometimes wanted to be Jaclyn Smith and I just didn't dare to say it in case you didn't want to swap and wouldn't want to play with me."

And then she takes my hand and I can feel the charms on her bracelet tickling my little finger.

"I don't know what took the Jaclyn Smith out of you but she's still in there, I think."

I'm not sure what to say next. I feel a bit awkward. I didn't expect her to hold my hand. I don't want her to let go but I don't know what she wants me to say.

"A bit," I say, "but the hair could do with a bit of work!" and I flick my still damp hair and she laughs and takes her hand away.

I want to tell her about work today too, about Mandy and the vanilla slice and all of that, but I've chattered on enough I think.

"I'd better go," she says. I've got a meeting in the morning and I'm useless at winging it. Do you need a lift?"

"I'm in the car too," I say. And we both rummage for our keys and drink the last drops from our glass and look towards the door.

"Easy does it on that stool," she says.

"Less of your cheek."

In the car park she points to her car and I tell her 'I'm over there.'

"I'll see you soon," she says. "I'm away this weekend but we'll have to arrange a proper evening out or something."

I just nod and then she hugs me. I never would have thought she was the hugging type. She's all bony and her arms seem unfeasibly long.

"You can always ring me," she says as she walks backwards towards her car, putting her hand to her ear like a telephone. "Or text me and I'll call you back," she says even louder because she's further away.

"Thanks," I mouth back at her. And I get in my car and go home.

When I get back He's already home and his friend Jimmy is there with Him. They're having a can of lager and there's a big tin of chocolate biscuits on the kitchen table.

"You're late back," He says.

I put my swimming bag on the chair next to Him so that he can smell the chlorine.

"Yeah," I tell Him, "there was a bit of a kerfuffle at the pool. Some lads were messing about and pushing each other in and generally making a nuisance of themselves. And guess who went up to the pool attendant and told them they should be sorting it out?"

"I'll bet they loved that," He says. "And guess who valiantly came second in the quiz!"

"Was it you by any chance?"

"It was." And He presents me with the tin of biscuits with a big aren't-I-clever grin on his face.

"We should have come first but I persuaded him on a couple of the answers and they turned out to be a bit of a bum steer," says Jimmy. "Sorry about that."

"So what was the first prize?"

"A bottle of Champagne," He says with mock anger in Jimmy's direction. "Never mind. You can't beat a couple of chocolate biscuits when you've been for a swim, can you love? Put the kettle on then."

20

I'm in the kitchen peeling apples to make an apple pie. I can remember watching my grandma doing this, with a knife just like this one. I can remember gathering up all the peelings and sprinkling sugar on them and eating them and persuading myself it was the most delicious thing on earth. My mum says I have my grandma's gift for pastry but I don't think I'm quite there yet. Nothing I could ever make could possibly taste as good as my grandma's apple pie.

It's Saturday and it's been a funny kind of week. He's been nice since the pub quiz on Monday. Super-nice, in fact. On Tuesday, instead of just leaving me flowers on the table He actually gave them to me and He told me he loved me and that it will all be all right. He asked me if I want us to do anything to remember the baby by, like plant a tree or something, and I ended up crying and He just put his arms around me while I sobbed. I thought He'd get cross but He didn't. And on Wednesday He didn't even go out. He always – pretty much always – goes out on a Wednesday, but this Wednesday He ordered take-out and He made me sit down while He pretended to be the waiter and put on some completely ridiculous foreign accent. He made me laugh and we laughed together. We looked like some sitcom couple off the telly. We looked like an ordinary couple, just sitting at home, having a laugh. I don't know why He's being like this and I don't know how long it will last. It's happened before. There have been other times when He's been lovely for weeks at a time and maybe this time it will be for good.

I'm standing in the kitchen peeling apples and willing Him to have turned over a permanent new leaf. If the peel I'm peeling off this apple comes off cleanly in one, long, curly, green coil then I'll know that everything will be fine, happily ever after, Mr Nice Guy and Mrs Domestic Goddess in wedded bliss 'til death us do part. If the peel breaks before I've shaved all of it off the apple I'll take it as a bad omen that the personality transplant is temporary and all will not be well. I peel extra carefully, extra slowly. I peel as though my life depends on it. When I am almost at the end, at the prickly bit, the apple's bottom, the peel breaks and the long snake lands on the floor, leaving me with just an almost-naked apple in one hand and a knife in the other. I could try another apple. I could tell myself not to be so stupid because believing in the power of the peel is just bonkers. But I know the apple is right. Even more bonkers than that, I think my grandma might even have made the peel break on purpose – I was so close to getting it all off in one, and so slow and careful. She always did say that you should be honest with everyone, including yourself. She died when I was eleven so she never met Him. I'm pretty sure she wouldn't have liked Him if she had.

So the apple peel has spoken. It's made its prediction and it's made me feel all uneasy, but it's not like it's told me anything I didn't already know. But, anyway, it's not exactly scientific. It could still be OK or, given that I managed to keep it all in one piece until almost the end of the apple, perhaps it will be almost OK. Ok-ish.

It's Saturday. Supermarket day. I have to get the pie in the oven, get the washing machine on, hoover the stairs and landing, clean the toilet, get the pie out of the oven and pick Him up from squash so that we can go to the supermarket. He thinks I should make a list but I know it's all in my head. I know what we bought last week and I know what I've used since last week but He likes a list, then He can go round with a pen ticking things off as I put them in the trolley. So somewhere between the pie and the toilet I also need to make a list. It doesn't matter if it doesn't have everything on it, as long as we have a list.

It really has been a funny week. Two bunches of flowers. One from work, which is still at work – I don't need the questions or the stress over whether he believes the answers, even though they're true – and one from Him, which is on the dining room table. Four texts from Julie, the latest one this morning: "Arggh! Weekend from hell. Drink after swim on Mon?" One swim, one drink after swim, two new friends – Julie and Mandy – six recipe suggestions for Mandy and her vegan boyfriend crisis – dinner party part 2 – none of which she seemed to like. I suspect it's the boyfriend that she doesn't like but apparently the sex is fantastic and it certainly sounds it when she's giving me a blow-by-blow account of what she's been up to. It's a wonder she can manage to get up for work in the morning. It's a wonder he's got the energy on a diet of couscous and mung beans; she reckons lentils must be some kind of aphrodisiac. No lentils in my house (He says they disagree with Him) but one shag of my own – not disclosed to or discussed with Mandy – but only of the conventional in-the-bedroom-in-the-actual-bed variety, so much too boring to be of any real interest to Mandy anyway.

By apple number four when I don't have a single piece of peel intact I just stop trying to peel them all in one. Instead, I am breathing in hard to soak up the lovely fresh smell of the apples. Much fresher than the supposed 'fresh pine' that awaits me in the bathroom once the pie is in the oven. I love the smell of apples. It's the smell of picnics and school trips and walks home from the park with my dad when a dull-looking green apple would miraculously appear from his coat pocket just when I thought I might collapse with hunger and he'd rub it on his coat like a cricket ball to clean it and it would go all shiny like a picture in a magazine. It's the smell of nostalgia.

I slice the apples into little slivers and I can't help myself from eating a few before I put them in the pie and sprinkle them with sugar then cover them over with a blanket of pastry and tuck them in with a fork all the way around. I paint egg all over the top then cut three quick slashes in the top – Father,

Son and Holy Ghost – and pray to the god of all good things that the pie will be the best one ever. Then it's in the oven and off to fill the laundry basket.

By the time I go to pick Him up from squash the kitchen is bursting with the smell of my freshly baked pie and I smell of bleach and synthetic pine trees. I'm a couple of minutes late driving into the car park to get Him and I can feel that rising panic in the back of my throat in case He's standing there tapping his foot in the foyer with a face like thunder. But it's Him that's all apologetic: He's had to wait for a shower because two of them were out of order. Can we drop Jimmy home on the way to the supermarket? His car's in for a service.

So Jimmy gets in the back and they dissect the game while I drive and I feel like a mum ferrying her teenagers around. Jimmy's house is more-or-less on the way and he asks us in for coffee and I think it might be nice to go in and chat for a bit, but He says no.

"Jimmy was just being polite," He says as we pull away from the kerb with Jimmy smiling and waving as though he doesn't expect to see us again for months and months. "Let's get to the supermarket."

Then a minute later he says: "Did you make a list?"

"Yes!" And I dig it out of my coat pocket while we're stopped at the traffic lights and He reads it all the way there.

It's busy in the supermarket and the trolley's steering isn't really up to swerving round the crowds. Of course it's busy, it's Saturday lunchtime, it's full of people doing their weekly shop: harassed-looking mums with their kids; old ladies who've had all week to go to the supermarket while it's quiet but like to pop to the shops every day and young, hungover couples who've dragged themselves out of bed just long enough to go and buy something to eat. They'll toss a coin to decide who makes the toast and who gets to snuggle back down under the duvet first before they both abandon their plates on the bedroom floor and retreat to their crumpled, crumb-filled bed for the rest of the afternoon. I was like that once, a long, long time ago. Not in this supermarket, not with Him, but I was definitely like that and I can just about remember it.

"I wish I could read your bloody writing," He says, clutching my list as though it's some essential guide to navigating your way round the supermarket. "Why don't you write the bloody thing so that I can read it?"

"Why don't *you* write the bloody thing?" I actually say that. Out loud! But He doesn't hear me, He's too busy staring at the woman who's pointing at me.

"Marion! Oh my God, Marion." It's Mandy. She's excited. She's very excited and quite a lot more dishevelled than I've ever seen her. "I was just talking about you this morning and telling Guy about the recipes you've given me and he says we should make the lentil and Marmite thingy so we've come to get the Marmite. Evil stuff," she turns to Him, assuming since I gave her the recipe and Guy wants to make the thingy that He's the only potential anti-Marmite ally available. "But you know, what my gorgeous man wants my gorgeous man gets!" And she lets out a filthy cackle and pinches his bum while Guy tries not to look embarrassed and He throws me a 'who-the-hell-is-this?' look.

She catches the look and thrusts her hand out towards Him so that He has no choice but to shake it.

"I'm Mandy," she says. "I work with Marion. She's probably told you about me. We sit together. We bonded over a vanilla slice."

He gives her the kind of look He usually gives people who come to the door selling broadband or loft insulation.

"We're friends," she adds, and that makes me smile. I have a friend and here she is and there's nothing He can do about it.

"Well, it's great to meet one of Marion's work friends," He says, looking her up and down. His eyes rest on her cleavage for a few seconds, long enough for her to glance down and wonder if she's got a stain or something on her T-shirt, and then the awkward silence comes back.

"I'll see you Monday," I say. "Good luck with the lentil bake."

"Why don't you come and help us eat it?" she says. She looks at Guy to back up the invitation and he nods.

"Yes," he says. "Come and eat with us. We've only got one other couple coming: Mandy's cooking put my other friends off for life. If nothing else, you can help her rescue the dinner when things start to go pear-shaped. I believe you're a dab hand in the kitchen."

I assume it will be like Jimmy's coffee, just a thanks-but-we're-a-bit-busy style polite no, but He can't resist the chance to snoop around the life I have away from Him.

"That'd be great," He says, apparently forgetting that lentils don't agree with Him. "Shall we bring the pudding? Marion's made an apple pie this morning."

"I'm vegan," Guy says, "but bring it anyway, no reason why you and Mandy shouldn't have some." And he puts the palm of his hand on the back of her neck so that she kind of shrugs her shoulders and smiles at him for giving her the pie to look forward to after the Marmite concoction.

"Great," He says.

So before I know it He's scribbling the address down on the back of my shopping list along with some directions and slapping Guy on the back as though they've been great mates for ages.

"Any idea where they keep the Marmite in this godforsaken place?" says Mandy.

"Near the jam, I think, way down there."

"Thanks," she says. "You're such a lifesaver." And she kisses me on the cheek and grabs Guy's hand and the two of them literally skip off to finish their shopping.

"She seems nice," He says.

I wait for the barbed comment but He doesn't say anything else. He's waiting for me to volunteer some information about her.

"Have you still got the list?" I ask. "What's next?"

So we wander round as usual, me pushing the trolley and putting things in it, Him clutching the list as though it's a coded message he must crack before we get to the checkout, giving me instructions about where to go and what to get.

When we get to the wine aisle He stops, even though I didn't put wine on the list. I never do. It's not like you'll forget to get some wine if you fancy some wine. It's not like you can't live without it, like milk or bread or toilet paper.

"We should get some wine to take with us tonight," He says.

That's right, we're going out to a friend's house for dinner. We'd better get some wine. We'd better had get some wine. I look at the shelves and all I can see are bottles and bottles and I have no idea what sort of wine we should take.

"What do you think, red or white or one of each? Or maybe some wine and some beer?"

"Maybe it needs to be vegan wine?"

"Vegan wine? There's no such thing. There's no such thing, surely?" He's clearly outraged at the possibility that there might be such a thing as vegan wine and that we might have to find a bottle of it amongst the several million bottles of wine in front of us.

"I'm sure there is," I say, "I think they use animal guts or something."

"Nice," He says, sticking his tongue out like a kid pretending to be sick. "I'll ask someone."

So He looks round and sees a guy in a fleece turning bottles round on the shelf to make the labels all face forwards.

"Excuse me, this might sound like an odd question but can you tell me which of these wines is suitable for vegans?"

"Sorry, mate, I don't work here," the guy says turning round to face us. And then he spots me and says. "Hello love, good to see you've not managed to get yourself run over yet. I bet your sister wasn't impressed with your jay-walking antics."

It's the lorry driver that dropped me off at Julie's. I feel like I've been caught in the bank vault wearing a stripy jumper with a big bag marked 'swag'.

"Sister?" He says.

"Julie," I mumble.

"Oh, that sister," He says.

"Well, we'd better get that wine, thanks anyway mate," and He smiles at the lorry driver, takes hold of me by the elbow and pushes the trolley with the other hand.

We go to the checkout in silence, put the groceries through, pack the bags and pay. All without a word. I don't look at Him and He doesn't look at me, we just get the shopping sorted and leave without even buying any wine.

21

The worst thing about the silent treatment isn't the silence itself. That's fine. That's actually quite nice. The worst thing is not knowing when it will end. The worst thing is not knowing what He's going to say when He finally starts speaking to me again. It's not going to be anything I'm going to want to listen to, let's face it.

But I know how this plays out. I've heard it before. When He starts speaking to me again it will all be completely innocuous to start with. It will be a silence that ends with no real noise. Your average fly on the wall would wonder what all the fuss was about: "No cabaret here boys, moving on." He'll just ask me if I know where the phone is or whether I've seen the weather forecast. He'll just pretend like He's not spent the past few hours ignoring me. He'll expect me to think that it's all over, like He's moved on and we should just put it behind us and get on with the day. Then He'll pounce.

So I'm playing his game. I'm pretending that nothing's going on either and just getting ready to go out to Mandy's for dinner. I may not be able to convince myself that there's an enjoyable evening ahead, but I'm not going to give Him the satisfaction of watching me squirm. He won't have much fun giving me the silent treatment if I'm not even in the room, will He? So I've ironed Him a shirt and ironed me a dress. It's not the dress I want to wear, that's still in the wardrobe, with a cardigan hung over the top of it so that it looks like a second choice, shoved-to-the-back kind of dress that I wouldn't choose for myself. So He'll see which one I've spent time ironing, tell me I'm not to wear that and dig out the other one from under the cardigan.

He'll think He's won and I'll know I have. One nil to me. I iron the stuff and just keep ironing and ironing until He comes in the room and switches the TV on, then I unplug the iron and pack it away and leave Him in the room not talking to me all by Himself.

Normally I would take a bath, but baths are interruptible, especially when you have no lock on the bathroom door. There used to be a lock there when we moved in. There was a lock there for quite a while afterwards. I used to lock myself in there when He yelled at me and He would bang on the door and rattle the handle and I would have to wait it out until He calmed down or slammed out of the house in a huff. And then one day He just took it off. No big drama, no kicking the door in. He just decided I wasn't going to have anywhere to hide myself away any more, so in the calm after a row He took a screwdriver to the door and removed the lock. So now we have a bathroom door without a lock and with a big round hole that you could peep through if you were that way inclined. Baths are not private any more. Nothing's private. Except inside my head. Except at work and at Julie's house. I'm in for a shitty evening but I am standing stark naked in the bathroom about to get into the shower and grinning at myself in the mirror. He won't open the door to the shower because he might get wet. And He can't open the door to my head because I can lock it whenever I feel like it.

But, sure enough, when I step out of the shower He's there in the bathroom waiting for me, sitting on the toilet with the lid down with my freshly ironed dress all screwed up in a heap by his feet. He says nothing.

"Sorry," I say, "were you waiting for the shower?"

"No."

"Oh, well I just need to get dry and then the bathroom's all yours."

"I don't want the bathroom," He says. "It's not the bathroom I've been waiting for."

And without another word He gets up and picks up the towel I'd left on the floor by the shower ready to dry myself and He dries my skin. Not gently like you would for a little kid, more like He's drying the pots or wiping a dirty mark off a table cloth. And when He's satisfied that I'm dry He takes me by the shoulders, moves me across to the bathroom wall, pulls his pants down and fucks me right there in my own bathroom.

I don't say anything. What am I going to say? There's nothing much I can do about it. But inside my head I'm saying the words as loud as I can, again and again and again.

"I hate you, I hate you, I hate you, I hate you, I hate you." And I don't look at Him and I don't make a sound.

When He's finished He says: "You'd better get dressed. We'll be late. I've put a dress out for you in the bedroom."

Getting back in the shower to get myself clean again is not an option. But it's OK. When I walk into the bedroom I can see straight away that He's pulled my under-the-cardigan dress out of the back of the wardrobe and laid it out for me. I close the bedroom door behind me, stick my tongue out at Him through the door and get dressed.

He's still in the shower when I finish getting ready so I go downstairs and potter. I've made some baked apples to take with us as a vegan alternative to the apple pie. I've put them in a bowl and wrapped foil over the top so that Mandy can just pop them in the oven to warm them up when we're ready for dessert. He said I shouldn't bother, and when I peel back the corner of the foil to admire my handiwork I can't help wondering if maybe He's right. They looked nice when I first took them out of the oven. They smelt gorgeous. But now they look like shrivelled little shrunken heads with their skin all leathery and discoloured like it's been sitting in a peat bog for the past two thousand years. I wonder if there's anything I can do to make them look a bit nicer – it's not like I can cover them in cream or custard – or perhaps I should just leave them behind. Or pretend I've forgotten them. But maybe my shrunken heads have a little voodoo magic and they'll be my lucky charms for this evening. I could pluck out a hair and slip it inside one and He could choke on it as the slippery flesh slides down his throat and by the time the ambulance gets there He'll be dead on the dining room carpet, killed just like that by a baked apple.

But He's alive and well in the car on the way there and my wizened, mushy apples and my beautiful pie are balanced one on top of the other while I drive and He sighs every time I change gear.

He's alive and well as I park up in the rain, as we dash from the car to the front door, me now holding my apple concoctions, Him holding my umbrella.

He's alive and well as we ring the doorbell and Mandy opens the door with a massive grin and He lunges in for a peck on the cheek that becomes a peck on both cheeks and a well-practised accidental hand on the bum.

"Guy's in the living room," she says to Him, "go on through. It's just us, I'm afraid: Ben and Izzy have cried off." We wait for Him to do as He's told and go and make polite chitchat with Mandy's boyfriend.

She turns to me. "Is he always so friendly?" she asks in mock embarrassment, as I wonder whether to proffer my cheek or my desserts.

"Oh yes. Always. More so, sometimes. How's the lentil bake?"

"Don't ask," she says, and bends forward, covering her head with her arms.

"Have you been at the cooking sherry?"

"Not at all," she smiles. "Just a little bit of medicinal red wine to help me through the whole cooking-for-guests trauma. Come and have a look!"

So she takes me by the elbow and leads me into the kitchen which looks as if it's been ransacked by a gang of ravenous wolves.

"I know," she says.

"Oh my God!"

"Yes," she says, "I know! Let's see what you've brought"

So she looks at my apple pie and says "Maybe we could just have dessert and then coffee and mints and vodka cocktails." Then she looks at my baked apples and says, "OK. Mine doesn't look any worse than yours. We could be OK. We could eat blindfolded."

And we're laughing in the kitchen and I wish that He would just go home. Or just disappear in a puff-of-smoke-type magic trick where he lands in someone else's living room and we get some unsuspecting guy in his slippers reading a newspaper and going 'where am I?'

"I think I'm a bit hysterical," says Mandy. "I think cooking gives me post-traumatic stress disorder and my brain just ceases to function properly."

We're laughing and Guy shouts in from the next room "What are you two up to in there?"

"Just experimenting with lesbianism while the potatoes finish roasting," she calls back to him and bursts into another wave of giggles.

"God," she says when she finally recovers the power of speech, "I really need a wee. It's in there," she nods her head towards a tin with foil wrapped over the top. See what you can do with it, will you, and we'll eat in five."

So she rushes off to the loo and I'm in the kitchen looking at the orangey coloured mush in the tin. I cut it into slices and put them under the grill. It's the only way to go. And as I'm doing it I can hear Him talking to Guy in the room next door.

He's telling Guy about my mental health issues. He's telling Guy that I struggle to keep friends for very long because I can't control my jealousy, so I always end up trying to ruin their lives by coming on to their boyfriends or getting them into trouble at work or spreading rumours about them amongst their friends. And then He tells Guy that it's been a tough couple of years because He's had to come to terms with the fact that I'm just not the person that people think they see before they know me properly, but that He knows the real Marion is in there somewhere, we've just got to work through my issues together and hopefully come out the other side.

I would like to walk in there and hand Him an Oscar for his excellent performance as the long-suffering husband but I'm far too busy trying to overcome the urge to inflict some actual suffering with the hot grill pan. Luckily, Mandy reappears before I do anything rash.

"You're a genius," she says as I serve up the now vaguely edible-looking slices of lentil bake. "I totally love you."

And she grabs me round the waist and plants a big kiss on my cheek, just in time for Guy to walk in and say: "Wow, you weren't kidding about the lesbian action!" The two of them fall about laughing.

But no-one's laughing at the dinner table, which is more of a coffee table with a table cloth and we're all sitting cross-legged on the floor.

"Sorry we didn't bring any wine," I say as Guy fills up my glass.

"Oh, that's fine," Guy says, reaching across to fill the other glasses up too. "I only drink vegan wine and it can be a bit tricky to find in the ordinary supermarkets."

"Yeah, we thought that, didn't we Marion?" He says. And He leaves it at that. Innocuous enough that it can't mean anything, but said in a tone that clearly tells everyone that He's accusing me of something.

Sod Him. Change the subject.

"So, how long have you been vegan, Guy?"

"All my life...."

"Poor thing!" Mandy interrupts and He guffaws like it's the funniest quip he's ever heard.

"My parents were total hippies. Grew their own veg, made their own clothes. It was like The Good Life without the pigs. Not that I knew about The Good Life until I was much older, we didn't have a TV."

"God, Marion would never have survived," He says.

"Neither would I," says Mandy.

"Neither would you," I want to say but I don't, not this time. This is not my house and I'm not going to let Him make me into the paranoid hysterical one.

"So you've never, ever eaten meat?" I ask.

"Never," he says, actually puffing out his chest in pride.

"Marion'd never survive that either, would you Marion?" He smiles. "You like a bit of meat, don't you love? And she's not fussy, any old meat will do."

Mandy gives me one of those I'm-on-your-side smiles and I wonder what Jaclyn Smith would do now. Karate chop Him through the window perhaps? Stab a fork in his hand and pour a glass of wine over his head? I go for the advice my mum always used to give me when I came home from school complaining that other girls were teasing me because I had knee socks and they all had ankle socks: just ignore them and they'll go away.

"So did they meditate and have crystals and all that?" I continue to Guy.

"Not so much crystals," he says, "but definitely meditation. We used to meditate together every morning and I still do that now. It gets you in tune with the day...if that doesn't sound too off-the-wall."

"Not at all," I say.

"Not much sounds off-the-wall to Marion, does it love?" He says. "In fact, the more wacko the better: it makes her feel like she's the normal one."

"She is the normal one in our office," says Mandy. I'm glad she's on my side.

"You must be a funny old lot then."

"Less of the old, if you don't mind," says Mandy, who must be ten years younger than me. Or at least eight.

She's good at shutting Him up. She's good at changing the subject. She's good at talking.

And that seems to be her strategy from here on in. Just keep chatting, don't let Him get a word in edgeways and He can't be obnoxious.

But she doesn't know Him. He can still be obnoxious. He can drink all the wine. He can yawn in their faces. He can drum his fingers on the table. He can stare at her tits while she's talking.

Eventually, she stops talking about nothing in particular and says "pudding?" and I get that sinking feeling when I think about my voodoo apple heads.

"Give me a hand will you?" she says, and I stand up to help her clear the plates and bring the pudding in but sitting on my own ankles for the best part of an hour has cut off my circulation and when I stand up the pins and needles have got to me and my jelly ankles won't take my weight.

I stumble forwards, fall onto the table, land with my arm on Guy's plate and it flips up in the air and crashes down right in front of Him, spattering Him with bits of half-eaten lentil and Marmite bake. It's worthy of Laurel and Hardy, or Frank Spencer or the Chuckle Brothers. I couldn't have choreographed it better if I'd spent a decade at RADA.

There's a comedy silence. I look at Him, He looks at the mess all over his trousers and they look at me. And then they laugh like maniacs and I can't help but join in.

He hesitates. He clearly doesn't find it funny. He clearly doesn't want to laugh. But I can see Him weighing it up. Laugh at Himself and give them permission to laugh or refuse to laugh and let them think that he's a dickhead with a chip on his shoulder and no sense of humour. He laughs. Half-heartedly, but He laughs. And then He asks where the bathroom is and excuses Himself for a quick wipe down.

"I'm sorry," says Mandy, pulling herself together as we take the plates into the kitchen. "It was just so comical, I couldn't not laugh."

"Why shouldn't you? It's your house and it was funny."

"Yeah, but he didn't seem to think so."

"He'll live," I say, knowing that He'll be in the bathroom trying to dream up ways of getting his own back.

And He does try. When I bring out the baked apples, all nicely re-heated and smelling delicious, He says: "I thought this was a vegan meal – didn't know internal organs counted as vegan."

But Guy says, "They smell gorgeous, I love baked apples." And I think 'ha ha, one nil to me.'

Then when I bring in the pie, with a jug of 'cream' made out of oats provided by Guy, He tries to trip me up so that I'll drop it and I do stumble but I manage not to fall or drop the pie. Two nil to me.

"Great save!" says Guy, "you could be an air hostess!"

"She'd have to brush her hair first," He says.

"Shall we tuck in?" says Mandy, smiling at me. And she and Guy make appropriate noises over their baked apples and I pour oat cream all over mine and am just about to start eating when He pulls a hair out of his bowl.

"Speaking of Marion's hair," He says. "Bit of extra protein in mine, love – d'you want this back?" and He puts it on his spoon and then holds the spoon out to me as though He's found the most revolting substance known to man in his pudding. So, it looks like the voodoo gods were not on my side after all.

"Oh God, I think that's one of mine," says Mandy. "It must have fallen in when I heated them up. Give me yours, there's another couple in the kitchen, I'll get you a fresh one." Three nil.

So then He gives up. He just eats his replacement apple and tries a change of strategy. Compliments Mandy on her flat. Enthuses about the oaty cream. Offers to cut the apple pie and tells them that I make better apple pie than any restaurant in the country.

They must be wondering what's going on. It's like the man who was here a few minutes ago has been snatched by aliens and replaced by a physically identical version with a much pleasanter disposition. But I've seen Him play this game before, the 'I'm Mr Wonderful and it's all in her head' game. He can play whatever game He wants, I'm still three nil up and they're still my friends and there's no-one in this room that's gullible enough to be taken in by his charm offensive, even if Mandy is a flaky pastry and her boyfriend was raised on space cakes.

I just want to go now, but if I let Him see that then we'll be here all evening. So when Mandy suggests we put some music on, I jump up to go and rummage through her CDs with her and he takes that as a cue to say that we should be going now.

"What about the washing up?" I say, "I'll need to give Mandy a hand with the washing up."

"Oh, don't worry about that," Guy smiles. "We normally just shut the door on it and tackle it in the morning."

"What he means is I normally just shut the door on it and he tackles it in the morning," laughs Mandy.

And I smile at her and try not to feel jealous of her confidence and her happiness and her lovely boyfriend.

"Right then," He says.

"Right then," I say back.

"Right," He hovers, waiting for me to move us out of the house.

"Thanks for a lovely evening," I say, and give Mandy a hug and a kiss on the cheek. She whispers "Don't let him bully you" in my ear, then says, "Thanks for coming. See you on Monday."

"Thanks," I nod to Guy and he comes over and hugs me and kisses me on the cheek too.

"Any cooking tips you can give her, that'd be great," he says.

"Right then," He says again. He gestures towards the door, we pick up our coats and we're gone.

22

It's something past two in the morning and I can't sleep. That's well over two hours of listening to Him snore and trying to reclaim anything vaguely approaching half of the bed. It's not really the snoring that's keeping me awake. If anything, it's the spaces in between the snores, the waiting for the next one, the rhythm that keeps my thoughts flicking from one thing to the next...wait a moment...to the next...wait a moment... to the next. So my head is full of stuff, full of things that don't matter, but the thoughts take no notice when I try to tell them that. They're like double glazing salesmen, brazening it out even when it's been made perfectly clear to them that they're not welcome.

And I've tried all the usual tricks. I've been for a wee. Twice. I've had two paracetamol and a bowl of Rice Krispies. I've opened a window. I've checked all the doors are locked, looked outside to see that the car's still there and felt in my handbag for my keys, zipping up the pocket to make sure they stay put. But I still can't sleep and now the sound of His snores is saying 'caaaaaan't... sleeeeeeep, caaaaaaaan't... sleeeeeeeeep'.

So instead of thinking about what I can do to help me sleep, I start thinking about what I can do while the rest of the world is sleeping. Might as well make best use of the time. And before I know it I'm on my hands and knees in the bathroom, cleaning the toilet with infinite care and attention as though I'm expecting a visit from the Queen. My mum always says that you can tell a lot about a person from the state of their bathroom. She says you should never eat anything in the house of a person who has a dirty toilet or no soap on the sink, because they're dirty people who don't clean up after themselves and don't wash their hands after they've been. My entire childhood was spent proving that I'd washed my hands and my adolescence was an apprenticeship of helpful household hints and tips, all delivered with the words 'you'll have to do this in your own home one of these days.'

So, just like my mum taught me, I'm taking out an old toothbrush from the cupboard under the bathroom sink and squirting bleach onto it and using it to scrub under the rim of the toilet. In the bit where it's too narrow for the toilet brush to fit, the bit where the germs sit. And I'm killing them, every last one of them. Dead germs. They don't stand a chance against me and my toothbrush of doom. They're gonners, every last one of them.

There's something kind of addictive about cleaning once you get started, and here in the silence of the night it feels a bit illicit too. "Nobody cleans the bathroom in the middle of the night," He would say. "Are you bonkers? Get back to bed." But there's no danger of that. He's had more than enough wine to keep Him asleep until morning; He might notice the smell of the bleach when He wakes up but He won't notice that the bathroom's any cleaner. So I just keep brushing away with my worn-out old toothbrush, from the rim to the bit under the seat and the bit round the hinges where the dirt and the splashes of piss collect, and the underside of the lid, and the cistern and the base.

I should feel tired after all that scrubbing but the bleach is like smelling salts, and anyway I'm not doing this to feel tired. I don't want to feel sleepy any more. I want to feel wide awake. I want to clean and clean and clean until there is not a single germ left here. I want to be like the cleaner after a Mafia hit, removing all evidence of everything.

I move on to the shower. I move all the bottles out, and the soap and the loofah, and I start at the edges with my bleachy toothbrush and brush it down the plug hole and pull out bits of hair and scum that I rinse off down the sink until the toothbrush looks clean again. Then I step into the shower and get going on the tiles, every last grouted groove and mildewed corner is scrubbed with my toothbrush until it's white, white, whiter than white and smelling like the changing rooms at the swimming pool. This toothbrush has seen more active service in this one night than it ever did when it was actually used for brushing teeth, and produced whiter results, that's for sure. But this could be its last stand. The bristles are all splayed out to the sides now. I need an upgrade.

I also need a cup of tea, so I wander downstairs to make one and bring it back up with a couple of custard creams, just to keep me going. But when I eat them they're tainted from the bleach that's on my hands. It doesn't taste great but it doesn't burn. You'd think from the big skull and cross bones and POISON in capital letters on the bottle that you'd keel over dead if you let so much as let a drip past your lips but maybe you'd need to drink more than that for it to actually hurt you.

I lift up the bottle and hold it to the light to see how much is still left inside. It feels quite heavy; it must be about three quarters full I think, so about a bottle of wine's worth still in there. Would it hurt? Would it be worth doing if it didn't hurt? At school we only studied two Shakespeare plays, Macbeth and Julius Caesar, and amongst all the carnage I always remember the wives committing suicide and no-one seeming that bothered about it. I don't remember what Lady Macbeth did but the wife in Julius Caesar killed herself by swallowing hot coals. How could you do that? Could you actually do that? Even if you managed one, surely it would hurt so much that you wouldn't be able to swallow any more? How many would it take? How much bleach would it take? If I took a swig would I be able to swallow it? Would it kill me? Or make me ill? Or would it just make me clean on the inside?

I drink my tea. Drinking bleach is a stupid idea. Drinking tea might not solve all the ills of the world but it's comforting in its own way. It's the drink of ordinary days, days that pass and just get forgotten and it's the drink of awful days when people don't know what else to do, so they make you a cup of tea and look worried. And sometimes they put sugar in it, even if you don't take sugar, and then make you drink it, even though you don't like it. "It's for the shock," the neighbour told my mum when she asked why they'd put sugar in her tea when her mother died. There wasn't much of a shock about it: her mother had had cancer for eighteen months and no-one had expected her to last past Christmas, but my mum didn't argue, she just drank the tea and told me to close the curtains and hand round a packet of biscuits.

I've eaten both of my bleach-infused custard creams and so far so good. Not so much as a hiccough. I wonder if you'd be able to taste bleach over the taste of cool mint breath-freshening toothpaste. I wonder if He would notice if I just squirted a little on his toothbrush. It's petty, I know. It's futile. It's definitely futile. And if He realised I'd done it there'd be hell to pay. And if He didn't realise I'd done it, what would be the point?

The point would be I'd know. I'd be able to make Him do something vile and He wouldn't be able to stop me. I take his toothbrush and I squeeze a little bleach out of the bottle onto the bristles. It's a shame I didn't think of this before I cleaned the bathroom from top to bottom. There's no scum for me to scrape off with the brush now because I've done all that. There's not a single germ left in the room for me to invite onto his brush because I've already killed the lot. I can't believe I'm doing this. Maybe I should wash it off. I turn the tap on to wash the bleach off again. It's not worth it. But that's what He wants me to think. She won't argue because it's not worth it. She won't fight back because it's not worth it. She won't kick up a fuss because it's just not worth it. I turn off the tap, I put a little more bleach on the brush, I scrub the floor with it where the toilet pedestal meets the lino and then I put it back into the toothbrush mug ready for Him to use in the morning.

In the morning He'll get up and He'll pretend that nothing's happened tonight. He'll probably make some comment about how awful the food was or how lovely my baked apples were. He won't mention the crumpled dress or the sex in the bathroom or what happened in the supermarket or what happened when we got home. He's saving the next helping of recriminations for round two. He's saving them for when Julie comes to our house for dinner next weekend.

I don't know whether He'd decided on inviting her in the supermarket or whether He just hit on the idea at Mandy's house when things didn't go his way. When we got home I tried to slope off for a shower before bed but He told me my shower could wait.

"You had a shower before we went out," He said. "It won't be too long before we all have to start being accountable for our carbon footprint, you know, and if you're having a bath or a shower every five minutes there'll probably be some kind of fine to pay, or you'll have to plant trees or something to offset your bad habits."

He thought He was still playing to an audience. He was playing it for laughs. I flattered Him with a smile but I wasn't laughing. I just wanted a shower. I just wanted a fucking shower and a long, deep sleep. But I wasn't going to say that to Him. He was waiting for the tears and the contrition and the desperate assurances that I have no more secrets and will never do anything without telling Him ever again. He'd have a long wait. I'd played along this far so a little compliant smiling and a sit down in the living room for five minutes was no great shakes.

"I'm appalled by your behaviour today," He said.

Quite an opener. What was I supposed to say to that?

"Not just today, Marion. These last few days when you've obviously been lying to me about your whereabouts and traipsing around here, there and everywhere behind my back."

Hardly!

He paused. I think He might have been waiting for my excuses, or maybe he was just pausing for dramatic effect. He does like a good courtroom drama. I just waited for Him to carry on; He clearly had a point to get to.

"I heard Mandy joking about lesbians tonight. Or maybe she wasn't joking. Was she? Is that the real story, are you and Julie having an affair?"

I laughed, which wasn't going to do me any favours but I couldn't help it, it just sort of tumbled out of me.

"Well?"

"No, of course not."

"Well you can't blame me for wondering."

"I'm sorry."

"I should think so," He said, getting to his point now, picking up the pace. "I've been worried sick. You pick up with someone that you vaguely knew years ago, that you hardly know at all. We meet a complete stranger in the supermarket who gave you a lift and thinks you and Julie are sisters, and you're clearly meeting up with her behind my back and getting up to God knows what!"

"We had coffee and baked beans on toast," I said. Probably not helpful and possibly quite unwise, but even if he couldn't see how ridiculous this all was, I wanted to remind myself that it's pretty tame as far as matrimonial disputes go. Hardly Jeremy Kyle material.

"Look," He said, "I don't care what you had to eat, the fact is that you lied to me about where you were and I'm worried about you. For all you know she could be some complete weirdo. She looks a bit weird. And you have to admit you're not a very good judge of character, are you? Remember that time you gave a tenner to that guy to help him get a taxi to his sister's house because his car had been stolen? Totally gullible. I just don't want you to be taken in by this woman just because you've got some misplaced feelings of guilt about blabbing to everyone that she was adopted..."

I shuddered. I still feel guilty about that, even though Julie's never mentioned it. I could strangle my mum for telling Him, I knew He'd file it away to use again.

"So anyway, I think we should have Julie round here for dinner so that I can check her out properly."

"But you've already met her."

"Only briefly, and I didn't know then that you'd be meeting up with her all over the place and trying to make out that she's your sister."

Bloody hell.

"OK, I'll ask her."

He passed me the phone.

"Not now," I said, taking the phone off Him anyway. "It's nearly eleven."

"It's Saturday night," He said. "No-one goes to bed early on a Saturday night."

"I'll have to find the number."

"Great," He said. "Find it."

So I rifled through my handbag and found the number and called her. She was asleep.

"Hi Julie, it's Marion. Sorry to ring you so late but we were wondering if you'd like to come to dinner next Saturday."

"What?" she said. "Marion, are you all right?"

"Not really," I answered. But He was looking at me and waiting for me to do the deal and get off the phone. "No, we're not really celebrating anything, we just thought it would be nice."

"Do you want me to have something else on?"

"We can postpone if you like," I told her, trying to ignore his eyes on me, "but we'll have to get you over sooner or later, so if you can make it this Saturday...?"

"OK," she said. "Is He there now?"

"Yes, that's right."

"Ring me when you can."

"Brilliant, about seven then, next Saturday. See you then."

"Take care."

I rang off before she did.

"Great," He said. "I'm going to bed." And He kissed me on the lips, took the phone from me, ushered me out of the door in front of Him and turned off the lights.

I wash the bleach off his toothbrush again. It will probably still taste a bit odd, but only a bit. It's poison, I can't put poison on my husband's toothbrush, what sort of mad cow would that make me? I'm not crazy. I'm not. What would Julie think? What would my mum say? I know what she would say, she would say never do anything that you'd be scared to admit to. Maybe that makes me a coward. I'd like to think it means I know who I am and what my limits are. I know who I am and I'm not that crazy. I'm a cleaner-up of messes, not a mess maker.

My bathroom is clean, my husband is still asleep, it's something past three in the morning and I need to get some sleep myself. So finally I run a bath and I take out the shampoo that I took from the shower at the hospital. The smell of it takes me straight back there and I am sitting in the bath with my hair covered in suds allowing myself to cry again, just a little bit. Crying for my lost baby and for myself, and promising my little one that I will, one day soon, do something about all this.

23

I'm sitting in the car. He's driving and I don't know where we're going. "It's a surprise!" He says. Fabulous. He can't half pick his moments. I feel like death after four and a half hours' sleep, my hands still smell of bleach, my hair's all fluffy and kinks in stupid places because I went back to bed with it still wet and I feel like bludgeoning Him with the Thermos flask for the way he behaved yesterday.

"Excited?" He says.

I just nod and smile. It's hard to be excited when you have no idea what to expect next.

Wherever it is that we're going, it's a fair old trek and it looks as if there'll be mud or water (or muddy water) involved because I saw Him put wellies for both of us in the boot. He does this every now and then. Decides we need to get out of the house, tells me we're going out for the day and expects me to be in the passenger seat with suitable clothing and a flask of tea five minutes later. But today he told me to forget the cagoule. "Just come as you are," He said. But I did grab the flask and put some mascara on.

The whole thing reminds me of the early days before we were married when we used to get up at lunchtime on a Sunday and drive out to the countryside just for a change of scene. We'd always set off in the same direction but never end up in the same place twice. I'd have a flask of tea and a couple of Kit Kats in a rucksack and we'd both still be a bit hung over from the night before. Eventually, He'd decide we'd driven far enough and find somewhere to park up and we'd laugh at the pensioners sitting in their cars, eating their sandwiches from their Tupperware boxes and admiring the view because it was much too cold to get out of the car. No doubt the pensioners had a good old giggle at our expense too, as they watched us head off in jeans and trainers up some hill or other with no map and no real sense of purpose, stopping after five minutes to fuel up on chocolate biscuits.

I look across at Him as we drive up a country road that I'm sure we must have been up before. He doesn't look back at me, He just puts his hand on my knee and carries on watching the road.

"Some of the bends on these roads are vicious," He says. "I swear they don't mark 'em just to put city folk off from driving round the countryside. Folk from round 'ere ain't from round 'ere!"

He laughs and I find myself laughing with Him. This is the man I fell in love with. He's still there. I don't see Him every day. I don't usually see Him at all. But He's still there.

"We're nearly there," He says.

I look around us and see nothing but bored-looking sheep and dry stone walls as far as the eye can see. Perhaps He's brought me here to do me in and leave me to rot where no-one will ever find me. Perhaps He plans to bundle me out at the next cattle grid and tell me I can walk home (and without so much as a flask of tea to keep me going). But suddenly, there's a pub with a sign that says 'Great Food Served All Day' outside. The sign has a drawing of two plates with steaming pies on them instead of the double 'o' in 'food'.

"This isn't it," He says, "But we may as well stop for some lunch while we're out, make a day of it."

Despite the total lack of all human habitation for at least a five mile radius outside, inside the pub it's packed out. There's a roaring fire, a dart board and a woman scurrying around delivering plates of food to people all over the place. She's either not wearing well for her tender years or is incredibly agile for her age. It's hard to tell which, but apparently it's her job to take the orders as well as bring the food because, as soon as we sit down, she's at our table like a shot asking what she can get us.

"Is there a menu?" I don't know why but I direct the question to Him rather than her; I feel like He's conjured up this Brigadoon and He's in charge.

"It's all on the board, love," she says, nodding her head towards an enormous blackboard right in front of me that I hadn't seen until she pointed it out.

"You'll have to excuse my wife," He tells her. "She doesn't get out much."

We both stare intently at the blackboard as if the correct answer will automatically jump out and present itself if we stare long and hard enough. I keep reading it, again and again, but I'm tired. When I get to the end all I can remember is sticky toffee pudding and as soon as I think of it I don't feel like having anything else.

"I'll come back," she says pointedly after about a minute and a half. I don't blame her. I'd be running out of patience with me too, if I were in her shoes.

"OK," He says, "I'll go and get us some drinks while you have a good look at the board and then when I get back we'll order."

"OK."

"OK. What do you want to drink?"

"I don't know."

"Awww, come on. What do you want?"

"I'll have a lime and soda."

"Don't you want a proper drink?"

"You might want me to drive home."

"I won't."

"Are you sure?"

"I'm sure. Have anything you like. What do you want?"

"I'll have a white wine and soda."

"White wine and soda," He confirms.

"Yes. No. Actually I'll just have a white wine."

"Sure?"

"Yes. Dry white."

"You're sure?"

"Yes, yes. I'm sure."

And He bows in mock reverence and goes to the bar, making sure He stands at the end where the twenty-something in the clingy T-shirt is serving instead of the end where the old fella with the drinker's complexion is in charge.

I look back at the board. Sticky toffee pudding is still the only bit of the menu that's calling to me but I suppose if I have a cheap main course, like soup of the day with bread roll, He might let me have the pudding too. There's no way He'd let me have just pudding, that might show Him up, so I need to figure out whether it's worth gambling on Him letting me have pudding if I've had a cheap main or if I should just go for the lasagne and salad and have done with it.

While I'm still weighing up the best strategy I hear my phone. It's a text from Julie. 'Not heard frm u since last nite. R U OK?'

I look round to see if He's watching. He's engrossed in conversation with Miss Clingy T-shirt and sneaking in a whisky chaser while I'm not looking.

I text Julie back. 'Am fine. Will call u frm wrk 2morrow.' I press send and put the phone back in my bag.

"Did someone call?" He says, arriving behind me with a white wine and soda and a pint of bitter.

"I was just checking the time," I say. "I think they stop serving food at two."

"Oh, it'll be fine," He says. "Have you decided what you want?"

"I was thinking maybe soup?" I say, testing the water.

"Soup? Come on, you'll be starving by the time we get home if you just have soup."

"Well, then I can maybe save room for afters and have sticky toffee pudding."

"I like your thinking, that sounds like a great plan!" And without another word it's a done deal. He turns round and spots the long-suffering waitress and then I cringe as he clicks his fingers at her.

"Miss," He calls, "We're ready to order now."

She makes a point of spending a few extra seconds chatting with the people she's already serving and comes over.

"Two soups of the day followed by two sticky toffee puddings," He exclaims, brandishing the words as though He's just figured out the winning answer in a pub quiz tie-breaker.

"What sort of bread would you like with your soup?" she asks. "We've got white, granary, wholemeal or sundried tomato."

"I'll have granary," I say, apologetically.

"Make that two," He says, impatiently.

"And what would you like with your sticky toffee pudding?" she asks. "We've got cream, custard or ice cream."

"Cream for me," He says.

"And would you like your pudding hot or cold, sir?"

"Hot," He says, "obviously."

"And hot for me too," I add quickly before He starts raising his voice. "With custard, please."

"Thank you," she says, smiling professionally at me, and scurries off.

We both sit there looking at the blackboard once she's gone, as though there is stuff written up there that we forgot to look at earlier. We dutifully check in case we've made some terrible oversight and have to call the waitress back immediately to change our order.

"Aren't you curious about where we're going after this?" He asks.

"Of course I am."

Silence. More looking at the blackboard.

"Do you want me to guess?"

I know even as I utter the words that this is a nonsensical question. He doesn't want me to guess. He is like Rumpelstiltskin: if I were to guess the right answer He'd be so mad He'd jump up and down so hard that his foot would go through the floor. But if I don't guess at all He will be so mad that He'll probably call the whole thing off. He doesn't want me to guess the answer. He just wants me to be excited enough to guess.

He says nothing.

"Is it a stately home?"

"No."

"Sculpture park?"

"No."

"Are we going to visit someone?"

"No. Well, in a way..."

Luckily, as though my guesses were some kind of prayer, the long-suffering waitress appears with two bowls of unidentified brown soup and two plates with bread on them.

"We've run out of granary so I've given you wholemeal. I hope that's OK?"

She doesn't want an answer, she just wants a polite thank you, but He gives her one anyway.

"To be honest, love, I don't think either of us would have noticed the difference if you hadn't told us."

He grins at her. She gives absolutely no facial expression back.

"Lovely," she says, "just let me know when you're ready for your pudding."

She scurries off to deliver the same bored but efficient service to some other indecisive couple and I'm left eating my soup, watching Him dissect his bread as though planning to feed it to the ducks and putting the chunks in the bowl to become soggy, disintegrating croutons.

My mum says you can tell a lot about a person by the way they eat soup. She says the same thing about gravy. It was a revelation to me the first time I went to France and saw a woman actively encouraging her child to mop up his gravy with a piece of bread. In our house that was high up on the list of eating taboos: my dad used to do it and I'm not sure whether that's why she hated the practice so much or whether he just used to do it to piss her off. A bit of both probably. On the soup front, her philosophy is that bread should always be dry, never buttered, and may be dipped but never submerged and it must never ever be used to wipe the remnants from the sides of the all-but-empty bowl. I'm not sure whether she's got an official line on the tossing of duck food into the still-full bowl: it's probably a practice so deviant that she hasn't even thought of it. He always eats soup like that and it's not only unpleasant to watch but quite revolting when you're the one washing up afterwards and you have to scrape out the bits of sodden, mushy bread that He's left behind. I think He does it because soup's just too liquid; he wants something more substantial in his bowl. We hardly ever have soup at home so that I don't have to watch Him eat it. Maybe that's why He's developed the bread confetti eating style, to put me off giving Him soup in the first place.

"I can't be doing with soup," He says, filling his spoon to the rim and then lifting it high above the bowl and pouring it back in. "It's like smoothies: what's the point? Why not just eat the fruit or the fucking vegetables?"

What's He getting so cross about? What are we doing sitting here in a middle-of-nowhere pub talking about soup, not talking about anything that's happened? Not talking about anything that either of us is thinking about. If He doesn't mention anything, then it didn't happen. That's what He does. That's what He always does. I just don't want to talk about it. I don't want to think about it. I'm not scared to, which is odd for me. I always have been in the past but today I'm not scared, today I just don't know where to start or how to put all of that into words. Those big words are too big, much too big for my little mouth today. I hope one day I might be able to get my tongue around them, and get them in the right order and spew them all out before I choke, but that day is not today. Today I will finish my soup, eat sticky toffee pudding and hope that my surprise is a nice one.

It's not the bored waitress that takes our soup bowls away and brings us our sticky toffee pudding, it's the guy that was behind the bar when we first came in. I wonder what's happened to her: is she sulking in a corner because He was so rude to her, or has she collapsed from exhaustion in a heap in the kitchen? Mine smells delicious and is dripping with custard. His has ice cream instead of cream and He sneers at it, but He says nothing to the guy that brings it over and says "enjoy!", so wherever the bored waitress is, at least she's been saved his sarcasm.

He checks his watch. It's half past two. Twelve hours since I was lacing his toothbrush with bleach and here I am tucking into sticky toffee pudding with Him and discussing whether we'd be able to have an open fire in our house like the one in this pub.

"We've got another half an hour before we need to be there, d'you want another drink?"

This is a mostly rhetorical question: what He means is that He is going to the bar and will get me another drink while He's there if I say I'd like one.

"D'you think they do coffee?"

He gives me the face but puts away the matching words and instead says, "I can ask."

So He does ask, and He brings me a coffee and then goes back to the bar to collect his pint and chat to the barmaid with the not-even-trying-to-look-natural hair colour.

So I wait until He finally decides to come back to the table and I nip off to the ladies before surprise time.

The waitress is in there sobbing her heart out and sitting cross-legged on the floor. I want to ask her what's the matter. I want to go over to her and put my arms around her and say it's OK, whatever it is, it'll all be fine. But maybe it won't. Maybe she'll be stuck taking orders for sticky toffee pudding from people who don't give a shit whether she cries every day in the toilets for the rest of her life. I go for a wee, I wash my hands and I just leave her to it. She doesn't even look up.

"Right then," He says when I get back to the table, "we'd better get going or we'll be late."

And He bustles me out of the pub and back to the car. He's had a couple of pints but He doesn't ask me to drive and I'd rather risk a multiple pile up than risk suggesting that I should be the designated driver.

The engine's barely warm when we stop again. It's just a house. Not the house of anyone we know but they're expecting us.

"Hello, hello, hello," says the buxom woman that greets us on the drive. "Good journey? Traffic OK? Find us OK?" She doesn't draw breath long enough for either of us to answer her. "Come in, come on in. I've got a nice fire going inside and the kettle's on. I've got the little fella all ready for you. You'll love him," she says to me. "You'll absolutely love him."

I feel like we've just walked into some kind of horror film where the seemingly nice but clearly bonkers psycho sits us down in the living room of her cutesy middle-of-nowhere cottage, bumbles off to the kitchen to fetch a cup of tea and then comes back with a chainsaw and a menacing cackle. But actually it's even crazier than that. She goes off to get us a cup of tea and comes back with a puppy, a fluffy little terrier that runs to the corner of the room and pees on a pile of newspaper as soon as she puts it on the floor.

"Milk and sugar?" she grins.

"No thanks," He says for both of us. And off she trots again for the tea.

I think I may actually have my mouth wide open in a cartoon-like catching flies pose.

"Well," He asks, "d'you like him?"

Failure to enthuse over the puppy could mean that the day takes a turn for the worse. On the other hand, it's an actual real live animal which He is clearly expecting us to take home and I will then have to feed it, walk it and pick up its poo.

"Go and have a look at him then," He says. And He nods towards the puppy, which has now given up peeing and is busy sniffing around the edges of the newspaper it's just used as a toilet.

I kneel down next to the puppy and, as though he's been trained to make my heart melt in an instant, he comes straight to me and crawls onto my lap and looks me straight in the eye. And that's it, I forget all about scooping shit into a little plastic bag and going out for early morning walks in the pissing rain. Instead all I can see is me watching TV with this little dog snuggled up to me on the sofa.

"What's his name?"

"Oh, we haven't given the puppies names," says the woman coming back in the room with three mugs of tea and a plate of biscuits. "People usually like to choose their own names. Anyway, the kids get too attached to the puppies at the best of times and if we named them they'd think we were keeping them. You can call him whatever you like. I'll put your tea down here."

I look round to see where she's putting my tea and I can see Him grinning from ear to ear. It turns out He arranged all this two weeks ago. Someone He knows from work has had a puppy from this lady before, so He called her and she had some that weren't quite ready to leave their mum yet, so He'd arranged for us to come today and kept it as a surprise. It was definitely a surprise.

I put the dog down to go and pick up my tea and the daft thing follows me. It sits by my feet playing with my shoes while I drink my tea and the lady chats on and on about the puppy, and its mother and father and the other litters they've had before and the other dogs they used to have that are now dead. And I must do a good job of looking interested because, as soon as I put my mug down, she takes me into the hall and shows me photographs hung in frames on the wall of all the dead dogs she used to have. I get a bit of the horror film anxiety back.

"So, shall we keep him?" He says, standing in the doorway with the puppy in his arms.

"Of course we're going to keep him," I smile. And I reach out and take the little dog and hold him on my lap all the way home, tickling him behind the ear until he falls asleep.

24

When I was little I always wanted a dog. Not just a dog: I wanted an Afghan hound and a chinchilla and a seahorse. Dad said no-one had seahorses as pets. Mum said no-one in our family had pets. I got my best friend to get me a goldfish as a 'surprise' for my fifteenth birthday and it died four days later. That's my only previous experience as an animal lover and now here I am walking a dog in the park at the crack of dawn before I go to work and willing it to poo while we're out, even though I know I'll have to pick up the poo using only the Sainsbury's bag that I've brought along for the purpose. But if it doesn't poo now, it's bound to poo on the carpet while I'm out and no supermarket carrier bag will save me then.

I'm not sure He's thought it through, the whole dog-owning thing. It was a nice thought, but we're not exactly a romantic walk in the park kind of couple.

I try to get some reassurance on all of this from Mandy when I eventually make it into work. She's always enthusiastic about everything; she'll make me believe that having the puppy will be great. But when I tell her all about the mystery trip to the countryside and the bonkers woman and her gallery of dead dogs she just nods at me blankly as though she's reciting her times tables in her head while I'm babbling on, and then when I say: "Obviously, He's just got me the puppy as a baby substitute which is a nice thought but He doesn't really get it," she starts crying.

It's a funny way of crying. She not sobbing, she's not making any real noise and she's rooted to the spot but there are tears and snot and she's breaking her heart.

"Let's go to the ladies," I say. I'm not used to other people crying but the loo is a far better place for all of that than the middle of the office.

"What is it? What's the matter?"

I put my arm around her and she hugs me like her life depends on it but she still says nothing.

"What is it? Is it Guy? Has something happened?"

And then she starts sobbing and she's trying to speak but I can't understand anything of what she's saying.

"You'll need to calm down and slow down a bit," I tell her and she looks at me like I'm all wise and grown up and we take a few deep breaths together and she tries again.

"It's not Guy," she says, "Guy's lovely. Guy's wonderful. Guy's much too good for me."

"Nonsense."

"It's true," she says.

"Because?"

"Because I'm pregnant and I can't keep it."

Silence. What am I supposed to say now? I don't know what to say. It doesn't matter, because Mandy's on a roll now. Maybe it's something on my face, or maybe she just knows what I'm thinking, but she just keeps talking.

"I've only known him for two months," she says. And she tells me that he's wonderful, he's amazing. She couldn't have found anyone more perfect if she'd written a job description and ticked off every last thing on the list before she'd taken him on. Apart from he doesn't want kids, she says. She tells me how he thinks we need to reduce the birth rate to preserve the earth's resources and how he says we in the West should be the ones to take action against overpopulation because we have the easiest access to contraception and the biggest carbon footprint.

"Bullshit," I say when she tells me that last bit. Maybe not the most useful comment, but surely one baby wouldn't make that much of a difference? And it'd be a vegan baby, let's face it.

"The thing is, that's what he believes. So I could have the baby and wreck everything with Guy or not have the baby and then..."

Mandy and Julie are my best friends. I haven't had best friends for years and years. But I realise that I don't know Mandy very well at all. I don't really know either of them. But just because we've never had long chats about babies and abortion and boyfriends and politics doesn't mean that we don't think the same way. While she stares at me blankly, hoping I'll have a magic answer for her, I know that her response to this is exactly what mine would be in her shoes. Except I'm not in her shoes, I'm in mine, and my baby has gone and I didn't want it to go but I couldn't stop it.

Suddenly I find myself crying too. Not very helpful. I feel sorry for Mandy, I do, and I'm upset for her but that's not it. I try to make a proper thought out of the stomach-churning feeling that's making me cry and when I do it's so ridiculous that I can't say it to her, so I just say: "You can't get rid of your baby. That's your baby!"

But what I mean is, that's my baby. My baby that couldn't stay with me has come to you instead.

She's blowing her nose on a piece of toilet paper that's disintegrating. It's time for me to be all grown up and take charge of the situation like she's been waiting for me to.

"Have you told Guy yet?"

"No," she says. "I only found out myself yesterday. I haven't told anyone yet. Only you."

"Right then," I say. "You need to take the day off sick and arrange to meet Guy and tell him. You need to tell him how you've been breaking your heart about how he's going to take the news. You're going to tell him that you know there's lots of big reasons why you shouldn't have the baby and that you've thought about them all. And then you're going to tell him that you love him and that you'll love the baby and that you hope he will too. And then you'll just have to keep your fingers crossed and see what he says."

"And what if he says to get rid of it?"

"Then he's clearly not quite as lovely and amazing as you think he is. But I think he is pretty special and I think you'll need to let him prove it to you."

She gets a paper towel and gives her nose an enormous blow and then gives me a massive hug. Heidi puts her head round the door.

"There are phones ringing out here and not enough people answering them," she says. "D'you think you two could have your bonding session some other time?"

"Actually," I say before Mandy can get a word in. "Mandy's grandma has just died and she's pretty cut up about it, I think we'd best just let her go home. She can't even string a sentence together without crying."

I've always thought of myself as a rubbish liar but Heidi just takes my word for it and tells Mandy to take the rest of the day off.

"And just let me know when the funeral is, won't you Mandy?" Heidi says as she holds the door open for Mandy and me. "Obviously you'll need to take that day off too and there won't be a problem with that. She must have been very special."

"Very special," Mandy agrees and squeezes my hand. Then I head off to my desk and she lets Heidi walk her to the coats.

Funny that Mandy should be crying because she's pregnant when I've spent so much time crying because I'm not. I wonder if anyone's life ever really goes to plan. Probably most people's goes to plan at some point, possibly more often than mine. But maybe I was over-ambitious. My plan was to elope with Michael Lowther, the most gorgeous boy at my sixth form. He had a leather jacket and a Led Zeppelin T-shirt and jeans with genuine, threadbare rips in them in the days before shops starting selling jeans with ready-made tears. Thanks to him

I went on an anti-fascist march and nearly got arrested for shouting 'Pigs go home' at a policeman. Thanks to him I read *A Farewell to Arms* and *To Kill a Mockingbird* during endless hours spent hanging around in the library hoping he'd wander in and find me there being all intellectual. Thanks to him I got an E in my geography 'A' level because I spent the night before the second exam sobbing my heart out because I'd seen him snogging Lisa Glancy after the first geography exam. I wonder where Michael Lowther is now. Maybe he's married with kids and a detached house with a double garage. Maybe he's divorced with a couple of kids and two mortgages and a big flabby belly from eating too many microwave meals for one.

I can't help thinking that plan A (Michael Lowther) would surely have turned out better than plans B, C, D, E and F. But maybe the planning bit is the problem. Maybe I should stop trying to make things go to plan and start learning from the complete shambles I've left in my wake.

"Is that your phone ringing?" asks Phoebe, the girl sitting behind me. "You should have it on silent in here."

Mandy's only been gone five minutes and I'm missing her already. That's the rule, that you have your phone on silent if you leave it on in the office, but no-one actually sticks to the rule. Not even me, and I'm Goody Two-shoes. Anyway, I've already had to deal with death, pregnancy and dog shit this morning. I turn round and smile at her with my best 'don't mess with me' grimace, but she clearly doesn't feel even slightly threatened because she just sneers at me and turns round again. Work's just like school, except this time it's a life sentence. No parole.

I check my phone. Missed call from Julie. I can't ring her now so I put my phone in my pocket and text her from the ladies. 'Will call at lunch. Weekend was crap. Got dog!' I'm about to press send and realise what a whinger I must seem to Julie. I delete the last couple of things. 'Will call at lunch.' Send.

The morning drags. I'm itching to call Mandy and find out whether she's spoken to Guy and what's going to happen. I can't let her get rid of the baby. She doesn't really want to. I can tell. She couldn't do that. I'm itching to call her but I realise that I don't even have her number. I've been to her flat, I know her secrets and she pretty much knows mine but we haven't been friends long enough for me to have her number. How crazy is that? I can hear my mum's voice at the back of my mind saying 'What do you know about this Mandy girl, Marion? What makes you think you can trust her? For all you know she could be blabbing everything you tell her all around everywhere. She could be stringing you along, just trying to see what she can get out of you.' That's what she said about Him when I first started going out with Him. When we'd been together for two years and there was no sign of an engagement ring she went into a blind panic, but we made it all official in the end. But the thing is, it's my mum that's a bad judge of people, not me. That's why she worries about me mixing with the wrong sort and being gullible and being taken for a ride, because she's a monumentally bad judge of people. She gets taken in by people who are rotten to the core and dismisses people who are great just because they look a bit odd or act a bit funny or have strange dress sense. I don't think she'd like Mandy. She'd think she's a floozy. Maybe she is a floozy but she's far and away the nicest floozy I know and her baby has been sent to replace the baby that I lost. I want to call her and say that her baby is there for a reason. But I don't have her number and it's probably a good job.

I take my lunch break early and call Julie from outside the sandwich shop. It goes straight to voicemail so I go in and get myself a ham salad baguette and a Kit Kat and try again. It goes straight to voicemail again so I leave a message this time. "Julie, hi, it's me Marion. Just thought I'd call while I'm on my lunch break. Had a pretty full-on weekend and He's gone and bought me a dog and now my friend Mandy is pregnant. Anyway, if

I don't hear from you before maybe we can meet up again after swimming tonight. Let me know. Hope everything's OK with you." The tone sounds before I get to the end of 'you': her voicemail clearly likes you to keep the message short and sweet.

Since it's sunny I decide to go and sit in the park to eat my lunch. Everyone calls it the park but it's more of a big garden. Just four benches, a couple of flowerbeds and some trees around the outside. They keep it nice, though – whoever 'they' are – and it's not the office, which is a big plus in its favour. I sit down on Moira's bench: it has a plaque on it that says 'For Moira, who always took time out to smell the flowers.' I wonder whether Moira requested these words on her memorial bench. I think if I were Moira I might feel a bit cross that the abiding message about me to a bunch of strangers as they sat eating their lunch would be that I ambled through life smelling flowers instead of getting stuff done. I wonder what they'd put on a bench in memory of me. 'For Marion, she made great pastry,' 'For Marion, she often sat eating her lunch here wishing she didn't have to go back to work,' 'For Marion, with love.' That would be the one I'd want. That should be the only one anyone should have. If it's not with love then why bother? But then, if your grand gesture of love is going to be a bench in a crappy little park littered with coffee cups, why bother at all?

My phone rings just as I'm trying to chew a too-big mouthful of baguette. It's Julie so I pull the big chunk of half chewed bread out of my mouth and put it on the wrapper on my lap so that I can speak to her. The woman on the bench opposite me gives me a disapproving look, but she's got crumbs all over her chest so I don't think I'll bother getting too upset what she thinks about my manners.

"Are you all right?" Julie asks.

I wish people wouldn't ask that question. No-one ever asks it when you actually are all right, just when they know that you're not and then you feel obliged to tell them that you're OK anyway.

"I'm OK."

"So what happened?"

I tell her about the supermarket and bumping into Mandy and Guy and then bumping into the lorry driver and about how cross He was that I'd lied to Him and about how awful the evening at Mandy's had been. I don't tell her everything. I give her the abridged version and I can see Crumb Woman eavesdropping as I speak. Her bench would read 'loved poking her nose into other people's business.'

"But you've not really lied to him," Julie says.

"Well I did," I say. "I didn't tell Him that I went round to yours for lunch or about getting the lift from the lorry driver, and I still haven't told Him that we met up after swimming last week."

"And do you normally account for all your movements?" she asks.

"No, of course not. No. But I suppose He usually knows where I am. I mean, I don't normally go anywhere that I don't normally go and He knows where I am, pretty much, most of the time."

I wonder if what I'm saying makes any sense to her at all. I don't want her to think I'm a complete saddo who does as she's told all the time.

"Sounds like he keeps you on a pretty tight lead to me," she says. "But he must be happy about us being friends if he's letting you invite me round for dinner."

I don't know what to say now. I thought Julie would just know how it is. I thought she understood how He does things but clearly she doesn't.

"Marion?" She's waiting for me to go on. Crumb Woman is also waiting for me to go on.

"He's not letting me invite you round for dinner, He's making me. He's making me invite you round so that He can spoil things."

"How's he going to do that?"

"I don't know, but that's what He wants to do. He doesn't like me having friends. He likes to just keep things how they are."

I can hear myself speaking and it sounds daft. Julie will think I'm paranoid, and Crumb Woman clearly already thinks I'm a bona fide nutcase.

"Marion," Julie says, "I'm on your side. That's all you have to remember on Saturday and all the days until Saturday, OK?"

"OK."

"So I'll see you after swimming tonight, same as last week and we'll decide on a game plan for Saturday."

"OK."

"Great. See you then."

I didn't even tell her about the dog and Mandy's baby but I can tell her later.

I look down at my lunch. I don't feel like eating it any more. I don't know why I get baguette sandwiches: so much effort involved and it's just bread after all that chewing. It's just to make it feel worth buying because it's not what I'd have at home.

I throw it in the bin and put the Kit Kat in my pocket to put in Mandy's desk drawer as a treat for when she comes back in tomorrow. Crumb Woman watches me as I walk out of the park.

The afternoon drags without Mandy, even though her not being there means I'm much busier than usual. At least three customers ask me where she is. I just tell them her grandma has died and we're hoping she'll be back in the office tomorrow. I hope Mandy hasn't got a real granny that might die anytime soon. I kind of feel as if I'm tempting fate with my spurious bereavement story. I don't want to be karmically responsible for killing her actual granny.

By the time I leave the office, all I can think about is my swim. I can't wait to be weightless in that water, to feel the shock of coldness when I get in and find my rhythm as I work my way through the pool.

When I get home, He's not there but the dog has made its presence felt. I put down newspapers all around the edge of the kitchen before I left the house this morning but the dog has managed to get into the living room and has peed up against the side of the chair and the settee and crapped in the middle of the carpet. This has got to be the most ill-conceived present in the history of the universe. Who thinks 'ooh, she's lost her baby so I'll get her a puppy and she'll be delighted'?

Given that it's already done enough wees to last a fortnight, taking the poor animal out for a walk seems a bit futile, but I don't want to start clearing up the mess until I'm sure he's not going to make another one. And I feel sorry for the little fella. He's probably missing his mum and just pissing for something to do.

So I take him to the park round the corner. It's a big park: people drive here to walk their dogs. There's a play area and a picnic area. There's even a duck pond. There are tons of people out walking their dogs and they keep stopping and chatting to each other. Some of them even say hello to me as we pass. People I've never met before. It's like having a dog with you makes you friends. You're in the same club. They too have cleared crap up off their living room carpet. Except I haven't... yet.

When I get back, He's there.

"D'you know the dog's crapped in the living room?" He says.

"Has he?"

"Yes he fucking has. And he's peed on the settee!"

"Now that is naughty," I say to the dog.

"I thought we were going to keep him in the kitchen during the day?"

"I thought we had," I say, "He was in here when I got home."

"That's probably because he'd got fed up with his own stink in the other room," He says, looking at me as though I'd encouraged the dog to make the mess. "Anyway, it needs cleaning up."

"What about the dinner?"

"Sod the dinner, you need to clean the mess up. That's what it's like having a dog, isn't it? You clean up the dog's mess and I'll take him to the chippy with me and get us some fish and chips."

So here I am again, on my hands and knees with rubber gloves and a bucket full of disinfectant. The living room will smell of fresh pine and not-so-natural lavender for weeks after I've finished with it. Still, it's not all bad: at least I don't have to cook before swimming.

The plates are on the table waiting by the time He gets back from the chippy; there's tea in the pot and salt and vinegar and ketchup sitting waiting. The dog runs in ahead of Him so it's dog, smell of chips and then Him. Chippy tea is still a treat. It takes me right back to when my dad used to get us chippy dinner every now and then, once in a blue moon, and it tasted like the best thing I could imagine. I had so many lovely dinners that my mum poured her love into as she cooked them, but nothing ever tasted of love and happiness as much as a surprise chippy dinner from my dad. I almost expect to see my dad walk in with the paper bundle.

"Some kid at the chippy has just asked me what the dog was called," He says, unwrapping the fish and chips and plonking mine on my plate. "You've not even given it a name. What are you going to call it?"

I say the first thing that comes into my head. "Geoff"

"Geoff?"

"Yeah. Like my dad."

"Geoff? Nobody calls a dog Geoff. Nobody calls their dog after their dad. Choose something else."

I don't see why people don't call their dog after their dad, but never mind.

"OK then, how about 'Chips'?"

"Chips, is that the best you can do? There you go Chips," and he gives the dog a chip. "It's a bloody good job we didn't get pizza instead, you could have found yourself called Pepperoni." He laughs loudly at his own joke and I laugh too. Fish and chips and a dog pissing on the furniture bring out the best in us. Maybe we should run our own takeaway and keep a menagerie in the back.

It's nearly eight by the time I screw up what's left of my chips in their wrapper and take his from Him to throw in the bin too.

"Have you seen the time? I'd better get ready for swimming."

"Surely you're not going tonight?"

"Why not?"

"What about the dog?"

"The dog's fine."

"The dog needs settling in properly. You're the one that's cleaned the shit up off the carpet, surely you want to make sure he doesn't feel the need to do that again?"

"But you're here."

"Pub quiz again," He says. "It's a grudge match, don't forget. Second last week. We're going for the winners' prize this time round. It's only one swim, isn't it? I'm sure you'll be able to go next week, little Chips will have settled in properly by then, won't you Chips? Here, give me those wrappers if you like, I'll put them in the outside bin on my way out."

So I hand Him the chip wrappers and off He goes, leaving me with the dog and the lingering smell of disinfectant.

25

As a teenager I travelled the world having romantic adventures in all the most picturesque locations with the most chivalrous of men. I rationed myself, stopping the daydream at critical points so that I could re-start it the next day, with a bit of a recap over the best moments. I left out the boring bits. I skipped past the bits that were difficult to explain and I never got past the bit where he asked me to marry him and we skipped off happily into the sunset together to lead a life of wedded bliss. It was all very chaste and respectable. It was all absolutely nothing like real life turned out to be.

By the time I met Him I wasn't expecting a tall, Swedish archaeologist any more, or a surfer from the South of France or even an Italian aristocrat whose family had long since lost its fortune but retained its title. Reality had set in by the time I was twenty, and by the time I was thirty reality had really started to bite. But I remember all those handsome suitors and the way they wooed me and the way, after playing pretty damned hard to get it has to be said, I'd finally cave, only to have to overcome numerous obstacles that I put in our way so that we could be reconciled again and again. I'd take things as far down the line as choosing a dress for the big day but never far enough that I'd ever have to wash his dirty socks or scrape his discarded half-eaten dinner into the bin.

I don't dream of those boys any more. I don't think they'd recognise me now. But I still daydream. I'm making the dinner – spaghetti Bolognese – and imagining that there's a knock at the door. I'm busy folding the clean washing upstairs and pairing up socks so I don't answer it straight away, I've got my hands full, and while I'm coming down the stairs the doorbell rings again. And then again. And I wonder who on earth it can be that's so keen for me to open the door. When I open it there are two police officers – a man and a woman – and I can see their car behind them.

"Hello", says the lady police officer, "is it Marion?"

"Yes," I say. "Is everything all right?"

"Can we come in Marion?" she says.

"Yes. Is everything all right?"

They come in to my living room and ask me would I like a cup of tea. It's my living room, surely I'm the one that's supposed to offer the cup of tea.

"I've just had one, thanks," I say. Or sometimes, just to string it out a bit longer I might say "How rude of me not to offer it. I won't be a minute." And I head off to make a cup of tea for each of us and come back with it all on a tray with biscuits on a plate and a sugar bowl and spoons like I never would normally.

"Sit down love," says the policeman.

I sit down.

"We've got some bad news I'm afraid," he says. And then he tells me that my husband has been killed in a car crash or has been murdered on his way home from work or died in a gas explosion at the office. I can change the story however I like. I can even make Him survive temporarily if I like and then die later in hospital. But He always dies at some point.

And the lady police officer comes and sits next to me on the settee and puts her arm round me and says, "I'm sorry love," and hands me a cup of tea with sugar in.

And then I have to try and look upset. They'd think I wasn't normal if I wasn't upset and things always get interrupted because I can't really imagine just how I would feel. I try to work out if I would cry or not. I just don't know.

It doesn't matter anyway. If I cry she just hands me a tissue and if I don't she just puts it down to the shock and tells me it will take a while to sink in.

And then I have to go and identify the body. And it's always a dark room and there's always plinky-plonky music playing as though we're in a spa or something. The man pulls the sheet back to reveal his face and He's grinning at me. I try to make Him look battered or miserable or nondescript, even, but He's always bloody grinning and I have to go back to the start.

"How's the dog been?"

He comes straight up behind me, pinches my bum, kisses me on the back of my neck and makes me jump out of my skin.

"Fine," I say, "fine. I think he's settling in now."

I don't tell Him that I've had to disinfect the carpet for the fourth night running. I don't tell Him that I went out at lunchtime today to buy more disinfectant in anticipation of the dog pee that would be all over the house when I got home from work. Luckily it was less than it has been. We have turned a corner. I hope.

Last night, He was threatening to send Chips back if he doesn't stop peeing on the carpet. He was fine about it on Tuesday night because He was still in a good mood after his pub quiz triumph on Monday. But last night He yelled at the dog and then yelled at me. It wasn't my idea to bring a dog into the house but He seems to have forgotten that. The dog was his gift to me and is therefore my responsibility. Fine. I missed my swim but I will get back to swimming and now I have something else too: dog walking. I can use the dog's calls of nature to go for a walk whenever I want and He can't find an objection strong enough to stand a chance against the possibility of shit on the living room floor.

I have lived less than five minutes walk from a park for almost five years and in all that time I've probably been there about three times. Until this week that is, when I've spent more time there than I've spent at home, more or less. I never knew what a lovely park it was and I never knew how many people spent so much time there, walking their dogs or their kids or their girlfriends. And I have found out one important piece of information known only to dog owners: all dog owners are automatically friends with all other dog owners.

In the past four days I've had more complete strangers say a friendly hello to me than I've ever had in my life. As a kid, I was always embarrassed by my mum's ability to strike up a conversation with complete strangers in bus queues or changing rooms or supermarkets, but with a dog by my side I've lost all of those inhibitions and it seems completely normal to chat to people that you've never seen before in your life – providing they also have a dog.

I'm now on first name terms with a golden retriever, two mongrels and an enormously fat and slow dog whose owner claims it's a Doberman but in Doberman circles it's probably ostracised for looking as far removed from vicious as it's possible to be without being a cuddly toy. The golden retriever is called Diana and is walked by a lovely old lady who lets the dog off its lead and sits reading on a bench while it goes off to do its business. The mongrels are Sam and Fido. Sam has a hassled housewife owner, who tell me that it's the kids' dog because they mithered for it but she's the only one who ever feeds it, walks it or cleans up its sick when it's been out eating all kinds of crap it's found lying around (which it frequently does, apparently). Fido is owned by a student type with a goatee and a pierced eyebrow. He's a lovely dog that gets very excited when he sees Chips. Not that Chips is bothered, he's far too interested in pissing up every tree he can find. And finally, the Doberman is called Jupiter and walks around incredibly slowly with an old fella who doesn't smoke a pipe but looks like he should. He seems quite friendly with golden retriever lady and I suspect there might be a little bit of a dog walker's romance there. Unrequited maybe. Perhaps they've both been married for fifty years or so and have had enough of their other halves but can't bring themselves to break free and start again at their age. Perhaps that's how I'll end up, traipsing round parks with a dog having polite conversations with people whose name I don't even know and feeling like we have something in common just because we know the names of each other's dogs.

Chips is settling in and I'm settling into being a dog owner. It seems ridiculous to say it but having a dog has given me a whole other life. A life where I'm walking not to get anywhere, but just to walk. A life where it's OK to talk to strangers and they become less like strangers by the day. It's not like the swimming pool where people see each other week after week but never say a word, never even nod at each other. In the park we don't have the embarrassment of being almost naked in front of people we don't know or having to shower side by side with someone we've never even said hello to. In the park we're all fully dressed and we have a prop with us as an icebreaker for conversation. The etiquette has shifted: in the pool it would be weird to suddenly start talking to a fellow swimmer; in the park, if you don't pass the time of day with your fellow dog walkers you're the weirdo.

It's been a pretty uneventful week apart from the dog walks and the dog-related cleaning. I've hardly seen Him between work and dog-walking and his pub quiz and his Wednesday night out. And when He has been around He's been nice. Not husband of the year material, no need for me to call the papers, but He's chatted to me, He's listened to me and He's even done the washing up. Twice!

The odd thing is, it's the niceness and the normalness that's making me miserable. That, and the lack of Mandy to chat to at work. That and the looming dinner with Julie, which could be lovely if He stays nice like, this but what are the chances of that? It's his niceness and normalness that makes me think: this is as good as it's ever going to get and frankly, it's not that great. It's not going to make me dash home from work because I can't wait to see Him. It's not going to make me leap out of bed in the morning because I want to put my face on before He sees me. It's not going to buoy me up for when it inevitably goes to shit again. If this is the best it's ever going to be, what the fuck am I doing here?

And then I hear my mother's voice. "Rome wasn't built in a day you know. Marriage was never meant to be a bed of roses. You have to work at it. You're in it for the long haul."

She was in it for the long haul. She was from a long line of make-your-bed-and-lie-in-it women who married young, got their lovely house in a nice area and cooked and cleaned and freshened up their make-up in time for their husbands coming home. She was part of a sisterhood of housewives who swapped handy household hints, swooned over Hollywood stars and only ever had good things to say about their husbands. So when her husband started shagging around she carried on washing his dirty socks and cooking his Sunday dinner and pretending that nothing was wrong. When I found an earring in the back of his car, she let him tell me that it must have been from when he gave some of the women from work a lift to the station. When he finally left, she told me that he just needed some space and would probably come back in a couple of weeks. And when he didn't come back she said she'd made some mistakes, they both had. Marriage was never meant to be a bed of roses.

She was delighted when I finally got married. She actually said to me on my wedding day that she'd begun to think that it would never happen and she'd had to avoid the subject with her friends. Not with Julie's mum, presumably, because Julie wasn't married, but they weren't what you'd call friends by that time, not after the whole adoption gossip thing. She gave me a pep talk while I was doing my make-up. She told me that men want to think that their wife is vulnerable and needy and relies on them for everything, but they don't want to deal with any vulnerability or neediness or responsibility in real life. "Be strong," she said. "Carry the weight of the world on your shoulders if you have to and learn how to seem fine even if you're not. But never be afraid to cry if he wants to see you upset and always be prepared to tell him how much you love him and rely on him, even if you don't feel it."

At the time I remember thinking that my mum was the anti-feminist. She'd lived through the great era of women's lib and come out the other side with Victorian sensibilities that would make even the Victorians dismiss her as a throwback. Meanwhile, my dad ended up moving to Australia and moving in with a woman who already had three kids. She had two more with him: Martin and Marina, the brother and sister I've never even met. The brother and sister I'm not ever allowed to mention in front of my mum. He is a chef and she is an architect. They send me Christmas cards. They have the same shaped face as me.

That's the trouble with a boring week like this week when you have no-one to talk to and too much time to think: you think. You think about all kinds of stuff and all that thinking never helps you find any answers, it just brings up more and more questions. Did I know He was like this when I married Him? If I knew, why did I marry Him? Why am I still married to Him? Why can't I get away? What do I have to do to get away?

I ask Chips: "What do I have to do to get away?" He doesn't answer me. Of course he doesn't, he's a dog. He just looks at me and then wanders off and cocks his leg up a tree. I can't believe it. I have been a dog owner for less than a week and I'm already one of those crazy people who talks to their dogs and expects a human response.

By Friday morning I'm on the brink of total doggy nuttiness, but when I get to work Mandy is at her desk eating a bowl of Rice Krispies and giving me a huge grin as soon as I walk through the door. I see the grin and hope that it means that the baby is here for keeps. I think it must be.

"The man from Del Monte, he say 'Yes!'", she says as I plonk my bag on the floor next to my chair.

"That's fantastic," I say and burst into tears like a complete idiot.

26

Sometimes I have dreams that start off as dreams and end up as nightmares. I'm in the swimming pool. Same old pool, same old stone steps into the water and same grubby changing rooms down each wall. Same old tiles and flying saucer lights hanging from the ceiling. But it smells lovely. You can't smell the chlorine at all, it smells more like a spa or some of that fancy handmade soap that you sometimes get as a present and put in your knicker drawer to make your smalls smell nice.

I'm the only person in the pool and it's lovely. No-one splashing me, no-one doing back stroke on a collision course, no-one jumping in, no-one chatting at the side of the pool and getting in everyone's way. Not everyone's, just mine. There's only me and suddenly that's not nice and quiet and peaceful any more. It's spooky. It's cold and much too quiet. And then I look up and the lorry driver is the pool attendant with his big fat belly squeezed into shorts that are way too tight. And my mum is there holding a life belt and I think she's going to throw it into the pool but it's tied to the wall. And then I can see all kinds of random people. Julie's mum, Heidi, the guy from the corner shop who always calls me pumpkin and nearly always has a toffee in his mouth. He's chewing; he has a toffee in his mouth, just like always.

They're all staring at me and I want to get away from them but I can't get out of the pool. The steps have disappeared and the water is suddenly much, much deeper. So I try diving down under the water. If I can stay down there, just for a few minutes, they might think I've gone and just go and leave me to my swim.

But the further down I go, the deeper the water gets and I can't get back up again and I can't breathe.

It's Friday night. Well, strictly speaking it's Saturday morning but so early that some people probably won't have gone to bed yet. Friday flew by in a bit of a blur. It was a great day. The dog didn't pee on the carpet – not even once – and I even let him off the lead for a bit in the park and he didn't run off. Mandy came back to work having apparently spent the last three days celebrating being pregnant with Guy who, after all her angst and soul searching, turned out to be thrilled at the news and has already moved in with her and opened a savings account for the baby. Julie texted me just after I'd got into work and asked if I could meet her for lunch.

We met at a cafe about half way between where I work and where Julie works. Closer to my work really, but it was her suggestion and it was fine by me. I've never been in there before. It's not the kind of place I'd go into on my own. I don't really go into places and sit down on my own. Julie looked tired but she said she was OK and I told her about Chips and about Mandy's baby and about the waitress crying in the toilets in the pub on the way to pick up the dog.

"I have absolutely no idea what she was crying about. It could have been anything. I feel quite guilty about it actually. What's the worst that could have happened? She could have told me to bugger off maybe. Big deal. But she might have really needed someone to talk to, or I might have been able to do something to help..."

I can feel myself wittering on while Julie is rifling through her handbag for something.

"Don't worry about it," she says, "I'm sure the woman was fine. The last thing most people want when they're upset is some complete stranger poking their nose in and making them talk about it."

And she finally finds the little packet of tissues buried at the bottom of her enormous handbag and pulls one out and starts blowing her nose.

Then I realise that she's crying quietly, like an old lady cries: no fuss, just tears.

"Are you OK? What's the matter? What is it?"

How stupid, of course she's not OK, otherwise she wouldn't be crying. I think back over what I've said to try and figure out whether there was anything in it that might have upset her. I think back over what she's said to see if there was something she mentioned that I should have asked her about.

"I'm fine,' she says.

Clearly, she's not fine.

"Obviously, you're not, are you?" I say, getting up and walking round to her side of the table and giving her a hug.

She gives me a polite hug back but she's uncomfortable. I can see her glancing to the side to see if anyone's looking at us and they are, so I go back to my seat and give her hand a squeeze instead.

"What's up?"

"I'm fine."

I wait.

"So?"

"My mum's died," she says. "Not my mum that you know: Linda, my mother. I found out this morning that she died two weeks ago and I didn't even know. I only found out when I got a letter from a solicitor telling me that I'm a beneficiary in her will. They're reading the will next week and I'm invited to attend. Her family don't even know who I am. How can I go and sit there with them while they read out her will and not tell anyone that she was my mother? How could she go and die just like that when it took me so long to find her? How could she be dead all that time and I didn't even know?"

Julie is really crying now and I don't know what to do. This feels completely back to front. I'm the one who cries and she's the one that's supposed to be sensible and know what to do every minute of the day.

"Let's have a drink," I say.

"Thanks, but I've got to be back at work in half an hour."

"So have I. Let's have one anyway."

So when the waitress comes over with the food I order us a glass of wine each and we have a toast to Linda.

"It's a shame you didn't get to meet her," says Julie. "You would have liked her. She was really calm; really... what's the word? I can't think of the word. Serene. That sounds cheesy, but she was."

"Like you then."

"Not like me," says Julie. "She looked like me, or I look like her, but we weren't really alike, she was more like you."

"Like me? I'm not serene. Nothing like."

"I think you are," she says. "I think Linda would have liked you."

It's time to take the compliment and move on.

We talk about the will reading and whether Julie will go. I think she should.

"The thing is her husband will wonder who I am. What if he asks me?"

"Tell him."

"But he doesn't even know that I exist. If he finds out, it could ruin Linda's memory for him."

"Or it could give him and you someone that was close to Linda to be close to now that she's gone."

Julie starts to cry again. "You see," she says "that's exactly the sort of thing that Linda would say."

So she decides that she will go to the reading of the will and she won't make a point of introducing herself but she will tell Linda's husband the full story if he asks.

"It's a plan," she says. And as if she's just pressed the off switch on her crying function, she changes the subject.

"So, what about the plan for tomorrow?"

With the arrival of Chips and all the stuff about Mandy's baby and then Julie's mum I'd forgotten all about the dinner we've invited Julie to tomorrow night.

"I haven't got much of a plan. Don't even know what I'm cooking. Are you going to bring someone?"

"Like who? Like a date you mean?"

"It might make things easier?"

"D'you think?"

"I don't know."

I tell her about dinner at Mandy's.

"Well, from the sound of it, whether I bring someone or not won't make much difference. I think I'll come by myself and I'll bring some nice wine and my best solicitor's poker face."

"OK, it's a plan. And I'll make Moroccan lamb and Tiramisu."

"And if he misbehaves we'll just get in a taxi and go for a night out on the tiles."

"Cheers!"

"Cheers!"

I love the plan. I love the bravado. I love Julie. I'm still dreading Saturday night.

Julie barely touches her food but we both finish our wine and she insists on paying.

"I invited you," she says. "My treat."

"When my granddad died, my mum and dad took me out for lunch as a treat," I say. "I always remember that. I was only little, only about six, but I can still remember what I had. Chicken in a basket with chips, and a knickerbocker glory for afters. I remember feeling excited that I could have whatever I liked off the menu and then feeling guilty for enjoying myself. I felt like I'd traded him in for a knickerbocker glory."

"But you hadn't. He was already dead. Refusing dessert wasn't going to bring him back."

"No. It'd be good if things worked like that wouldn't it?"

I'm smiling but Julie suddenly gets all serious. Not upset, just serious.

"The connections might not be as obvious as all that," she says. "But they're still there. It might not be that A happens because of B but sometimes, because A plus B happens and then C, D and E happen, then at some point Z can happen."

I start to remember why we used to call her the Weirdy Girl. I have absolutely no idea what she's going on about but it obviously makes perfect sense to her. Maybe I just don't get it. Maybe she's in a worse state than she's letting on.

I must look pretty perplexed because she stops trying to explain with the alphabet and she takes my hand and I can feel her bracelet tickling my wrist.

"Don't you ever think that things are interconnected and that one will only happen if something or some things have happened first? I feel like Linda could only die because I was fine and she had the opportunity to see that I was OK. I feel as though if I'd kept away, she wouldn't have been able to go just yet."

"That's more crazy than my knickerbocker glory and I was only six," I say.

She laughs. But she's not really laughing.

"I know it sounds nuts," she says.

"Yep. But that's fine. It's your turn to be the bonkers one. If she died knowing that you were OK and everything was fine between you, that's a good thing, isn't it?"

"Yeah." She still doesn't sound convinced.

"Yeah... but what?"

"Yeah but what's it supposed to mean for me? What's the message in it? What am I supposed to do next?"

"God, Julie, you really are weird sometimes. In a good way. Take your time to miss her and be glad that you got to spend some time with her first."

"You're right."

"Of course I am."

She looks at her watch.

"Bloody hell, I'm late! I've got a meeting that starts about five minutes ago." She starts walking backwards. "What time d'you want me tomorrow?"

"About seven."

"OK. See you then!" And she disappears round the corner and goes off to her sensible job in her sensible office with her not very sensible haircut.

I'm late back to work and as I step through the door I have a text from Julie. 'Client late thank God. Thanks for listening.'

I text back. 'No probs. My turn 2 b the shoulder!"

Heidi appears behind me.

"When you've finished arranging your social life, d'you think you could make it back to your desk? Poor Mandy is trying to manage your phone and hers."

Mandy gives me the look and then I have to apologise to Heidi without letting Mandy make me laugh.

"Where've you been?" asks Mandy.

"I had lunch with a friend. Her mum's just died so we took a bit longer than planned and had a little glass of wine."

"Don't mention wine," says Mandy. "I'm officially not allowed now and Guy's got me drinking these horrible green milkshakes with celery and parsley in them. He says parsley is the universal cure-all. This poor baby's going to come out all green."

Heidi looks daggers at us laughing and I feel like I've finally made it into the ranks of the cool girls. Suddenly, I am the kind of girl who bunks off school and sits on the back seat of the bus and has boyfriends and writes graffiti on toilet walls.

When Heidi backs off and there's a gap in the phone calls, Mandy turns to me and says: "You do think it will be all right don't you, Marion? Everything will turn out for the best?"

I wonder if she realises that I am probably the least qualified person in her world to give assurances that things will be all right.

“Honestly, I don’t know. No-one knows that.” Her face falls. “But you have everything to look forward to. I think it will all be fine,” I say. “I’m sure it will be.”

26

Slicing up the lamb makes me think about that episode of Tales of the Unexpected. I was just a kid when I saw it and I don't know how I came to see it, I wasn't usually allowed to watch that sort of thing. ITV was generally frowned upon in our house and my mum used to turn Tales of the Unexpected off as soon as the naked lady silhouettes started dancing because it was unsuitable. The lamb makes me think of the episode I saw when the woman kills her husband using a frozen leg of lamb and then cooks it and feeds it to the police that come to investigate.

We have been shopping for the ingredients today. We followed the full ritual. I made the list. He drove. I got the trolley while He parked the car. I pushed the trolley while He ticked things off the list one by one. I looked briefly at the special offers but didn't get any – going off list is not in the rule book. But He did okay the box of mint chocolates to go with after-dinner coffee: they were £1.50 off and there was only one box left on the shelf, so it would have been silly not to.

And now He's leaving me to it. That's what He said when He left the house.

"I'll leave you to it, love. I'm just going to meet Jimmy for a pint."

I turn round expecting Him to say something else but apparently He wasn't planning to.

"What?" He says, "It's only a pint. It's not like I'm going to be much use here, am I? I'll be back in plenty of time."

And for a minute I let myself think that maybe He won't be back in time for Julie to arrive and perhaps Julie and I will have a lovely meal together and talk about her mum some more and talk about any old thing.

I wash the herbs. My hands sting in the cold, cold water and I wish I didn't have to wash them because it takes away the lovely smell. But the flavour will still be there and the smell will come back as they cook.

And sure enough the cooking smells fill the kitchen and the hall and the living room. I wonder if people can smell the food I'm making as they walk past the house. I wonder whether it will make their mouths water. I wonder if the whole of Morocco smells like this or whether the genuine article smells nothing like it. I hope Julie likes it. I hold on to hope of a pleasant evening with nice food and my friend and my husband.

I leave the lamb in the oven and the Tiramisu in the fridge. It's only five and everything is all but ready in the kitchen. The table cloth is ironed and the wine is open and breathing, for whatever difference that makes. I have time for a shower and time to dry my hair and put on some make up and get dressed and set the table and put the rice on the stove before Julie gets here (He doesn't like the couscous that it says in the recipe book, He says it's like eating sand).

So I switch on the shower and brush my teeth while the water gets hot. I shake the bottle of shampoo that I took from the hospital. There's still a little left. There's still enough left for today and probably, just about, for the next time too. And the smell of it takes me back there again. Back to that curiously female place with its faint odour of boiled vegetables, and its disposable this and that, and its pastel decor. I watch the suds of expensive shampoo wash all the way down my body and rush to the plug hole and I think myself into tomorrow and imagine myself here again, still fine, still taking a shower, still friends with Julie, still this person with the lovely clean hair.

I'm clean but I can't quite bring myself to step out of the shower. The water is too warm, too lovely and I'm not ready to switch it off. From all warm and comforting to shivering with a towel wrapped round me, just like that. It doesn't seem right. It must be how it feels for a baby when it's just born. One minute all snuggled up and warm in the dark and the quiet and the next out in the world with the lights and the air con and everyone chattering away.

But then He's here. He's knocking on the side of the shower cubicle and pointing to his watch. It's quarter to six. He'll be wanting a shower and He'll want a walk round to check everything's sorted before Julie gets here. I switch the water off and He watches me as I let the last of the water run off me and open the doors and step out into the draughts and the steam.

He stands there while I get dry and I can't ask Him to leave me to it. So instead I just chat like it's fine that He's there, like it's a good thing I've got this five minutes with Him so that I can finalise plans for tonight.

"Nice drink?"

"Yeah. Jimmy's got some new girl on the go. Says he'd like you to meet her and see what you think."

"Me?"

"Yeah, yeah. He seems to think that you're a good judge of character. Goodness knows why!"

Indeed!

"So where's he found her, this girl?"

"Dunno. Picked her up in some pub or other, I think. Is everything ready for tonight?"

"It is. The food's all but done. The tablecloth's on and the wine's open. I just need to get dressed and everything and go and set the table and get the rice on."

"And I just need to get my shower," He says. "If you're finished."

"I am."

"Great. See you downstairs."

When I get into the bedroom the dress I'd put out has been swapped for something else. But that's OK. That's not the main thing. I put on the dress that He's chosen for me instead. I like it. I bought it. It's not as if there's much in the wardrobe that I don't like. Then I dig deep into the bottom of my jewellery box to find a necklace that my first boyfriend bought for me. It's a piece of old tat. It's the 'Love is...' couple holding hands in some kind of base metal that turns your neck green if you wear it too long. His name was Jason and I haven't thought of him in years. We only went out for a couple of months. We never even did it. But he was lovely and he meant it when he gave me the necklace and it will sit on my collar bone all evening to remind me that I am a real person with years behind me and more years in front of me.

I put my make-up on. I've always thought it's a shame for boys that they don't get to do this. Not your everyday average sort of bloke anyway. My mum always used to call it putting her face on and it was amazing what a bit of make-up could do for her. One minute she was super-banshee yelling at me, crying because she couldn't find the lid for the Tupperware box she'd put my lunch in. The next minute she was supermum with the perfect eyebrows and the immaculate lipstick, with a face that said, 'I am a perfectly calm rational human being', even though the inside of her handbag with its three half-empty packets of cigarettes, indigestion tablets and Post-it note reminders told a different story.

I have a rule of thumb with make-up. It needs to be obvious enough that I can tell I look better, but not so obvious that anyone would think I'm vain enough to have to wear make-up all the time. I smudge concealer all around my eyes and it's like rubbing out the pencil shading that was there before so that my brown eyes look lost like two little buttons on my pale, pale face. Then I draw their outline with a grey pencil and hold my mouth open while I brush mascara on the top and bottom lashes. I have a pot of pink stuff that does to liven up my lips and my cheeks and then that's it. I look just as I did before but like I've had some fresh air, or a drink or two, or a good, brisk walk in the country.

Jesus. I've not walked the dog. It's ten to seven and Julie could be here any minute and He's still in the shower and I haven't walked the dog. I could take it out now but she might get here while I'm out. I could just not take him out but he might crap on the floor while we're eating... not the most appetising of starts to a meal.

The door bell rings.

"I'm so sorry," says Julie. "I hate people who are early. It's so rude. I was trying not to be late and I think I tried too hard. You look nice."

She hands me a bottle of wine with one hand and a box of chocolates with the other and kisses me on the cheek.

"You look lovely. Where's...." and she silently mouths his name.

"He's upstairs. I think He's just got out of the shower. Everything's set, but I've just remembered that I haven't taken the dog for a walk."

And as though his little fluffy ears were burning Chips bundles through the kitchen door and scurries down the hall to greet Julie. Not exactly guard dog material, but very cute.

"He's so cute! What's his name?"

"Chips."

"Awww. That's so cute. Hello Chips, hello little fella." She bends down to fuss the dog and he runs round her ankles in excitement.

"I'd love a dog," she says, "I always swore I'd have one when I was a grown-up but with work and everything I've never managed it."

"I should have got him out for a walk so that he can do his business." I can feel the stress rising. I was so organised. I had everything under control and now it's all going to be ruined by the dog's bodily functions.

"I can take him out for a walk, then we can pretend that I wasn't early and I can arrive fashionably five minutes late."

"Are you sure? It'll probably mean picking up his poo and carrying it home to the bin."

"Will there be a gin and tonic in it for me?"

"For sure!"

"It's a deal!"

So I give her the dog's lead and off she goes with the dog, leaving me to put the rice on and set the table and pour her a double.

He need never know that Julie was here and that I fobbed the dog off on her. He need never know, but of course He does.

"Did I hear the door?" He asks. It's a rhetorical question.

"It was Julie, she was a bit early."

"So where is she?"

"She's gone for a wander with the dog."

He doesn't say anything. He just gives me the Explain Yourself face.

"It's OK. She was early and the dog needed to go out for a walk and she wanted to take him out for a walk and that's perfect 'cos now I'm making the rice."

I turn round and the pan with the rice in it is bubbling over, with thick white foam lifting the lid and white slime forming down the sides of the pan.

"Oh, is that what you're doing," He says. And he takes the G and T I made for Julie and leaves the kitchen.

I stick two fingers up at the door behind Him and turn the heat down on the rice.

Just as the rice is ready, Julie arrives back with Chips and a little black bag full of triumph.

"He did one," she says gleefully and holds it up for me to admire.

"How kind of you to bring it back for me. Put it in the bin outside, would you? Dinner's ready."

"Is my gin ready too?"

"Yeah, it was. It will be in a minute. You take the poo out and I'll sort the G and T situation."

I drain the rice, I pour drinks for Julie and me, and I give the dog a little cuddle and I put a couple of chunks of lamb into his bowl. I'm not sure how his stomach will cope with coriander but it seems to go down OK.

"You remember Julie, don't you?" I'm carrying the pot of lamb; she's carrying drinks for her and me. "I'll just go and get the rice."

By the time I go back into the room He's sitting next to her, pouring her some wine and thanking her for taking Chips out for a walk.

"I bought her the dog because I thought it might help her get over losing the baby," He says. "Looks like the baby had a lucky escape if she was going to be as eager to fob that off on someone else as she is that poor dog."

"Marion didn't fob the dog off on me, I asked if I could take him for a walk," says Julie. "I've always wanted a dog. In fact, one of my neighbours has a dog walking service to check on hers during the day, maybe I should just get one and hire someone to look after it."

"Like a childminder," He says.

"Exactly," she replies. One nil to her.

She loves the lamb and tells me so three or four times.

"Yeah, I'm a lucky man," He says. "She's a great cook." No irony. No crushing follow up. Just that.

"It's so good just to be out of the office and eating proper food," says Julie. "I've just had such a full-on couple of weeks. I've been working 'til seven or eight, getting home, having a couple of pieces of toast and getting some more work done. We've had a couple of people off sick and work's just been taking over my life."

And she delves into the pot for seconds without even asking and I just completely love her and He just stares at her and eats and stares.

"You do look like you've lost weight," I say.

"That'll be the stress," she says, mouth full, fork poised for the next one.

"Marion clearly has a stress-free existence," He chips in.

She shoots Him a look. Every woman He's ever met has been sucked in by his super-confident alpha male routine. Including me. Especially me. But not Julie. Julie doesn't give a shit. Her bracelet jangles with every mouthful she takes and I wonder about the charms and what made her choose each one.

"So, you're not married then, Julie?" He asks.

"Nope."

"Ever come close?"

"Close enough to know it's not for me."

If ever there was a polite neon sign saying 'that's enough, change the subject' Julie is flashing that sign now. But He takes no notice.

"So why's that?"

"I think I'd be more of a husband than a wife," she says, "and generally speaking that's not really what your average man is looking for."

I laugh so suddenly and unexpectedly that wine spurts out of my nose and I have to fake a choking fit to try and cover it up.

"Marion!" He says and suddenly I am my teenage self and my mother is standing there disapproving of me and telling me I'll never find a husband if I can't improve my manners.

"I was very lucky," Julie says. "My mum brought me up to be happy with who I was and to expect to make my own way in life. It must be much harder for girls who grow up waiting to be somebody's wife. Let's face it, whatever you dream of being as a kid always turns out to be not quite the fairytale you'd built it up to be, once it's real. If it's your job, at least you can console yourself that you're being paid for it and you'll get to retire one day, but if it's being a wife and things are not quite the Disney ending, what d'ya do?"

Obviously this is a rhetorical question but either He doesn't get that or He just doesn't want to let it go.

"Presumably you count your blessings," He says. "Presumably you stop being such a self-indulgent little miss and realise that it's not all about you."

He's talking to her but really He's talking to me.

"It's like fox hunting," He says. "You know," He pauses for a sip of wine, "the fox might not have a great time of it and it might look a bit unfair to the outsider that such a lovely, delicate animal is being chased by all those dogs and people and horses. But the fox is the predator and it's hard as nails. And there's a natural order to the way things are. And who's to say that the fox doesn't have the time of its life running away from the pack? It probably dies in an orgasmic stupor."

Julie looks at me. I look at my plate.

Silence.

"Don't you think?" He says.

"I think I need a cigarette," she answers. "D'you mind if I go outside for a minute? It's a horrible habit, I know. I only smoke a couple a day."

"It's fine," I say. "You have a cigarette while I get the afters."

"It's fine to smoke at the table," He says.

"It's OK," she says. "Shivering in the dark in the garden is part of the punishment for the addiction. If you let me smoke indoors I'll be on twenty a day by the end of next week!"

Julie and I both get up from our seats and head into the kitchen, her with her own plate in her hand, me with mine and his. She puts her plate on the worktop and then just stands there.

"The key's in the blue pot on the shelf." I gesture with my forehead while I open the bin with my foot and tip the remnants of my dinner in.

"Fox hunting?"

"He's just looking for something that will get your back up, so he can cause an argument."

"I argue for a living."

"But you've got a night off."

"Don't you ever feel like killing him?"

"Frequently!"

She laughs. She gives me a hug in her awkward way with her bony arms and takes the key from the pot, unlocks the kitchen door and disappears into the darkness outside for her cigarette.

"My mum used to call them cancer sticks," He says as I put his dessert down in front of Him and Julie sits back down at the table.

"Sticks and stones, I say to that," she smiles at Him. "Something's got to see you off at some point and if the gruesome pictures on the packet aren't enough to put me off, I don't think the odd heckler here or there is going to have much of an effect. I smoke two or three a day: frankly, I think I'm more at risk from the number of packets of crisps I eat and the distinct lack of anything green in my fridge than I am from the tar and nicotine in a packet and a half a week."

She plunges her spoon dramatically into her tiramisu, scoops out a massive blob of it and grins as she devours it in a devil-may-care-about-the-calories sort of way.

I feel like giving her a round of applause. But He hasn't finished.

"So what does your mum think about your smoking?"

"My mum? She thinks I'm a grown-up girl and she should probably not treat me like a teenager," says Julie with another dismissive spoonful.

"So was she bothered about it when you were a teenager?"

"She probably would have been if I'd been smoking then, but I was a speccy-four-eyed swotty type back then; I wouldn't have dreamt of smoking. It wasn't until I started working fourteen-hour days that I succumbed to the nicotine and, frankly, it's probably helped to keep me alive rather than killing me."

I daren't put any tiramisu in my mouth in case I end up snorting food through my nose again. I wonder if she can train me to talk like her. I wonder if she could give me a phrase book of smart one-liners that I can pull out of the bag when He gets like this. I put some tiramisu on my spoon and scrape the extra off the top so that it's perfectly flat. I sit with it ready in my hand and wait for Him to give up.

He's not giving up yet.

"So what about your real mum?"

"My real mum?"

"Yes, you know, your real mum. The one that gave birth to you, the one that abandoned you, the one you would never even have known about if Marion hadn't blabbed it all over the school."

I hold on to my spoon. I look at the hole I've made in the surface of my dessert and hold on tight to my spoon.

"Her name is Linda. Her name was Linda. She was amazing. She would never have dreamed of criticising me for something like smoking. She smoked like a chimney, and if there was ever anything that was going to make me stop it would be knowing that smoking probably helped to kill her. But d'you know what, it probably helped to keep her alive too. It probably gave her something to cling to when things were tough for her, and things were bloody tough for her sometimes."

Julie has stopped eating. We've all stopped eating.

"I'm sorry," He says. "I didn't know she'd died. Marion didn't tell me she'd died."

"It's only just happened," Julie says. "It's only just happened, you weren't to know, don't worry about it. You weren't to know, but I will tell you one thing that you should know. I am grateful, unbelievably grateful to Marion for letting the cat out of the bag about me being adopted all those years ago. If she hadn't talked about it my Mum, not Linda, you know, my Mum mum, she might never have talked to me about it. I might never have known. I might never have met Linda. I might never have spent time with her and I wouldn't be missing her now. But I would rather miss her like this every day for the rest of my life than have missed the opportunity to spend the bits and pieces of time we managed to get together."

"I'm sorry," He says quietly again. And he eats his tiramisu quickly and then yawns theatrically.

"I'd better take the dog for a last little wander before I turn in," He says and smiles vaguely at Julie as he leaves the table and wanders off into the hall to fetch the dog lead. The door slams shut and I can hear Him telling the dog to watch where he's going as he trips down the front step.

"Are you OK?"

"I'm not," says Julie. "I'm not and I'm not sure how to deal with it."

"You don't need to deal with it," I say. "You just need to keep going and wait for it to ease off."

"D'you think it will?"

"I don't know." Maybe that's too honest. Now is not the time for honesty. "I'm sure it will. You're still in shock. You're still getting used to the idea. You'll be OK."

It's more of an instruction than an assurance but it's as much as she needs to pull herself together.

"D'you mind if I just go?" she says. "I know it's rude to just eat and run and it was lovely, it was gorgeous. But I'm not the best company. I'm not in the mood."

I give her a hug and take the dishes into the kitchen on the way to fetching her coat.

"Thanks," she says, putting her coat on. "The food was lovely."

I give her a hug as we stand in the hall and she feels like an old lady in my arms, all skin and bone.

"I just need to nip for a wee before I go," she smiles, extricating herself from me.

And she bounds up the stairs taking two at a time.

He comes back in with the dog, who immediately races up to me with his tail wagging.

"I'm sorry, I should have told you that Julie's mother had died. I forgot."

"Some friend you are. Forgot? Yeah, right. You were just waiting to make an idiot out of me." He comes up close to me as He's speaking. He's standing more or less nose to nose with me.

"I did forget. I'm sorry."

"Sorry," He prods me in the chest with his finger. "Sorry," prod, "sorry," prod, "sorry," prod, prod, prod. The sorries get louder and the prods get harder and then Julie coughs theatrically from the top of the stairs.

"I'll be off then," she says. "I don't suppose you could come back to mine and keep me company?" she says to me, glancing at Him.

"I think you probably need some time on your own. Grieving's a very personal thing isn't it?" He says.

And He opens the front door and stands there like a bouncer while she leaves.

27

There are other women. Don't ask me how I know, I just know. Call me crazy if you like, call me a paranoid, fantasist bunny boiler if you want, but I know.

The thing is though, I'm not sure I actually care.

There's this one, Siobhan. She's young. She has red hair. What they call red hair, but really it's orange. It's the colour of sunsets on cheesy paintings. The colour of orange-flavoured ice pops. The colour of orange-flavoured anything. With a name like Siobhan you'd think it's naturally ginger but it's not. It's pure chemical affectation. There's not a single freckle on her anywhere.

There are piercings though. There are a few of those. One on her eyebrow with a little ring through it. A sleeper. Goodness knows why they're called that. There's a stud just under her bottom lip in the corner. From a distance it looks like a massive zit, or a wart or a beauty mark. It's small and round and silver and I'm sure it must catch on jumpers and T-shirts when she pulls them over her head. It's pointless. It makes her look worse, not better, and it's a man-made snagging device on her face. But to Him that's missing the point. To Him the point of the tiny little metal thing just under her bottom lip is that it's a great big juicy signpost to the other piercings she may or may not have in other places.

She has one in the middle of her tongue, that's for sure. And that's the one He's got his eye on. He's heard stories in the pub about girls with pierced tongues. He has plans for that bit of silver, an excellent conductor of hot and cold, a small solid object on a soft, mouldable tongue.

He met her on the bus. No, that's a lie. She was on the bus, He was on the pavement. They didn't so much meet as share a moment. The bus was stopped at the side of the road after some kind of incident with a bicycle. The driver had got out to check that the cyclist was OK and the cyclist was gesticulating and asking the driver was he blind, and telling the driver that he had a bus full of witnesses you know so he should watch what he said. And then the cyclist brought Him into it.

"You must have seen what happened, you were just walking up when the bus nearly wiped me off the face of the planet."

He had just been walking round to the garage to get my Tuesday night flowers. They're not normally from the garage, they're normally from the supermarket, but He hadn't had chance to pop out at lunchtime so last-resort garage flowers it was.

"Sorry mate," He says, "I didn't see anything. I was miles away."

The driver breathes a sigh of relief and the rest of the bus is staring at Him. A hotchpotch of faces: some delighted that something has livened up their tedious bus journey, some furious that the bus has come to a halt and may not be getting them to where they're going any time soon.

But she's not excited or impatient, she's just curious. She looks Him up and down like she's trying to read his life history on his face and, when He looks back at the double-deckered row of eyes all focussed on Him and the cyclist and the driver, hers are the only ones He sees.

He looks back at her and smiles. She laughs and sticks her tongue out at Him, showing Him the big silver stud anchored into it.

He smiles back. The bus shudders and grumbles back to life as the cyclist finally gives up ranting and opts to note down the number plate and cycle off with the words 'this is not over' instead.

He just stands there looking at Siobhan and her piercings – the ones that He can see and the ones that He can't – like that sappy posh bloke in Brief Encounter when the love of his life chugs off back to her husband on the train. And as the bus moves away He waves at her and she waves back.

So the next evening He goes out at the same time, says we need some milk for the morning and He'll just nip to the garage. He has never in his life checked whether we need milk for the morning. But He comes back with a litre bottle and sure enough it comes in handy.

He walks to the bus stop and makes sure He's passing at exactly the same time as the night before. The bus stops, and there she is, looking out of the window just like before. Smiling at Him just like before. But tonight there is no rattled bus driver or irate cyclist. The bus just stops to let two people off and one person on and then pulls out again. Barely time for Him to stick his tongue out at her by way of asking her to stick hers out back at Him before she's gone again.

For the next couple of nights He finds some pretext to go for a wander. He has indigestion and He thinks a stroll will help Him walk it off. He thinks he might catch the last post, He seems to remember there's a late collection at the post office on Bradshaw Street. He fancies fish and chips tonight, shall we have take-out? But however creative his excuses to be at the bus stop just at the right time, He doesn't get to see her. He sees the bus. He scours the bus for signs that she might be there. Maybe she's changed her seat. Maybe she's upstairs, or on the right hand side of the bus, or sitting right at the back where it's difficult to see her. But no. She's just not there.

So He waits. Maybe she's missed the bus and she'll be on the next one. No.

So He heads out earlier the next night. Maybe she's decided she needs to make it out of the house a bit earlier and she'll be on the one before. No.

And after nearly a week, when He's almost out of little ruses to make sure He's walking past the bus stop at 6.24, there she is.

He sees her before the bus has even stopped. He smiles at her, she pulls her tongue out at Him and without thinking about it He just gets on the bus, pays for his ticket and sits down beside her with a big 'Hi, how are you?' as though they're long-lost chums from way back.

"I'm good," she says in that American way that He always says He hates, but He doesn't seem too bothered by it when she says it.

"I've not seen you on the bus the past few nights," He says.

She smiles. "I only get the bus at this time on Mondays, Tuesdays and Wednesdays," she says. "I work in a bar three nights a week and in a shop at weekends. Different hours. What about you? Where are you going?"

Good question. Should He lie and pretend He's on his way somewhere, or tell her the truth that He's only got on the bus so that He can speak to her. So that He can chat her up. So that He can shag her.

"I'm not sure," He says, hedging his bets. "I thought I might just get out of the house for a bit and maybe go for a drink. I could go for a drink where you work maybe?"

Lame. Really lame.

"Yeah, if you like," she says. "It's usually pretty quiet on a Monday; you can keep me company while I'm working, if you like."

So she walks Him to the bar where she works and she leads the way down the steps into a cellar with chandeliers on the ceiling and stainless steel on the floor. He sits at the bar for three hours while she works and He drinks, first beer then cocktails. She makes suggestions from the menu that He's been idly browsing while she was serving someone else and each one is a different colour from the one before. He keeps offering her drinks to keep Him company and she keeps telling Him that she'll have one later when she's knocked off for the evening, and she puts some money in a glass behind the bar.

He watches as she flirts with other customers. Cocks her head to one side, flashes the piercing in her tongue at them, sticks out her chest and throws back her head while she laughs.

He asks her what time she finishes work.

Midnight.

And what does she do then?

She might go to a club. She might go home and sleep. Depends how she feels at twelve. Depends who comes in later and who's up for a late one.

"I'm up for a late one," He says.

"Who are you, her dad?" says a skinny guy with sticky-up hair standing next to Him at the bar.

"I'm a friend of hers, if you must know," He says.

The guy looks Him up and down, then looks at her, then looks at Him again.

"You've got to be kidding me!"

He looks at her and waits for her to come to his defence.

"We just got chatting on the bus," she says. Then she doesn't say anything else, she just goes to the other end of the bar. "What can I get you love?"

28

The funny thing about the morning after everything's changed is that you look out of the window and everything's still the same. All the houses are the same and all the people behind all those curtains are just carrying on in the same old way as if nothing has even happened. The birds are singing and the old lady next door is hoovering to pass the time as usual, even though no-one will see her spotless carpets.

Even in here, in this bedroom with its massive bed and fitted wardrobe, even in here there is the silence of a room where nothing has happened. He is still asleep, not snoring, just breathing. I am awake, wondering what happens next.

Nothing, apparently. I go downstairs and five minutes later I hear Him switch on the shower while I'm eating my breakfast and He finally makes it downstairs just as I'm pouring washing powder into the machine ready to switch it on.

He says nothing.

I can't stand this nothingness.

"I thought I'd put a wash on, it looks like it's going to be fine."

"Good idea," He says. And He pours some cereal into a bowl, takes a spoon from the drawer, grabs the milk from the fridge and wanders off into the other room to eat his breakfast. Just like He always does.

So I put the kettle on for a cup of tea and make a start on the washing up and He comes back into the kitchen, slips his bowl and spoon into the bowl of soapy water and asks me if I want a cup of tea.

"I've put the kettle on."

"Yes, but do you want me to make a cup of tea?"

"If you're making one."

"I'm making one for me, d'you want me to make one for you or d'you want to finish doing that first and then make one?"

"No, now is fine."

"Good. Fine. A straight answer at last."

"And then I'll take the dog for a walk."

"Hasn't he been out yet?"

"I let him out into the garden for a pee but he'll need a run around."

"D'you want me to come with you?"

"If you like. It's up to you...."

"Well I won't then. I think I'll get the grass cut while it's dry."

Result. Chips and I can go for a walk to Julie's and He's just told me to go. More or less. And that's how the end of the world turns back to normal. More or less.

I potter a bit, waiting for the washing machine to finish its spin so that I can do the pegging out before I go, but it's still mid-cycle even after I've finished the washing up, drunk my tea, brushed my teeth and put my shoes on. So He says He'll peg the washing out when He's finished mowing the lawn and I can't complain at that. I hate the way He pegs out the washing – not that He's had much practice – He does it all wrong, with things all bunched up so that they don't dry properly and too many pegs so that there's pressure marks all over everything when you take it down. But at least He's trying. At least He knows He needs to make a bit of an effort.

I take Chips to the park first, just in case He's watching which way I go. Anyway, the dog does need a walk and a comfort break and I'm getting used to the whole picking up poo with a plastic bag on your hand thing. It's not that bad really. It can't be any worse than changing a nappy and I was fully prepared to do that.

I see Jupiter's owner in the park and ask him where his dog is.

"Isn't he a bit old for hide and seek?" I say. And immediately I realise what a mistake I've made. The old man clutches my hand.

"Oh love," he says. "Jupiter's gone, love. I had to have him put down last night, sweetheart. You're right, he was old, and his body was riddled with cancer, there was nothing they could do for him, they said it'd be kinder to have him put down. But I'm lost without him. I'm lost. I don't know what to do with myself. That's why I had to come here, love. I always come here with him on a Sunday morning and he sees his little doggy friends and I chat to their owners. It's what we do."

I don't know what to say. I give the old fella a hug; there's not much else I can do. But that's even more awkward for him than it is for me. I'm more of a hug-ee than a hugger and he clearly isn't used to being hugged by anyone, probably not even people he's actually related to.

"I'm OK. I'm OK thanks love," he says, extricating himself from my well-intentioned awkwardness. "I just need to tell everyone. I mean if we both just disappeared they'd be wondering, wouldn't they? They might think something had happened to me. And it's nice 'cos everyone I've seen has been lovely and sympathetic and whatnot, you know. Not like my sons, they think I was daft to keep such a big dog at my age and carry on paying his vet's bills all that time. They don't get it, you see. They don't see what a big gap it leaves in your life."

I look at Chips. He's a lovely dog but I don't feel like that about him. I think I might cry if he died but I don't think I'd be in this kind of a state.

"D'you want a cup of tea?" I ask him. "I only live five minutes away, you're welcome to come back to mine for a brew if you want a chat and a sit down."

"It's very sweet of you love," he says, "but there's a few dog-walking friends I haven't seen yet this morning and I need to let them know."

"D'you want me to spread the word for you? It must be tough telling the story of it again and again."

"You're very kind love, but no. I'd like to see everyone myself, it's nice to hear how well thought of Jupiter was, you know. You just make the most of your dog and your youth while you've still got both." And he takes one of my hands in both of his and squeezes it tight and it's my turn to feel all awkward and not know what to say. But it doesn't matter, because he just gets up off the bench then and shuffles off for another circuit around the park. I look back as I'm leaving and he's sitting on a bench with Diana's owner, digging in his pocket for his handkerchief and passing it to her.

When I tell Julie about Jupiter and the old man and how the lady with Diana was sobbing when I left the park, I find myself stupidly, ridiculously crying in her living room. As if I knew the dog, or the man, or was a bona fide dog lover.

She proffers a box of tissues. I take one and then she takes one herself. She's doing that silent crying thing again with the tears and no sobs. I wish I could cry as elegantly as that. There's not much that's elegant about Julie: her hair's always a mess and her clothes all need ironing – she can make a £100 dress look like something she's just brought home from the 50p tub at a charity shop. But when it comes to crying, she's like a Hollywood star. She's Vivien Leigh in *Gone with the Wind* in that dress made out of the velvet curtains.

She smiles at me crying and I smile back and we both know that neither of us is crying for the dead dog, or for the old fella. I blow my nose loudly and she jumps up out of her armchair.

"I've got just what we need," she announces with her long, scrawny arms waving all over the place. And she disappears off into the kitchen leaving me to try and decipher the clanging and rustling.

On the table next to me is a pile of postcards, address side up and a pile of letters, all in their envelopes with the raggedy edge torn across the top. I look across at the desk to see that it's just plain glass: she's taken the postcards out to read them. No wonder she's crying.

But she's not crying any more. She reappears in the doorway with a tray full of stuff and a big grin.

"OK, we've got crisps, we've got Jaffa Cakes, we've got pickled onions, we've got Dairylea Triangles, we've got dandelion and burdock and we've got genuine Russian vodka that was sitting on a supermarket shelf in Moscow until last week when a friend of mine brought it home and gave it to me!"

I can just about cope with the Jaffa Cake and pickled onion combination and I'm quite excited about the dandelion and burdock, but the triangles? I'm not sure that's legal once your age is bigger than your shoe size.

"Dairylea Triangles?" I raise one eyebrow at her in a party trick manoeuvre it took me years to perfect.

"No, honestly," she says. "You think they're going to be revolting but they are seriously delicious. I would have osteoporosis if it weren't for these little calcium-infested triangles. I promise you, it's all the nutrition you'll ever need in one little round box of silver-coated triangles."

She pours me a glass of dandelion and burdock with a hefty slug of vodka in it and places a cheese triangle in my hand.

"Doesn't it make you think of kids' parties and school picnics?"

It kind of does. But it's not the dandelion and burdock and the Dairylea that I'm thinking of. I'm thinking about my mum. When I was a kid and my dad had stormed off in a huff or had taken to his bed all day because he was 'ill', my mum would go into just the same cheery overdrive that Julie's in now. She'd take me to a cafe and let me have ice cream for lunch and we'd skip down the road together and pick daffodils in the park to bring home and put in a vase.

"You don't have to be cheery for my sake, you know."

"I know," she says. "I'm not."

Chips is sniffing at my Dairylea triangle so I just let him eat it and Julie peels another one and gives it to him.

"I mean, I know you must be feeling crap with your mother... with losing your mum and everything."

"I didn't lose her," Julie says, pouring herself another dandelion and burdock and vodka. "I lost her years ago and now she's died and it's not fair."

I don't know what to say. How can I know what to say? Julie's the one who always knows what to say. Julie's the one who's calm in a crisis and now look at her.

"It'll be OK, you know," I say. Bloody lame but I have to say something. "I mean, I always try to think, 'it's like this now, but it won't be like this forever'. One day I'll be looking back on this and it'll be in the past and I'll just be able to think, oh yeah, that's what it was like and that's what it felt like then but I won't feel like that forever."

"No offence Marion, but you've got no fucking idea what you're talking about." She leaps up. "Doughnuts!" she says. "I forgot the doughnuts. Fancy forgetting the fucking doughnuts!" and she lurches forwards towards the kitchen, taking her drink with her. She comes back a minute later with a bag of doughnuts in one hand, her almost empty drink in the other and a doughnut stuffed in her mouth.

She flops down into the chair, plants the bag of doughnuts on my lap and takes the doughnut out of her mouth.

"You know," she says, chewing as she talks. "I was never allowed doughnuts as a kid. My mum, the mum that you know, always said that stuff like this was full of the wrong sort of fats and would end up killing you if you ate too much of it, so better not to have any at all. I bet my real mum would have let me have doughnuts. What a stupid thing to say: too much will kill you so better not to have any at all. I think that's stupid don't you? I think that's absolutely the most stupid thing I've ever heard."

I look at my watch: it's 12.15. He'll be wondering where I am. Frankly, I'm beginning to wonder what kind of parallel universe I've stumbled into and, more to the point, where the exit is so that I can stumble back out again.

There's a voice at the back of my head saying just give her a big hug and tell her it'll all be all right and then it will all be all right.

I try it. It doesn't work.

"It won't though, will it?" she says and stands up to pour herself another drink. "My mum is dead and I have to go and hear them read her will in a couple of days and I hardly knew her and she won't be coming back and I'm not ready."

I try the hug thing again but she's not letting me. She's not interested in my little hugs.

"God Marion, you're so grin and bear it. In fact, not at all grin and bear it. Whinge and bear it. I think you must actually like it. I think you must enjoy being the martyr. Where would you be if you didn't have something to whinge about? What on earth would there be to you if you didn't have a crappy husband and a miserable marriage to harp on about? Poor old unfortunate Marion. And we all look after you and sympathise with you and listen to you and the record never changes and the ending is always the same and it's all so predictable and boring, boring, boring. My mum let me be adopted and I didn't have a choice, she kept me at arm's length and I didn't have a choice, she's fucking died and left me for good and I didn't have a choice and now I have to go and find out what she's left me in her will and whatever it is I don't want it but I have to take it because I haven't got a fucking choice."

She pauses for breath and I think she might be about to stop but she isn't. She's just putting her drink down and hauling herself up out of the chair to stand over me.

"But you, Marion," she's whispering now, but in a whisper louder than any shouting I have ever heard. "You," her hands are on my shoulders. "You do have a choice. You can choose to leave the bastard and get yourself a fucking life. So why don't you?"

She stares at me for a moment and for a moment I can't break her gaze. Her hands are on my shoulders and I look down to see her wrists all sinewy and strong with the charms on her bracelet swinging slightly to and fro. There's a shoe and an owl and a tiny silver post box.

She lets go.

"I'd better go. He'll be wondering where I am."

"You'd better had," she says.

And she marches out of the room and goes to open the front door for me. I pause to put Chips' lead back on and follow her into the hall.

"I'm sorry if I've upset you," I say.

"You know what? You're the least of my problems."

I walk through the door and before I have chance to turn round and say anything else she closes it behind me and instead of her face I just see the beautiful stained glass panel that made me know that we both like the same things.

When I get home, the washing is on the line and He's made me a sandwich.

"Nice walk?" He says, putting the kettle on.

"Yeah. Except one of the old folks that I've met out dog walking told me his dog's died."

"Oh dear," He says. "That's a shame. I've made you a sandwich. I made one for me too but I've not waited, I'm afraid. I was starving and I didn't know what time you'd be back so I just ate mine."

"Thanks," I say and I sit and eat my sandwich slowly while He makes me a cup of tea and I get on with the post-normal, super-normal, everyday afternoon.

29

The water is cold tonight. Much colder than usual. It seems it to me, anyhow. It's OK for those people who dive straight in at the deep end and go for immediate submersion: they have the cold sharp shock then the immediate distraction of having to swim before they sink. But I'm not one of them. I can't do that. I don't like to get my face wet and I don't like to be out of my depth unless I'm already swimming first.

I get changed in my usual changing room. Number five, like the perfume. Marilyn Monroe said that No. 5 was all she slept in: when I heard that I tried it, but the smell of perfume put on freshly to go to bed just kept me awake. Anyway, my number five isn't always empty when I get to the pool but tonight it is and I see that as a good sign. The swimming gods are smiling on me because my changing room is available, so I'm in for a good swim. But the minute I step onto the first stone step into the pool I can tell that the smiles are more like smirks. The swimming gods are laughing at me, taking the piss with this freezing cold water that has me covered in goose bumps before I'm even in to the knees.

But Tattoo Woman smiles at me and Gammy-leg Man is here, so it's all OK. Just a bit cold.

"It's fine once you're in!" Tattoo Woman calls to me and I give her a grimace.

"Honestly," she says.

I step slowly down into the pool, wincing and sucking in breath as I go.

"Just get yourself in," says Tattoo Woman.

I think I preferred it when no-one here ever spoke to each other. Post-thug incident she seems to think she can badger me like an old friend. I'll do it in my own time, thank you.

I smile at her and carry on inching my way down the steps. Eventually I take a deep breath and push off into the water. It is freezing. It's like I remember the sea being as a kid, when you ran out from behind the windbreak and splashed all the way in to the waist, screaming. I can't really scream here but I struggle to breathe for a minute and I'm shocked wide awake like I haven't been all day; like I was all night last night.

The water moves differently when it's so cold. Or perhaps it's just me that moves differently. There's more splashing and it feels like there's more water than usual. It takes me longer to get to the other end of the pool and after five lengths, when I'm usually just getting started, I feel really tired. Really, really tired. But I'm here to do forty lengths: I should be able to do thirty-six… thirty at the very least.

So I swim on. I swim on and I just keep swimming. Counting and swimming. I try to focus on counting and not thinking, counting and swimming, not thinking, not thinking, just swimming and swimming and counting and swimming.

Twenty-one. I spurted wine out of my nose. What an imbecile. Twenty-two. What did Julie say when I spurted the wine out? What did her face look like? Twenty-three. Fox hunting. What did He say about fox hunting? She thought that was ridiculous didn't she? Didn't she? Twenty-four. Did He mean for her to see Him prodding me? Where was she when He did that? What did she say then exactly? I can't remember what she said. Twenty-five. Twenty-six. Twenty-seven. Twenty-six… No, twenty-eight. How did we get on to the subject of Linda? Twenty-nine. Did that make her angry with Him or angry with me? Was she angry with me for letting Him bring it up in such a crass way? Is that it? Was she still angry when I went round yesterday? Thirty. That's it, that must be it. She was angry with me and when He prodded me like that she just thought I deserved it. I handled the whole thing all wrong. I shouldn't have let Him upset her. No wonder she disappeared so quickly. No wonder she was so cross with me when I turned up at hers with Chips. Thirty-two. But she said she was grateful to me for being the one to bring it all out into the open about her being adopted. She did say that. She definitely said that. Thirty-three. But she was angry at me yesterday. She was definitely angry at me. Thirty-four. Thirty-four. Thirty five.

I can't remember what number I'm supposed to be on. I can't remember what I was just thinking. I can't think at all and then everything goes bonkers all at once. The pool attendant comes running up and jumps in the pool fully clothed and splashes across to me and grabs my chin and pulls me to the side and hoists me out onto the side and lies me face down with my arm under my head and I'm being sick and there's a strange kind of shushing noise all over me.

"Are you OK love, are you OK?"

I'm cold. I'm really, really cold.

"I'm fine," I say. "I'm fine. I'm cold though. I am quite cold."

Out of nowhere, someone puts a towel over me and I can't see who it is. I try to look around but all I can see is the big flying saucer lights above me and they look much bigger and much closer than usual.

And suddenly I'm sitting on a chair and Tattoo Woman is handing me a glass of water.

"Try and have a sip love. Have a little sip."

I sip the water and look up. It's not just Tattoo Woman, it's the manager guy and the lifeguard and the woman from the front desk. The lifeguard is fully clothed but wet through with a towel round his shoulders. In the pool there are still people swimming but they're all slow and quiet.

I take a sip of the water.

"That's the ticket, love. How ya feeling now?" says Tattoo Woman.

Confused, mostly.

"Fine, I think."

"Are you sure?" says the manager guy. I don't like him. There's something unpleasant about him. He sweats too much.

"I'm sure," I say. "I'm just a bit embarrassed. What happened? What on earth happened?"

Tattoo Woman smiles at me. "You seemed fine one minute and then the next..."

"I think maybe you fainted or something," says the lifeguard. "You just sort of sank in the water and I jumped in to get you and then you passed out again on the side of the pool."

"We were wondering whether we should call an ambulance for you... Or maybe there's someone you'd like us to call?"

"God no!" I say, mostly in response to the ambulance question and I try to get up out of the chair and I try to tell them that I'll be fine now, thanks very much for all their help. "I'll just get dressed, my car's in the car park, I'll be fine now, sorry about the drama."

But the manager puts his clammy hand on my shoulder and Tattoo Woman shakes her head gently.

"There must be someone we can call?" Front Desk Woman chips in.

I think about the options: He'd be mortified and less than impressed that I'd embarrassed myself. Anyway, He will have had too much to drink by now to come and pick me up. Julie? Not sure she'd be that keen to come to my rescue after yesterday. Mandy? Not sure dragging a pregnant woman out to rescue me would be fair. And anyway, it's all just so embarrassing and, stupidly, I just want my mum.

"There isn't. And there's no need. Honestly..." I look up a Tattoo Woman for a bit of back-up and she must be able to read my face.

"How about if I give you a lift home and you come and collect your car in the morning?"

"Really? That'd be so kind. That'd be great."

"You'll have to fill in an incident form and sign off to say that you didn't want an ambulance to be called," says the manager. I dislike him more with every syllable he utters.

"Fine," I say, "That's fine. Can I get dressed now?" I feel as if I'm at school, asking permission to go to the toilet.

"As long as you feel OK."

"I'm fine."

"Good. Well, I'll go and get the form and Peter will fill it in with you when you're all ready." The manager nods at the lifeguard and wanders off with Front Desk Woman, whispering his disbelief that Peter's had to jump into the pool loud enough for me to hear him.

And by the time I've got changed, Tattoo Woman is standing fully clothed at the edge of the pool chatting to Peter the Lifeguard who's now wearing dry clothes and sipping a cup of tea. He hands me the incident form on a clip board, some of which he's filled out already, and shows me where I have to tick boxes to say whether his response to the incident was unsatisfactory, satisfactory, good or excellent and where I have to sign to say that they offered to call an ambulance or a family member and I refused.

I thank him again and I feel like I should give him a hug, or something a bit more substantial than the kind of thanks you give in a shop when the girl on the till hands you your change, but I'm just not one of those women that can hug people I don't know. I settle for an ordinary thank you and a mental note to bring him a bottle of wine or something. That's if I ever decide I can show my face in here again.

As we walk to the car park Tattoo Woman tells me that Peter the lifeguard is a PhD student researching something to do with speech development in infants and he's worried about getting his thesis finished because they keep giving him extra shifts at the pool. He's got debts to pay off, she says, so he takes the work because he can't afford to turn the money down. I wonder how on earth she's managed to get so chatty with the lifeguard in the ten minutes it's taken me to get changed and fill in the incident form. I think how odd it is that everything I know about the person who's just more or less saved my life (God, that sounds so melodramatic) can be summed up in about two sentences – three at a push if I added in a physical description. Weird.

It turns out that Tattoo Woman lives only a few streets from me and she swims at the pool three nights a week. She knows my road so I don't have to give her directions, and she just chats and chats all the way to the house. Perhaps she thinks she's got to keep me awake by chatting. Perhaps that's what Peter and the sweaty manager told her to do.

When we get there I say goodbye and thank you as she pulls up to the kerb but she switches the engine off and tells me she's coming inside with me.

"And I'm not taking no for an answer," she says. "I won't sleep tonight if I'm not convinced that you're perfectly all right before I go home."

That's fine. That's not so bad, but when she marches me through to the living room and insists that I sit down and then goes off into the kitchen to make us both a cup of tea I start to feel a bit manhandled.

The dog shoots through the kitchen door as soon as she opens it and she lets out a loud 'fuck me', then he comes bounding in to see me and jumps onto my lap uninvited. It's like he knows I need a bit of TLC, I think. Then I have to tell myself not to be so bonkers: he's just had a strange woman open the kitchen door for him, nearly trip over him and then swear at the top of her voice; he's come looking for reassurance, not offering it.

I can hear Tattoo Woman clattering cupboard doors in the kitchen, looking for mugs and teabags and everything. I wonder what I'm going to tell Him if He comes back now. What will He think if He walks in through the back door and finds there's been a coup in the kitchen?

She comes back in with tea in a teapot (which I never use, not even when my mum comes over) and a packet of chocolate biscuits that I didn't even know we had.

"My mum always said you need something sweet after a shock. I'd rather have a biscuit than sugar in my tea, wouldn't you?"

"My mum says you should have a nip of whisky in your tea after a shock," I answer. And I just want my mum. I wonder if I should phone her. I definitely shouldn't: the idea of her being here is definitely more comforting than the real thing.

"Well, if you've got some whisky?" Tattoo Woman says, clearly quite keen on the idea of a nip in the tea.

"Don't think so."

"Well, chocolate biscuit it will have to be then," she says. "I'll be mother. You just relax." She pours me a cup of tea and offers me one of my biscuits on my plate and refuses to put the plate down until I've had two, then takes two for herself. "No choccie for you!" she says to Chips, leaving him to gaze longingly and fruitlessly at me.

"How're you feeling now, love?" she asks me, gesturing at me to eat my chocolate biscuit by pointing at it with her own."

"I'm fine." I say, "I'm fine. I'm honestly fine. Honestly."

She doesn't say anything; she just raises her eyebrows and takes another bite of her biscuit.

We crunch our biscuits. Chips gives up on getting in on the biscuit action and skulks back into the kitchen for a lie down. I look at the clock on the bookshelf: 9.20, way too early for Him to get back from the pub quiz.

Tattoo Woman finishes her second biscuit and puts her cup down on the coffee table.

"The thing is, love. What's your name again?"

"Marion."

"Marion. The thing is Marion, you're not fine are you? I mean, tell me to mind my own business if you like. I don't want to interrogate you or anything, but I know what it's like to spend the whole time making out to everyone that you're fine and everything's all right and you're clearly not. I mean, in my opinion, I don't think you seem like someone who's all right."

She waits. She takes another biscuit. I don't know what to say. I feel like I've been caught cheating in an end-of-term spelling test. Any minute now she's going to tell me that I've let myself down and let the whole of the class down and then send me off to see the head.

"The thing is," she punctuates her sentences with little flicks of her biscuit in my direction. "The thing is, Marion, that fainting in the swimming pool isn't nothing: it's a big fat sign telling you that something's wrong."

"Nothing's wrong, honestly. I've never fainted before in my life. I'm fine. I'm absolutely fine. I just didn't sleep very well last night and I haven't eaten that much today. That's all."

The trouble is I'm trying to sound convincing but I can feel that burn at the back of my throat that you get when you need to cry but you don't want to let it out. I know it must show on my face. I know I won't be able to hold it in much longer if she doesn't leave me alone. But I don't want her to go.

She takes hold of my hand.

"Let me tell you a story," she says. "When I left school I went to secretarial college, the same as my mum had, the same as my sister did and my auntie, come to that. I was good at typing, and shorthand and all of that but I hated the smart clothes and the office and the making the tea for all the men in suits. I hated all of it. I got a good job and I hated that too. I used to cry every Sunday because I had to go back to the office on Monday morning and I used to drink too much every week night to help take the edge off the monotony of going back and doing all the same stuff the next day. And then one day my boyfriend died. Just like that out of the blue, he fell off some scaffolding on a building site and that was that. And that was the kick up the arse I needed. At his funeral the vicar warbled on about the waste of life and knew that I had to do something to make a change if I didn't want to waste the whole of my life doing a job that made me feel miserable."

"Actually, I quite like my job."

"Love," she says, "I'm not telling you to jack in your job. You could easily have died in the pool tonight if Peter, God love him, hadn't been so quick off the mark. That's all I'm saying. It's the kind of thing that makes you think, don't you think? If you knew you were going to drown this time next year, what would you want to change between now and then?"

"Those curtains, for sure." I nod in the direction of the living room curtains, cast-offs from my mum that have always made the room a bit too middle-aged.

She smiles at me. She smiles at me in the way that you'd expect to come after a wink and I see her for a minute as a plainclothes fairy godmother. She might wave her magic wand and replace my awful curtains with made to measure blinds. She might bring Chips in from the kitchen and turn him into George Clooney.

"The secret to not drowning," she says, "is to get out of the pool before you get too tired to keep swimming."

She takes one last biscuit, twists the top of the packet and pats me on the shoulder.

"I'll just take one more for the road, as long as you're sure you're all right. Make sure you see a doctor though, won't you? I'm sure it's something and nothing, but it's always best to see a doctor and put your mind at ease."

"I will," I reassure her, wondering if I'll bother. "I'll give them a ring tomorrow."

I get up to show her out.

"Thanks. Thanks ever so much... I don't even know your name."

"Toni."

"Toni. Thanks ever so much, for everything."

"All right, love. See you next week."

"Thanks again."

"Bye, love."

"Bye."

I close the door behind her and go back into the living room. I think about calling Julie. I think about Julie's mum. I leave the tea things sitting there on the coffee table and go to bed.

30

It's quiet in the house when I wake up and quiet outside too. There are no cars on the street yet, and in the bed He has his back to me and his breathing is slow and silent. It's the third time I've woken up since I went to bed last night but it's almost half past six so this time it's OK to get up. It's officially morning.

I have a cup of tea before I get in the shower, and a bowl of Rice Krispies and a piece of toast. I make two pieces but I only eat one. 'Your eyes are bigger than your belly' my mum would say, but that's the great thing about having a dog: nothing goes to waste and nothing's left behind as evidence. I know I should take Chips out for a walk, but I just let him go for a wander in the garden for a few minutes in the rain and he's happy with that. He has a wee and a quick sniff round and he's straight back inside to see if there's any more toast I don't want.

The shower sounds ridiculously loud in this quiet, quiet house but I know it won't wake Him. There's an empty Champagne bottle on the kitchen table so the pub quiz clearly went well and the spoils were clearly instantly consumed by the winners. He'll sleep until the alarm this morning, and probably through a repeated snooze button too.

The water is warm and lovely at first, but it suddenly goes cold without warning just when my hair is full of shampoo and I'm covered in soap all over. I want to scream. I want to scream out loud, the water is so cold. It's stinging me and making me gasp but I have to get the shampoo out of my hair and the soap off my skin. It's unbearable. And then it's warm again and by the time I step out and wrap the towel around myself I feel like I even quite enjoyed the freezing cold bit.

At twelve o'clock I woke up to the sound of his key in the door and Jimmy's voice and the sound of the pair of them staggering around and singing 'We are the Champions.' I could smell chips, I could hear the telly and when Jimmy finally went home and He came up to bed I lay as still as I could like a game of sleeping lions until I could feel his sleep beside me. And I lay there for ages and all the time all I could think was: 'you could easily have died in that pool tonight. You could have died in that pool tonight. For fuck's sake Marion, you could easily have died in that pool tonight, sort your fucking life out before your number's up.'

So I lay awake and made a plan. You get up in the morning and you go to work and then you tell Heidi that you fainted last night and you need to go and see the doctor this morning and then you go home and pack your stuff and you get on a train and go to your mum's and get her to help you make a proper plan of what to do next. And you can ring in sick before you catch the train and tell Heidi you've been signed off for a week – better make it two weeks – and then you've left your options open about going back or not going back. It was all just like that. Like a proper to-do list, tick off a few little things and then move on.

But I woke up again just before four. I woke up with that niggling feeling that you have when you know something's not quite right. That did-I-leave-the-iron-on feeling. That aren't-I-supposed-to-be-somewhere feeling. What about Chips? What about Julie? What about Mandy? What if my mum tells me not to be so stupid and just sends me home? What if He won't let me back in when I get here? What if Heidi sacks me and I end up with nowhere to live and only a suitcase full of clothes to my name? The night threw everything it's got at me until I was struggling to breathe with the panic. Staying is easy: I just get up in the morning like I always do and keep waiting for something to change. Leaving is hard. Leaving is not hard, it's impossible. I decided not to go. I decided not to be so stupid.

And now it's morning again. Now it's getting light and his shoes are in the doorway to the living room and I pick them up and put them in the hall. I could easily have died in that swimming pool last night. Julie's mum's died. My baby died. Chips comes in and sniffs at the shoes and I can hear the alarm clock upstairs. It switches the radio on and then seconds later He turns the music off again. It's just a few notes but it's so, so familiar. It's one of those lyrics that we sang endlessly on the school bus. "Wake me up before you go go," and I had the T-shirt to go with it. A massive baggy affair that said 'Choose Life' across the front. I used to wear it with my leg warmers and a scarf tied in a bow on top of my head. Today I feel like the universe is sending me a great big neon sign and the sign is telling me what to do next. My plan might be crap and I might have half baked it in the middle of the night, but it's a start.

I'm dying to tell Julie so I call her. Straight to voicemail so I leave her a message. "Hi, Julie. I'm so sorry about the argument and everything. I'm sorry. I'm thinking of going away for a bit but you can speak to me on this. I hope we can speak soon."

It sounds rubbish. I wish I could change it but that's voicemail for you. Everyone sounds crap. I sit down for a minute. I'm not sure what to do next and Julie might call me back. Or she might text.

"Marion. Marion. Marion, are you downstairs?"

"Yes."

He leans His head over the banister. "I wasn't sure if you'd left for work already. Any chance you could iron me a shirt before you go? I've only got the cufflinks one left in the wardrobe."

"Yeah. Just chuck one down and I'll do it for you."

"Thanks. You're a star. Did you see the bottle in the kitchen? We won. I knew we would."

"I saw it," I say. "Well done!"

What else am I going to say? 'I saw it and would very much like to smash it over your head before I leave'?

So I iron his shirt and, while I'm ironing it and pressing the steam button on the sleeves and the collar, I'm trying to make up my mind whether I should leave Him a note when I go. If I leave one what will it say? I might be back? I won't be back? I have no idea what I'll be doing? And if I don't leave one will he think I've gone missing? Will there be a police hunt for me? Will they put Him on TV to make a tearful appeal while a psychologist watches Him for signs that it was Him all along that did me in? Could I get Him framed for murder?

Clearly not. I can't even get myself out of the house without having a million panics on how to go about it and whether I should actually go or not. I check the shirt and go over the sleeves again where they're still a bit crumpled on the back, and then I take it up to Him.

He's in the bathroom shaving, so I go and hang the shirt up in the bedroom and go back into the bathroom, put down the toilet seat and sit down.

"My mum rang while you were out last night," I lie. "She's not feeling very well."

He doesn't say anything because He's shaving but He turns to me briefly and raises an inquisitive eyebrow to show me He's listening.

"Actually," I go on, "She thinks she might have shingles and she's asked if I can go over and just give her a bit of TLC for a few days. It's knocked her for six, I think. You know what she's like. You know how independent she is. If she's asking for help she must be in a really bad way."

He nods at me his agreement and carries on shaving.

"So I was going to ask Heidi if I can have a few days off work to go and help her out. If Heidi okays it, is that OK with you?"

He puts down the razor, splashes his face with water and covers it in a towel, drying it slowly and looking at me over the top while He does it. He's pausing for dramatic effect like the hosts on those TV talent shows. He knows He's going to say fine. I'm pretty sure He'll say fine but He wants to keep me guessing.

"Will you be taking the dog with you? I haven't got time to walk him."

"I'll have to check with my mum that it's OK, but I'm sure it will be. I'm sure that'll be fine."

"Fine, then. It's fine with me. You go and do your Florence Nightingale bit and I'll see you when you get back. My shirt's in the bedroom is it?"

"Yes."

"Great, thanks." He hangs the towel over the radiator, gives me a kiss on the cheek as He walks past and leaves me standing there in the bathroom wondering what I need to do next.

31

"Come on in then," she grins when she opens the door. "I've put you in your old bedroom upstairs but heaven knows where that's going to sleep."

I rang my mum as soon as He'd gone to work, just in case He decided to call her and check what I'd told Him. I'd expected it to be a tough conversation but it was just bonkers.

"Hi, mum, it's me, Marion. I need to come and stay with you for a few days."

"Marion? What time is it?"

"It's quarter past eight."

"In the morning?"

"Yes mum. It's Tuesday. Tuesday morning. Is it all right if I come and stay with you for a few days?"

"Why? What's so special about Tuesday?"

"There's nothing special about Tuesday. Is it all right mum? Is it OK if I come and stay for a few days?"

"Yes I don't see why not, but I don't like your tone very much. It was you that said 'it's Tuesday', like there's some great significance about Tuesday."

"I'm sorry if that's what it sounded like mum, there's not. I just need to get away for a bit."

"A bit of what?"

"A bit of space."

"Space. That's a laugh. This place is still bursting at the seams with all your stuff that you don't want to take to yours but can't bear for me to get rid of."

"Well this will be a good opportunity for me to sort through it, won't it? Is it OK if I bring my dog?"

"Since when did you have a dog?"

"Since about a week ago."

"Well I suppose so, as long as you don't expect me to clean up after it or feed it or anything."

"No, that's fine. It'll just be me and the dog."

"Oh, is that all?"

"Actually, there is just one other thing. I've said I'm coming to stay with you because you've probably got shingles and you need someone to look after you for a bit."

"Oh, thanks very much. Well I'll know who to blame if I do get shingles, won't I?"

"Sorry."

"And why've you said that? Do you need to have an excuse to spend a bit of time with your own mother?"

"No. It was just easier. I'll explain when I see you. I'm planning to get the train at ten past two so I'll be with you –"

"Just in time for dinner!"

"About five-ish, yes. Don't forget, if anyone rings you've got shingles and I'm coming to look after you."

"OK, Marion, I've got it. It's shingles I've got, apparently, not dementia. Do I need to find a red biro and draw spots on myself in case the police call round? Or will it be MI5?"

"Bye Mum. I'll see you around five," I say and put the phone down.

And by the time I've sat down on the train with my cup of coffee and a newspaper and Chips sitting on my foot keeping it warm, I'm half wondering why I've never done this before and half wondering why I've done it at all. I look out of the window and one field looks pretty much like the next but they're all quite nice. And the train goes so fast that they merge one into the next, making one big green line that's pointing me in the direction of home.

I could just get off at the next station and disappear. I could dare myself to do it. No matter where it is. I could start a new life and reinvent myself. But the next station is one of those depressing places where no-one ever gets on and no-one ever gets off, and I can just see myself in some awful Christmas dinner photo smiling out from a billboard on the dual carriageway with a big 'missing' caption above my head. I can't really do rebellion. I feel guilty if I accept the leftover half an hour on someone's pay and display ticket at the multi-storey.

I have that everyone's-looking-at-me feeling. I don't think they're really looking at me, I think they're looking at Chips because he's all cute, but it feels like they're looking at me. I should read my newspaper but I keep reading the same few lines over and over and then I can't remember where I'm up to and I end up reading them again. I think I might ring Julie. Or I could just text her. Or I could text Mandy.

I ring Julie. She answers but she can't hear me. I'm yelling 'Hello. Hello can you hear me?' down the phone and everyone is looking at me now but Julie still can't hear me so I hang up and then I get a text.

"Soz was so grumpy. Jst in a mess bout Linda. Will call soon xx."

So I send one back: "Gone to mum's 4 a bit. Hope ur ok. Ring me if u wanna chat."

I hold on to my phone in case she texts back. But it just sits there in my hand. I want to text Mandy but I can't think of anything to say. I just put it into my bag. I have a go at the crossword and eat a packet of mints. That's what train journeys are for.

I told my mum she needn't meet me at the station but when I step off the train I'm wishing she'd ignored me and turned up anyway. But she hates train stations. And she hates surprise visits. I prepare myself for a face like thunder, but when she opens the door she grins at me and summons me into the living room where there's a big bunch of pink gerberas.

"He rang to see how I was and to tell me he was getting these delivered for you because it's Tuesday," she says. "Aren't you pleased?"

I feel like He's followed me here. I've only just stepped through the door and He's here before me, sitting on the mantelpiece staring at me from under his pink petal lashes.

"Is it a special occasion? Are you celebrating something?"

"No Mum, He just buys me flowers every Tuesday. It's a kind of routine."

"Nice routine. You're a lucky girl."

I'm still wearing my coat and she hasn't even put the kettle on for a cup of tea yet but the words are out there before I even know it.

"Actually, Mum, I'm here because I want to leave Him and I didn't know what else to do apart from come here and have a think about it and a chat with you."

"Shouldn't it be your husband you're talking to? That's the only way you can work it out, you know."

"If I talk to Him, He'll convince me I'm being an idiot and it's all in my head and I won't be able to go."

"I see. And are you so sure that going is the best answer, Marion? Marriage isn't all flowers and Champagne you know. It's not easy. It's not a fairytale. It takes hard work. It takes a bit of give and take."

I want to scream at her. I want to rant. But I know that won't do me any favours. From somewhere I manage to find my inner calm.

"Shall I put the kettle on for a cup of tea? Have you got any biscuits?" And I leave her to sit for a few minutes rehearsing her lines while I hang up my coat and wait for the kettle to boil.

"The thing is," she says, snapping her chocolate bourbon in two, "The thing is, every marriage has its ups and downs. That's part of the deal. But if you take all of this too far, you'll have gone too far. That'll be it."

So I try to explain to her how things are. I try to explain how He keeps me in a box and doesn't let me out. I try to tell her that He makes me forget who I am. That He's cruel to me. That He makes me miserable.

But she doesn't get it. And when I say it all like that I don't get it either. I sound like a spoilt brat complaining about my parents. Any minute now she's going to tell me that there are children starving in Africa and I need to count my blessings and think myself lucky.

"He can't be that bad. He sends you flowers every Tuesday. That doesn't sound like someone who's cruel and nasty, that sounds like someone who loves you and wants to remind you how special you are."

Nope. That sounds like someone who wants to remind me where I stand.

"He made me eat them once."

"Eat what?"

"The flowers. He made me eat the flowers. I can't even remember why, but He made me eat them and He sat there watching me chew the flowers He'd bought for me just to prove that He could make me do it. Just to punish me."

She doesn't say anything. Perhaps she thinks I'm making it up. Perhaps she thinks I've finally lost the plot. I have turned up more or less unannounced with a dog and enough clean knickers for a fortnight. It's not like me, even I have to admit that.

"So how long has it been like this?" she asks.

I don't know.

"And why haven't you told me before?"

"I don't know."

And then suddenly, I do know. I know why and I feel stupid.

"I do know. I didn't tell you because I didn't want to feel like a failure. I didn't want you to think I'd messed it up. And I didn't think I could do anything about it anyway, so what would have been the point? Then I would have been rubbish twice, once for not telling and once for telling and then doing nothing about it."

She looks at me like I'm speaking Swahili and I feel like crying but I don't want to. I really don't want to.

"I always brought you up to be a strong woman," she says. "Maybe a bit too strong, after all... but when your dad left..."

And she rattles on about her life story and I want to yell at her that it's not strength but cowardice that's made me keep it all tucked away for so long. But I don't. I just let her finish speaking and I absolve her from her guilt and regrets and I tell her it's all fine and it's not been too bad, but I just need to think about what to do next and I just feel tired.

And then suddenly I feel very, very tired. Like I might fall asleep sitting upright in the chair. I tell her I'm going to get an early night and get up from the chair only for the world to disintegrate into a million tiny pieces that dissolve as I fall and she catches me.

I wake up on the floor with my mum stroking my hair and crying. She never cries. Perhaps I'm dead and I only think I'm alive, but that seems unlikely.

"I think you fainted," she says. "Have you been eating properly? Have you been sleeping properly?"

Of course I haven't.

"Of course I have!"

Clearly there was never any question of a career on the stage, the lie isn't even remotely convincing.

"Have you fainted before?" she asks.

Should I tell her? The thing is if I lie she'll probably know I'm lying and then she'll wonder why.

"Last night," I tell her, "in the swimming pool. But it was OK, I was fine. I ended up having a cup of tea with a nice woman. Surprisingly nice."

"Marion," she says, "people don't just faint in swimming pools." I can't decide whether she's concerned or just embarrassed that I've shown myself up.

“The only time I’ve ever fainted was when I was pregnant. Are you pregnant?” she says.

“No.” Bloody insensitive question. And then I remember the night of Mandy’s meal and I count up the days since then and I let myself wonder if I might be.

“Marion?”

“I suppose it’s possible.”

“Right then. It’s off to bed with you. A proper breakfast and off to see Dr Swift in the morning. I can ring at eight o’clock for you and I’m sure we’ll be able to get you in.”

I know it’s pointless to argue and before I know it she’s handing me a toothbrush with the toothpaste already on it and telling me not to mess about reading but to go straight to sleep.

***

In the doctor’s waiting room I try not to think to the rhythm of the tick from the clock on the wall but apparently that’s impossible. I might be pregnant – tick – what if I am? – tick – what shall I do? – tick – what will He say? – tick – what if I am? – tick- tick – tick.....

I wonder if my mum chose her doctor for the aesthetics of her waiting room. We’re not sitting on chairs: we’re on huge comfy sofas, the kind you sink into and can’t get out again. There’s a TV on the wall with the news channel on but it’s switched to mute and there are subtitles that move way too fast for you to read them so I try not to look but it’s pretty much impossible to pull my eyes away when it’s there and I’m sitting here trying not to think, trying not to listen to the tick, tick, tick.

There’s a water cooler and a vending machine for hot drinks, but if it weren’t for them I might think we’d stumbled into someone’s living room by mistake. The walls are covered in big swirly florals, there are ornaments on the fireplace and there’s a massive bookshelf full of books with a big red tub of kiddie books and another one full of toys just next to it on the floor. For my mum this probably says ‘homely and welcoming’. For me it mostly says 'expect a long wait, have a plastic cup of cappuccino and a read of *Pride and Prejudice* while you're waiting.'

But in the corner there's a woman peering through a glass window that gives the game away. She has a little medical alcove with wall-mounted leaflet holders jam-packed with all kinds of gruesome information about what you might have if you're sitting here and how to cope or how to avoid stuff that's catching. She's mostly shuffling papers and tapping her keyboard but every now and then she stops for a slurp of coffee and a good old peer through her sliding window and when the phone rings she chirps, "Hello, Doctor's surgery."

I'm wondering whether the cappuccino will taste of coffee or chicken soup and if I should risk it when the peering receptionist calls out my name.

"Marion, that's you." My mum nudges me with her elbow.

I jump out of my seat and knock my knee on the coffee table. My mum stands up with me and tucks the label back into the neck of my T-shirt.

"Shall I come with you?" she asks.

"No, you stay here, it's fine."

"I don't mind. I'll come with you."

"Mum, I need to go in and you need to stay here."

She looks at me crestfallen but this is not about her.

I go through the door in the corner of the waiting room and into a corridor and it's a bit like stepping through the wardrobe into Narnia. Suddenly I'm in a proper doctor's surgery with a doctorish smell and plastic chairs and serviceable carpet tiles. I want my mum, but it's too late to run back into the waiting room and get her now. I could just make a run for it and nip to Boots and pee on a stick like any normal person... but a door opens and a woman who looks more like Cinderella's ancient and slightly eccentric godmother than an actual doctor sticks her head around it.

"You must be Marion. Come on in."

32

It's raining when I get on the train. And even though we're technically still inside the station it's freezing cold and the dampness is everywhere: there are puddles on the ground, there's moisture in the air and the rain sounds like lentils being poured out of a packet into a big metal pan.

My suitcase is safely tucked away on the luggage rack and I'm standing by the door while my mum stands on the platform. She delves into her handbag and brings out a plastic bag and hands it up to me. There's a sandwich wrapped in silver foil, an apple, a carton of Ribena and a bar of chocolate in the bag.

"You need to keep your strength up and your blood pressure on an even keel," my mum says and I could swear she's going to cry.

"Thanks, mum."

"I couldn't find the flask but you can always get a cup of tea on board. Mind you don't scald yourself though. They always make it too hot."

The door beeps and closes.

My phone rings: "You're doing the right thing Marion. Just remember. This is for the best."

I nod at her through the window but say nothing. She starts to walk alongside the train as it begins moving.

"Give me a ring and let me know you're home safe."

"I will!" She's practically running now to keep up with the train. "Don't worry mum. I'll be fine. Thanks. I love you."

But she's gone. Even an Olympic sprinter would struggle to keep up with us now and within seconds the platform is behind us and I am on my own again. Except I'm not... quite.

It's been almost two weeks since I got on the train at the other end and headed over to see my mum, and in that small time everything has changed. Now, I am an expectant mother and I keep telling myself that it may not last and this baby may decide I'm not a great candidate for motherhood, just like the last one did. Or maybe this one will stick around. Maybe it's made of stronger stuff. Maybe I'm made of stronger stuff than I was when my lost little baby bowed out.

I haven't spoken to Him since I left. He rang a couple of times but I didn't answer, and in the end my mum told Him I needed a bit of time on my own just to clear my head. She told Him I was exhausted and emotional. She didn't tell Him about the baby – I made her promise not to – but she dropped plenty of hints about how I was tired and emotional and irrational and hormonal. The thing is, He's never been very good at hints: a giant banner and He might just get the message, but hints are just background noise as far as He's concerned.

Anyway, He knows I'm on my way home and He knows I'm back at work on Monday and the rest is for Him to find out when I get back.

I'm a bit surprised that I'm going back, to be honest. I didn't think I would be, but I'm not sure what else to do. I have a baby and a dog and it's like my mum says... you have to take the rough with the smooth.

The rain is making horizontal lines on the train window as we speed along but it's unbearably hot in the carriage and Chips has just gone to sleep under the table, knocked out by the lack of air. Just as well, probably. I lean on the window to absorb some of the coolness from outside and put my feet up on the seat opposite – if anyone complains, I'm a pregnant woman and I absolutely have to put my feet up: doctor's orders. I'm in a fantastically stroppy don't-mess-with-me mood, but no-one on this train seems even to have noticed I'm here, let alone be up for a fight. Which is probably just as well.

I have a newspaper and I open it and read a couple of headlines but I can't focus. I'm not really interested. In the back of my mind somewhere there is a thought that I can't quite get hold of. It's making me uneasy. Its making me annoyed. I look out of the window and everything is grey and wet and the same. So I'm sitting watching drips of rain on the window trickling down and the trickles join into each other like streams joining a river and eventually the one, fat, community raindrop gets to the bottom of the window and is gone. So I start again at the top of the window and follow them down and start trying to guess which one will be the dominant raindrop. Which one will be the one that accepts the others into it. But the one that's the big king of raindrops one minute just merges into an even bigger and fatter one the next.

This is my raindrop. This one here in the top right hand corner. If this one makes it all the way to the bottom without disappearing into another, bigger raindrop then it's telling me that I should think again. This raindrop is me. This raindrop will tell me whether I can make it on my own. If it needs to join with another blob of water that will tell me that I need to go home and make the best of it.

"Excuse me love..."

The ticket man taps my shoulder. "Sorry love, I wasn't sure whether you were asleep. I just need to check your ticket."

I rummage through my bag and then remember that I've put it in my pocket so that I can find it easily. He looks at it, clips it and gives it back to me. I look back at the window but I can't find my raindrop again. It's just one of a thousand raindrops on the window. They all look the same.

I put my ticket back into my coat pocket and feel something else in there. I take it out. It's a folded piece of thick cream paper and it says:

"Once I was a princess and my grandpa handed me the best rose from his garden when I went round to visit. I remember that I am a princess."

I fold it up again and put it back in my pocket. It reminds me of the Princess and The Pea, when she arrives at the prince's palace in the rain and she's so wet that the rain is gushing out of her shoe at the heel and she just stands on the doorstep saying 'I am a real princess, I am a real princess.' Of course, I know that I'm not a real princess. I tried the dried pea under just one mattress when I was about seven. It didn't work, I slept like a log. I am not a princess and I am not a Charlie's Angel and I am not a raindrop. But as the train rushes me back home it says to me 'you are a mum, you are a mum, you are a mum' and the rhythm won't let me have a single other thought.

It's still raining as the train approaches the station and, just as I'm clearing my bits and pieces off the table and into my bag, my phone starts to buzz and flash its little light.

His text reads; "Running 5 mins late. W8 on platform 4 me. X'

Typical. He's probably sitting, engine running, in the waiting-only short stay, trying to park for free for fifteen minutes instead of paying £1 for an hour.

My phone buzzes and flashes again. It's Julie: "U coming home 2day? Am in all evening if u want to talk/pop round."

I start to text her back but I'm not sure what to say. I'm sitting with my phone in my hand with my finger hovering over the keys, wishing myself back to a time when phones were only for making calls and only worked when plugged in to a socket in a wall. Then you knew if something you said sounded stupid from the silence or the sigh of the person on the other end. Back then you made arrangements and just stuck to them.

There is a man sitting across from me looking at me as I hesitate with my phone. He knows that I can see him looking at me from the corner of my eye but he's looking at me anyway. So I do something I never do: instead of pretending that I haven't noticed I look straight at him and almost make eye contact and he smiles at me and I think he might even say something before he looks back down at his newspaper and takes a sip of coffee.

"Thanks. Ur a star. Will catch up soon xxx."

Not exactly Nobel Prize winning stuff but I think it was the right thing to say.

It's still raining as the train pulls in at the platform. I have no umbrella and no proper coat, just a cotton jacket with no hood that soaks up water like a tea towel.

I check my phone again. No update. He must be on his way. So I get off the train with my suitcase and my dog and stand on the platform next to a bench that's too wet to sit on.

I have always loved railway stations. They are magical places. Places with endless possibilities. Perhaps he just won't turn up. Perhaps he'll get here and be that skinny bloke from years ago and stay that way for good this time. Perhaps I could just be gone by the time he gets here.

And then I see him. He's behind the barrier at the end of the platform, arguing with a woman in uniform and waving at me and pointing at me. He's beckoning me to him and she's looking at me too, waiting for me to take this bolshie fella off her hands. So I take my dog in one hand and the handle of my suitcase in the other and walk up the platform towards him, trying to control Chips' little legs and the suitcase's wonky wheels.

"She wouldn't let me on the platform without a ticket," he starts to tell me before I even get to where he's standing. "How ridiculous is that?" And he waits for me to be on his side while he gives this woman a dressing down for her unforgiveable conduct.

"Come on then," he says, "I'm in the restricted stay car park, I'll have a ticket by the time we get back if we don't get a move on."

He reaches over to take my suitcase and I hand him the dog instead. And then I do something that I didn't know I was going to do and even as I'm doing it I feel like it's not really happening. I might suddenly wake up on the landing and be guided back to bed at three in the morning.

I turn with my suitcase to the next platform, where the guard is getting ready to blow his whistle. I step onto the train just in time for the door to close behind me. As I hear the 'beep beep beep' to warn me that the doors are locking, I turn to see him running up the platform with Chips' little legs running alongside him. He bangs on the button to open the door but it's already locked. He keeps on banging as the train starts to move but it's not going to open and the train is not going to stop moving.

"For fuck's sake!" I see him say through the door.

There are plenty of seats to choose from in the carriage and I put my suitcase in the luggage rack and choose a seat with a table by the window. I don't know where this train is going and I don't care. We don't care.

There must be fifteen people in this carriage, maybe even twenty. But only one of them is me. I'm the only one who doesn't know where I'm going and doesn't know what I'll do when I get there. I'm the only one who will find out.

Acknowledgements

I'd like to thank Kevin, Lin and the team at Bluemoose, not least for smoothing out the rough edges with such patience and enthusiasm.

I'd also like to thank Commonword, whose workshops and First Three Chapters competition gave me the kick up the bum I needed to write this. In particular Martin De Mello for his kind but uncompromising criticism.

Thanks also to Emma Howard and Margaret Jaskulski for being my guinea pig readers.